Haley Hill is a fresh new voice in romantic fiction who has previously found success in the self-publishing world. Prior to launching her fiction career, Haley founded and ran the Elect Club dating agency—and is an expert in all things dating! Haley lives in south London with her husband and twin daughters.

IT'S GOT TO BE
Perfect

HALEY HILL

Published in Great Britain 2015
by Mills & Boon, an imprint of Harlequin (UK) Limited,
Eton House, 18-24 Paradise Road, Richmond, Surrey, TW9 1SR

© 2015 Haley Hill

ISBN: 978-0-263-25408-2

097-0815

Harlequin (UK) Limited's policy is to use papers that are natural, renewable and recyclable products and made from wood grown in sustainable forests. The logging and manufacturing processes conform to the legal environmental regulations of the country of origin.

Printed and bound by
CPI Group (UK) Ltd, Croydon, CR0 4YY

To all the fabulous clients who laughed, sobbed and, on occasion, vomited their way into my heart. And to James for bearing with me.

'If you look for perfection, you'll never be content.'

Leo Tolstoy, *Anna Karenina*

A Note to the Reader

PART ONE

Chapter 1

IT WAS A bitter November evening when I found myself in Be At One in Covent Garden, sitting opposite a man whose head was too small for his body. Below a gelled curtain fringe were squinty eyes, shiny skin and bushy hair sprouting from one nostril.

'You're the only girl I've met online who isn't a fatty,' he said, getting up from his chair and sitting down next to me. 'But I'd say you're more a size ten than an eight.'

I forced a smile.

'I don't mind a bit of meat though,' he said, his fingers creeping onto my thigh, tongue edging out in anticipation. His breath smelled of coffee and pickled onions.

I glanced at my watch and then downed my mojito. This date hadn't even made it to eight p.m.

The bar's heavy door slammed shut behind me and the icy air hit me like a slap in the face. I don't know why I hadn't just told him the truth, protected my online dating sisters. Instead, I'd found myself garbling an implausibly long-winded excuse, involving a twenty-four-hour veterinary surgery and a fictional cat undergoing pioneering bowel surgery. I pulled up my scarf and began the familiar trudge to Charing Cross station, wondering what crimes I must have committed in a past life to warrant such karmic retribution.

Eight months prior, spurred by heartbreak and lured by the promise of meeting thousands of 'like-minded singles', I'd embraced online dating with gusto, envisaging it to be like shopping for a husband: ooh, add to basket. But after what can only be described as intensive participation, I'd begun to learn that the slick profiles—comprising impressive credentials and enticing photos—often omitted pertinent details such as a clubbed foot, sexual deviance. Or a wife. Occasionally, I'd found one who walked and talked like a normal boyfriend, only to reveal a deep dark shadow that would have even sent Dr Phil running for the hills. And after tonight's offering of a misogynist with hair from the nineties, I knew it was time to call off the online search.

I let out a succession of sighs as I traipsed through the streets. It seemed that while I was being groped in Be At One, London's entire population had paired off, and then gone on to organise some kind of flash mob snog-a-thon. Couples criss-crossed my path and flaunted their love.

Enter besotted duo from the left. Cue loving gaze in restaurant. Candlelight, please.

Despite auditioning for roles such as 'happy bride' and 'woman in love', it felt as though I had inadvertently secured the lead in a new blockbuster entitled: *Everyone finds love...except for you.* Even my name, Eleanor Rigby, the lonely subject of a Beatles' song, would have been perfect for the credits. By the time I'd reached Charing Cross station, I was humming 'all the lonely people' and wondering if anyone would come to my funeral. I leant back against a railing and stared up at the sky. It was only two years since Robert had proposed, on bended knee in the pouring rain, declaring that he would love me for ever. We would have been married by now. I watched the stars glinting in the distance and willed fate to rethink its plan for me.

A man, seemingly oblivious to miles of unclaimed railing, came and stood right next to me and began noisily eating a Big Mac. I glared at him, then stared back up at the sky and began to wonder more about love. I'd spent my entire career analysing chemical reactions, albeit from behind the shield of polycarbonate safety goggles, in the controlled environment of the laboratory at ChemPlant. There, the outcome was predictable. I understood the variables and had learned precisely what it took to create an unbreakable bond, a bond that could withstand all manner of tampering. The elements didn't need a dating website. Carbon and oxygen didn't need to make small talk over the gentle flame of a Bunsen burner to determine whether they were right for each other.

'So how do you feel about polyamory?' asks carbon, eyeing up oxygen's electrons.

I glanced back at the man just as he shoved a fistful of fries into his mouth. I tutted. Perhaps I'd been naive to think it was possible to manipulate chemistry outside a laboratory, and maybe an online enhancement of the Collision Theory wasn't really the answer for me, or for all the other singles in the world.

When I eventually arrived home, I found Matthew, my long-term friend and short-term flatmate, lounging on the sofa, glass in one hand, wine bottle in the other, a wildlife documentary flickering in the background.

'So, how was the six-foot-two international entrepreneur?' he asked, sitting up to pour me a glass.

I snatched the glass and took a sip. 'Turns out, selling T-shirts in Thailand was the pinnacle of his entrepreneurial endeavours.'

He smirked. 'Well, there are around seventy million people in Thailand and they all need T-shirts...'

I unravelled my scarf and collapsed down next to him on the sofa. 'Yes, but I suspect they knew better than to buy them from a guy on a beach working to pay off his drug debt.' I took another sip. 'And he was about half my height. Like he wasn't going to be found out.'

Matthew laughed. 'Maybe he was planning to win you over with his personality?'

'Indeed. Now, was it the tales of childhood animal torture? Or perhaps the moment he almost stabbed the waitress with his fork? I just can't decide which indicator of mental instability it was that won me over.' I wriggled out of my coat and then threw it on the floor. 'No more internet dates. I'm done.'

He topped up my glass. I took another glug and then stared helplessly up at the ceiling.

'Where have all the good men gone?' I sighed.

He slapped his hand to his forehead. 'Ellie, please, no. Not Bonnie Tyler.'

I laughed. 'I don't need a hero, just a decent guy.'

'And what, pray tell, is a decent guy?'

'One who doesn't have nasal hair, a porn addiction or a personality disorder.'

He raised an eyebrow. 'No nasal hair? That would be a tricky one.'

'You know what I mean, tufts sprouting out of nostrils. Or one nostril even, that was weird.'

He laughed.

I turned to him. 'What? What's so funny?'

'Do you realise that every time you come back from a date, you've added something else to your tick list?'

He picked up a pen and notebook from the coffee table in front of him. 'Symmetrical nasal hair,' he said, pretending to write.

I heard a strange groan. A quick glance at the TV implied that either it came from me or a horny hippopotamus.

'But I have to discriminate somehow. I mean, look at my choices so far. It couldn't really get any worse, could it?'

'The male attracts the female by using his tail to spray her with faeces,' David Attenborough announced proudly.

Matthew raised his eyebrows at the disturbing image on the screen. 'See, it could always get worse,' he said, and flipped his legs up onto the sofa. 'So, where were we? Yes, your tick list. When we met, you must have been, what, fifteen?'

I nodded and took another gulp of wine.

'Well, back then, you said that the only thing you looked for in a boyfriend was a cute smile.'

I laughed.

'Then,' he continued, adopting a bizarre cover-girl-like pose, 'after a month or so, your requirements had progressed to a boy with a cute smile *and* a car.'

I could see where he was going with this.

'And now, let me think, what are your requirements now?' He moved his hand over his mouth in a dramatic shock gesture. Before I had a chance to respond, he continued. 'He has to be aged between thirty and thirty-five (preferably thirty-three), over six feet tall, good-looking, successful, independently wealthy, fit and sporty, confident (not arrogant), intelligent, interesting, well educated *and* have a great sense of humour.'

'Well—'

He put his hand up in a flamboyant stop sign. 'I haven't finished yet. In addition to that, he has to be sensitive yet masculine, affectionate and attentive, but not clingy. He must think you're the most beautiful woman he has ever seen, cherish you for eternity and have *manly* hands.'

I tried to speak, but Matthew rattled on.

'And now, since your recent bout of internet dating, you're discounting men for the most trivial of things.'

'Like what?'

'Tapered jeans.'

'Trivial?'

'Deck shoes.'

I screwed up my face.

'Triangular shoulders.'

'Bad.'

'Skinny calves.'

'Yuk.'

'Lumberjack shirt.'

'Seriously?'

'Flat bottom.'

'Eew.'

'Furry neck.'

'Nasty.'

'Whiny voice.'

'Worse.'

'Pointy fingernails. Head like a grape. Hyena laugh. Upside-down eyebrows. And what about the guy with the goatee?'

'He looked like a gnome.'

'He could have shaved it off.'

'That's not the point. He chose to grow it in the first place. I couldn't trust a man with such bad judgement.'

He sighed and lifted his arms above his head.

'Don't you think I deserve to meet a great guy?'

'Well,' he said, planting his feet on the carpet, as though reverting to his default sexuality, 'I think I deserve a room full of Playboy Bunnies and a permission slip from my girl-friend. But I'm not going to get that though, am I?'

I lunged forward and slapped him on the arm. 'You shouldn't want Playboy Bunnies. You're supposed to be in love.'

'Oh, yes, I forgot. You also believe that a man who loves you should never so much as imagine having sex with any-one else because that's disloyal.'

'I have good values.'

'You have idealistic values. There's a distinct difference.'

I sighed, feeling like a deflated balloon at the end of a party.

Matthew's expression softened as he shuffled up next to me and wiggled his fingers in my face. 'Are my hands manly?'

I inspected them and then laughed. 'You've had a mani-cure?'

He frowned. 'Well, what about your feet, Miss Perfect?' He glanced down at my size eights. 'They wouldn't look out of place on a seven-foot basketball player.'

I kicked off my shoes and wiggled my long toes.

'Seriously though, no one is perfect. You have to abandon your quest for the ideal man or you're only going to be disappointed. And even if you do find a man possessing *all* your requirements, who's to say he'd want to date a banana-footed fussy pants?'

I huffed and then folded my arms. 'So, instead, I'm supposed to settle? For someone I don't fancy or even like?'

He took a sip of wine and stared at me.

'Or should I have stayed with Robert, forgiven him for calling off our engagement? Because, yes, of course, every relationship has its ups and downs. And as for his webcam chats with naked Ukrainians, and his extensive porn collection, well, I should stop being such a fussy pants. I need to adjust my expectations.'

Matthew's expression suddenly morphed into his newsreader face. 'That's not what I'm saying.'

'So, what are you saying?'

He looked me in the eye. 'If Robert didn't look like your perfect man, if he wasn't a good-looking investment banker who drove a Ferrari, would you have fallen in love with him?'

I took another large gulp of wine, swished it around my mouth and considered what he had said.

'The issue is,' he went on as though having been chimed in by Big Ben, 'you made too many assumptions based on the fact that he looked perfect to you.'

I nodded, taking in the headline but wanting the full story.

'So, my wise guru, if my perfect man might not look like my perfect man, then how am I supposed to know who he is?'

'Well, firstly,' he said, raising a finger, his face fighting a smile. 'We've already established that there are no perfect men. That's error number one in your pursuit of love. You really must pay attention.'

I rolled my eyes. 'Okay, then. I stand corrected. As you are the fount of all knowledge on this matter, are you going to find Mr Not-so-perfect-but-right for me?'

He laughed. 'What, like your personal matchmaker?'

I nodded. 'You know me. You know what I'm looking for. So go find him. I'll pay you in wine,' I said, before refilling his glass.

Matthew stared at me for a moment, then pulled his glasses down to the end of his nose and picked up the notepad and pen from the coffee table.

'Right, young lady,' he said, adopting a matronly voice. 'You say you want to meet a wealthy man. Could you explain why this is so important to you?'

I giggled. 'So I can live in a big house and have a nice lifestyle, without having to worry about money.'

The cringe crept in as soon as I had said it.

'Well, madam,' he began, peering over his glasses, 'in this day and age, a lady can go out and achieve such things without the aid of a man. So, you're just being a lazybones. I'm going to cross that one off your list.'

'Er,' I said, trying to interrupt but he—or she—was in full flow.

'And what's all this about appearance? You say you want a handsome man. Don't we all, dear?' he said as he hoisted up his imaginary bosoms. 'But those good-looking ones are often a bit full of themselves and rather high maintenance, don't you think? I'll cross that off too.'

In quick succession Matthew's alter ego went on to annihilate every characteristic on my tick list. When he began to question whether it was essential that my soulmate be a *man*, I downed the last of the wine and took myself off to bed.

Later that night, while I was trying to sleep, images flashed through my mind—goatees, tapered jeans, naked Ukrainians, hairy nostrils—and I began to wonder if Matthew was right.

If I *had* been deluding myself by expecting the perfect man to give me the perfect life, and to behave perfectly at all times, then what was I supposed to do instead? I couldn't talk myself into fancying someone, and besides, I knew no matter how rational the argument, I'd rather remain single than settle for someone who smelled of pickled onions.

I pulled the duvet over my head and wondered if I really had believed that love would come packaged as a six-foot-three investment banker. Perhaps it wasn't as simple as having not yet found the right man. Maybe it was me? Maybe my judgement was off.

Throughout the night, the questions kept coming. I lay there, tossing and turning. And thinking.

I wanted answers. I needed answers.

Just before dawn, a shimmering light suddenly filled the room. It could have been a street lamp, either that, or Eros had been sent to summon me. I sat up in bed and rubbed my eyes. It was then that the idea came to me, flitting through my mind at first, skittish like a butterfly, but then it settled and I couldn't shake it. When my focus eventually adjusted to the bright white light which was pouring through the window, I realised that the path to my destiny had been lit up like a runway.

It was up to me to find the answers. Not only for myself but for others too.

I would begin by reclaiming Cupid's bow from soulless software. Then, using Matthew's questionnaire as a template, I would lead an army of matchmakers across the land. Noisy eating and tapered jeans would be banished for ever and unconditional love, shared values and mutual respect would glisten in our wake. I smiled and gazed up at the ceiling. No longer would I be confined to a lab, staring at a titration beaker, pondering the most cost-effective way to synthesise fertiliser, instead my days would be spent nurturing budding romances from under a pile of thank you notes, and my nights sleeping soundly, content in the knowledge that I had helped unite all the lonely hearts of the world.

All I would have to do is quit my job at ChemPlant, figure out how to survive on a maxed-out overdraft, then set about discovering the formula for love.

I'm going to be a matchmaker, I decided, throwing off the duvet, *I'll start today*.

And so, I did.

Chapter 2

'WHAT ABOUT THEM? They're cute,' I said, pointing to a group of men by the bar.

'I don't think so,' Cordelia replied with a dismissive flick of her Jennifer Lawrence hair. 'Your first clients have to be *super* eligible.'

With her sleek frame encased in a Vivienne Westwood pinstriped dress and her long legs elongated further with red Dior stilettos, she looked the image of timeless elegance. I couldn't help but feel inferior. My ensemble wasn't dissimilar, albeit a high street version on a high street body, but for me, it didn't come so easily. With a smudge of Benetint and a light dusting of powder, Cordelia personified Hollywood glamour. However, my less-impressive result required hours of prep, more foil than a Christmas turkey, and a paranoid avoidance of neon lighting. People who loved me, or those who saw me in candlelight said I looked a bit like Holly Willoughby. The rest said Beverley Callard.

Cordelia slipped her arm through mine and led me away

from the men—who she had culled for 'drinking pints in a champagne bar'—then marched us on to a balcony which afforded a panoramic view of the bar.

'No. No. And no,' she said, scanning the crowd and dismissing everyone in sight. 'Where have all the hot men gone?'

I laughed. 'That's what I've been asking for the past two years.'

'They must be hiding out somewhere,' she said, craning her neck around a gilt pillar. 'This is supposed to be the champagne bar of the moment according to the *FT*.'

I checked my watch: it was six o'clock on a Thursday evening. We were in the heart of the financial district and the bar was jammed, teeming with enough men to send the Weather Girls into cardiac arrest, but, according to Cordelia, no one was good enough.

'They don't have to be outrageously good-looking, do they?' I asked, feeling far less discriminatory since my dressing down from Matthew. 'All I need are normal people who are single.'

She tossed a sheet of golden hair behind her shoulders. 'You want to avoid the stigma that other agencies have, don't you?'

I nodded.

'Well, the only way to do that is to have the uber-eligible as your first members. It's a bit like a celebrity endorsement. You know, if they're doing it, then it must be good.'

'But no one really believes that Cheryl Cole dyes her own hair over a sink at home? Why would they believe that a gorgeous man has trouble finding love?'

'Because he does. Everyone does. That's the reason you have decided to become a matchmaker, is it not?' Her voice was sympathetic, but the pinched expression betrayed her impatience.

I nodded again, looking around the bar at the seemingly contented patrons. What if it was just me? What if no one wanted or even needed my help?

'Ah, here we go,' she said, gesturing towards two men who had just swaggered through the doorway. 'That's more like it.'

Both well over six feet tall with dark hair, and wearing Savile Row suits, they sauntered in like they'd stepped off the cover of *GQ* magazine. One of them glanced my way and flashed a smile. I took a deep breath, sucked in my tummy and weaved my way through the crowd towards him.

'Well, hello,' he said, when I'd reached him.

'Well, hello yourself,' I replied, attempting a Cordelia-style hair flick which resulted in several drinks being spilled behind me. He laughed: a soft, sexy, George Clooney drawl, not the high-pitched Road Runner warble that appeared to be coming from my mouth.

'So, what brings a gorgeous girl like you to a place like this?'

Back straight, tummy miraculously still in, I looked him in the eye and declared my purpose. 'I'm headhunting for eligible men.'

He raised one eyebrow, and his friend, who was standing beside him, leant in closer.

'You're what?' the friend asked, head cocked like a befuddled puppy.

'I represent an exclusive dating agency,' I explained, easing into character, 'and I'm looking for men good enough to date our female clients.' Technically, I decided, that wasn't a lie.

They both laughed, but were clearly intrigued.

'This, I absolutely *have* to hear,' George Clooney drawl said. 'Have a drink with us. If your female clients are anything like you then I could be persuaded.' He waved a fifty at the barman. 'I'm Mike, by the way, and this is Stephen.' He nodded vaguely in his friend's direction.

'Ellie,' I replied.

He slipped his arm round my waist and kissed me on the cheek. When Stephen stepped in to repeat the process, I wondered why I hadn't considered this career change years ago.

'So, you headhunters, do you hunt alone? Or in packs?' Mike asked, handing me a glass of champagne.

'In pairs,' I answered, glancing over my shoulder, wondering where Cordelia had gone. 'I'm here with my friend.' I stood on tiptoes to look above the heads. 'Cordelia. Now where is she? Ah, over there.'

I pointed her out. She was immersed in conversation with a tall olive-skinned girl who was blessed with the rare combination of endless limbs, tiny bottom and big boobs. As if to add further insult to the rest of the female population, she had also been awarded a super bonus prize of waist-length glossy brown hair.

'So, you do the boys and she does the girls?' Mike asked with a wink.

'No, we do both,' I replied, waving Cordelia over.

Mike raised his eyebrows. 'You do girls *and* boys? Excellent.'

He smirked and then topped up my champagne.

Moments later, Cordelia returned and introduced her new

acquaintance, Megan, whose bee-stung lips and emerald-green eyes now made the rest of her attributes seem decidedly average. Mike nudged me and then laughed. Stephen was transfixed, as if the befuddled puppy had encountered his first T-bone steak.

'We're not supposed to pair them off before they sign up,' Cordelia said, pulling me away from Mike. 'Or spend the entire night talking to one guy,' she whispered in my ear.

Mike reached for the champagne bottle. Just as he went to top up my glass again, Cordelia placed her hand over the top.

'We can't stay,' she said, before handing me my coat.

Mike's brow creased, his expression revealing something more than simply a dent to his ego. Although he'd already made it clear that he would never need to use a dating service, he was quick to add that he'd be happy to 'help me out' if I couldn't find any men for my female clients.

'Only if you get desperate though,' he added, pressing his business card into my hand.

I nodded and smiled, before hurrying after Cordelia.

'Right, be completely honest with me,' Cordelia said as she marched into the night. 'Are you really doing this dating thing for the good of the people? Or...' She let the door swing shut in my face.

I heaved it back open, with the aid of a slow-to-respond doorman and then glared at her. 'Or what?' I asked.

'Or,' she began, marching along the pavement, 'are you looking for a man for yourself?'

I scrunched up my nose. It was a valid question, and one that I wasn't quite sure I had an answer to.

'I want to help people,' I said, tottering behind her.

'Since when?' she asked, turning to face me and throwing up her hands. 'You know I love you to bits. You're my best friend.' Her expression softened. 'It's obvious you have a good heart: you donate to charities, you adore animals, you help old ladies, you even smile at ugly babies. But people—' she looked around as though searching for an example '—the unimpaired, adult kind—' she pointed vaguely at the pedestrians around us '—you've never really had much time for them.'

I frowned, wondering what had prompted such dramatics.

'Come on. They irritate you. With their eating in public, dithering on pavements, wearing bad clothes and saying inane things. People get on your nerves. You spent the past five years hiding from them in a lab. So why now, suddenly, do you want to help them?'

I squinted across the street at a man grappling with a cumbersome kebab, and I wondered if she was right.

'And then in the bar,' she said, pointing back as if to remind me of its location, 'with that guy. You had that smitten look you get.'

'Oh, come on,' I said. 'It's not as though I can prevent my most base level desires from reacting to a stimulus. Pupils, cease dilation, for now I am a matchmaker, born of higher purpose.' Then I glared at her shoes. 'And besides, it's not like you haven't exploited the perks of your job at Dior, is it?'

She looked down and smiled. 'Fair point,' she said, admiring her red Mary Janes as if for the first time. Then she looked up and her eyes met mine. 'I just want to make sure you're doing this for the right reasons.'

I watched Kebab Man, now heading towards us with iceberg lettuce stuck to his chin, and I mustered a smile.

'I'll make a good altruist,' I said, before leaning into the road to hail a passing taxi. Next stop, the Royal Exchange.

When we arrived at the eminent sixteenth-century building, Cordelia pointed up at the Duke of Wellington statue, in the manner of a tour guide. 'He defeated Napoleon, was Prime Minister twice and still managed a twenty-five-year marriage,' she said.

'Well, he deserves a statue, then,' I said, striding up the stone steps.

'Although he was shagging around the entire time,' she added with a smirk. 'Dirty bugger.'

I tutted and shot a disapproving look back at the statue, wondering if his wife had regretted the choice she'd made: assuming love would come packaged as a duke on a stallion.

Once inside the courtyard, we made our way past Bulgari and Boodles and upstairs to the lounge bar. Immediately I felt as though I should be negotiating the terms of a FTSE 100 company buyout, rather than contemplating the least embarrassing way to approach potentially single strangers. Cordelia and I perched on some upholstered bar stools and glanced at the wine list, which according to the barman comprised those made exclusively from ancient vines. Once he'd wandered off with my credit card, I decided that if I was to be mingling with city workers, I should at least have the vaguest comprehension of what a FTSE 100 company was. Cordelia, who had once dated a trader, offered me a crash course on city finance.

When she'd concluded with a dubious interpretation of the stock market, I peered around the room to look for potential clients. Straight away three men approached the bar. They stood right next to us. I hoped they hadn't mistaken us for call girls.

The oldest one, who had a bit of a paunch, purposely bumped Cordelia's knee.

'Oh, I'm *so* sorry,' he said with a lecherous smile. 'Now, the least I can do is to buy you a drink to make up for my clumsiness?'

'I already have one, thanks,' she replied, and swivelled her bar stool away from him.

Undeterred, he walked around the other side and wedged his paunch between us, and then leant in towards Cordelia.

'How else could I apologise? Dinner?' A dribble of saliva hung off his bottom lip.

'No, thanks,' she said, swivelling her bar stool back the other way.

He grabbed the seat and spun her back towards him. 'Diamonds? There's a jeweller's downstairs. Pick anything you'd like.'

'I'm fine. Thank you,' she said, peeling his hands off her chair, an action which only seemed to embolden him further.

A few minutes later, following what amounted to a clockwise–anticlockwise bar stool spin-off, he thrust his leg through the foot stand to anchor it and deposited a sloppy kiss, complete with blob of saliva, onto her hand.

'I'm Timothy,' he said, platinum wedding ring shining for all to see.

'Cordelia,' she replied, wiping her hand on a napkin, 'and this is my friend Ellie.' She waved him on to me as though he were an annoying fly. 'She's a matchma—'

'Gorgeous,' he said, looking me up and down, 'but obvious. You're much more interesting.' He leant back towards her.

I laughed, relieved to have escaped the slimy hand kiss.

Although after her blatant attempt to offload him onto me, I was struggling to decide whether she deserved rescuing. Just as I was weighing it up, one of his friends stepped forward.

'Sorry about him,' he said in a gentle American accent, his smile confirming teeth too perfect to be British. 'I'm Nate.'

He offered me his hand. I took it, reciprocating the firm grip.

'And this is Josh.' His other friend moved forward with his hand out too. I was mildly perturbed by the level of hand-shaking involved but quickly realised it was an excellent opportunity to check for wedding rings. These two were in the clear. I looked more closely at their all-American faces, the sort that seemed instantly familiar. Did I know them from somewhere? They didn't seem to recognise me, so I went on to explain my plans to reintroduce the world to deep and meaningful love. Nate looked fascinated, but Josh looked terrified, as though implementation of my business model necessitated the distribution of nuclear warheads to the Middle East.

'How will you match people?' he asked, brow furrowed.

I looked around the bar, hoping Eros's messenger might appear with a comprehensive matchmaking strategy inked onto a scroll.

'Various methods,' I said eventually and with surprising conviction.

'And your marketing strategy consists entirely of tapping people on the shoulder and asking if they're single?' Josh asked, studying my business card.

I nodded, realising how implausible it sounded out loud.

'But how will you discriminate?' Nate asked, brow furrowing further.

I glanced over at Timothy, who was now attempting to mount Cordelia on the bar stool and we all laughed.

By now, Cordelia's handbag was no longer functioning as a makeshift shield and her facial expression had shifted from disgust to one resembling genuine fear. My laughter quickly subsided as I watched his stubby fingers pawing at her thigh.

I prodded his upper arm. 'Excuse me, Timothy, isn't it?' I said.

He looked startled as though I had interrupted him mid-copulation.

I glared at him. 'You're obviously an intelligent man.'

He smirked.

My anger welled. 'So I'm surprised you have failed to pick up on any of the glaringly obvious signs that my friend here would rather lick the inside of a Delhi toilet bowl than remain in your company for a second longer.'

He leant back against the bar and thrust out his gut. 'She seems to be enjoying herself—'

I stared at his belly, trying not to imagine him naked. 'Enjoying herself?'

He nodded, still squeezing her thigh.

I knocked his hand away from her leg.

'Enjoying what exactly?' I continued, hands on hips. 'A middle-aged, married man trying to bribe her to have sex with him? Yes, that must be it. I mean, what girl wouldn't be tempted by the exciting prospect of all the glittering diamonds she could acquire simply by straddling your flabby paunch and pretending your piddly cocktail sausage was a donkey schlong?'

Timothy's eyes widened.

'And what about your wife?' I continued, gesturing to his wedding ring. 'Does she know you're sleazing around bars groping any body part you can get your doughy little digits on? Or more likely she's relieved that she doesn't have to have sex with you any more. Grateful for the fact that you can't get it up, unless you're with a girl who's half your age and half your weight?'

I paused for breath, keen to continue, when suddenly I felt Cordelia's grip on my arm. She led me towards the staircase, then tossed my coat at me.

'A simple goodbye would have sufficed,' she said.

I glanced back. Josh was giggling and Nate gave me a thumbs-up.

I shook my head. 'Men like him think a restraining order is playing hard to get.'

She laughed. 'You can't be a matchmaker if you're going to shout at everyone who isn't behaving how you'd like.'

'Yes I can, when it's *my* business.'

She laughed. 'Dictator dating. Love it.'

I huffed, wondering if it was feasible to restrict my services to those I felt morally deserving. 'But those other two, they seemed nice—looked so familiar.'

She paused on the step below me, and looked up. 'You're having a laugh, aren't you?'

'Or is it that they all look the same, those American preppy types?'

'You're seriously telling me you don't know who they are?' she said, striding ahead in her structurally engineered Diors.

I followed her down the stairs as speedily as my Primark peep-toes would allow. 'What do you mean? Who are they?'

She shook her head. 'You'll have to figure it out.'

'Fine,' I said, folding my arms, which was a brave move considering my questionable stability.

She smirked, clearly entertained by my wobbly sulk. 'So where to next?'

'The target was fifty men and women by the end of the night.'

'Right,' she said and glanced at her watch. 'Let's head to Apt.'

A three-tiered bar in Mansion House, Apt was where all the office workers within a half-mile radius ended up for 'one more drink'. After which, the original plan was generally abandoned in favour of an alternative, which most likely involved sambuca shots, a few grams of cocaine, terrible dancing and inappropriate liaisons with colleagues.

'But we'll have to go right now though,' Cordelia said, 'before they're too wasted to bother with.'

We flagged a cab. Although we were within easy walking distance, Cordelia insisted Dior heels were not made for walking, especially in the city, where she was convinced cobbles and cobblers were in a conspiratorial partnership.

When we arrived at Apt, there was a queue around the block and a one-in-one-out entrance restriction. Having decided that it was imperative, in the name of love, that I find a way to push in, I made a beeline for a group of men who were swaying precariously at the front of the queue. Thrusting my shoulders back, I adopted my most convincing smile and paired it with a less clumsily executed Cordelia hair flick.

'Like your style,' said the most sober one, after I'd explained how, by allowing two girls to push in, he was actually increasing his chances of entry. Rugged and stocky, and with a thick Irish accent, he seemed decent enough, although obviously unaware that the door policy was in no way as discerning as I had implied.

'These girls with you?' the towering doorman asked him.

He slid his arm around my waist.

'She's my fiancée,' he said, his hand inching down as we walked in, clearly aiming for a bottom grope. When I blocked its path and placed it back on my waist, he turned to me and frowned.

'A fair exchange, do you think?' he said. 'You get the front entrance, and I get the back entrance!'

The entire group erupted in a simultaneous belly laugh. I glared at him, opened my mouth to say something and then immediately closed it again after thinking better of it. His point was valid. Accepting diamonds for sex was much further along the spectrum, but hair-flicking for door entry was most definitely in the same category.

Leaving them still sniggering and inwardly apologising to my better self, I followed Cordelia through to the main bar area, down the staircase and into the darkness of the basement.

Two hours later, as shirts were being shed and coked-up city workers danced their interpretation of Michael Jackson's 'Thriller', Cordelia and I retreated up the stairs and out of the bar.

'That's the hard part over with,' she said, handing me a stack of business cards.

The beat of the music faded into the distance and the faces of all the people we'd met that night flashed through my mind. I gripped the cards tighter, wondering if, when it came to it, they would trust me enough to put their hearts in my hands.

I was hoping Matthew would still be up when I arrived home, but the flat was silent apart from gentle 'beer' snores coming from his room. He only ever snored after he'd been drinking beer, never wine or spirits. I'd always thought that was odd. I flopped down onto the sofa in the lounge, realising that it was the small intimacies in a relationship that gave it meaning.

Just as I was drifting off to the hypnotic rhythm of Matthew's snores, something on the coffee table caught my eye. It was the property magazine that thudded through our letter box every month. Usually I binned them straight away, but, for some reason, I felt inclined to pick it up. There was something familiar about the house on the cover.

Right away, I sat up. My stomach churned as I stared at the wisteria-cloaked walls and beautiful bay windows. The gravel driveway. The willow tree in the front garden. I flicked through the pages to find a photo of a slick-haired estate agent wearing an oversized tie and a capital growth smile. I had never met the man, but I knew I hated him. According to the quote above his portrait, he was delighted to present to the market…my house. Or rather, the house Robert and I were once planning to buy. I sank back down into the sofa and let the publication fall onto my chest. Suddenly, as though the street lights were on a dimmer switch, the room darkened. I felt a heavy weight bearing down on me. I knocked the magazine onto the floor. It made a loud bang and Matthew's snores momentarily paused. I closed my eyes tightly, willing him to wake up, but he didn't. When his snores resumed, I sank my head into my hands and let out a deep sigh. It was the first time since I'd packed up my car and wheel-spun out of Robert's life that I'd felt truly alone.

Until now, I thought I'd been riding the wave of resilience. As it turns out, drinking every night and suppressing three years of memories hadn't been an ingenious way to avoid the pain. Instead it had only delayed it. I ran into my room and pulled out a box from my wardrobe. Until now, I'd been too scared to open it. I tipped it up and the photos spilled onto my bedroom carpet. I'd heard people say that when you face the enemy, the fear is gone. I never would have believed them until I stared at my old life. The life I'd always wanted, the life I'd almost lived, scattered around me: Robert and I snorkelling on the Barrier Reef, wine tasting in South Africa, skiing in Verbier, laughing and drinking as though our happiness would never end. A tear trickled down my cheek, then another and then, finally, the grief came, like a tsunami crashing through a flood barrier. This time I knew I couldn't fight it. I threw myself onto the bed, burrowed my face into a pillow and sobbed. My chest heaved as my mind flashed through the scenes that led to our break-up. The feigned look of innocence when I'd uncovered his online indiscretions. The seemingly limitless adult chat sites he'd registered with. Trawling through his messages to other girls. The photos on his phone. He'd told me he would love me for ever. Did he even know what love was?

When there were no tears left, I looked up, expectantly. But nothing had changed. There had been no apocalypse. The world was still turning, Matthew was still snoring. I wiped the remaining tears from my cheeks and then picked up a photo: one a waiter had taken of us tucking in to a candlelit dinner on a beach in Mexico. I looked closer. I would have said this was one of the happiest moments of my life. But looking at it now, through puffy, yet sharper eyes, my smile seemed false, as though instead of sharing a precious moment with the man I loved, I were auditioning for a low budget toothpaste ad. And Robert's expression looked creepy, as though he were biding his time before he could nip off for a webcam chat with a naked Ukrainian.

At the time I'd felt beautiful, like a goddess. And Robert had been my god. Now, my dimpled cellulite and giant nose seemed to jump out at me and Robert looked like a cross between a Tory MP and a frog. I stared at the image some more, wondering if love could ever be real, or if instead it were something we craved so deeply that somehow we found a way to construct it in our minds.

Although I knew I was a long way from finding answers, that night, after I'd packed away the photos, I slept more soundly than I had done in months.

Chapter 3

BARRISTERS, ADVOCATES, SOLICITORS, heads of PR, heads of HR, heads of marketing, marketing consultants, business consultants, business analysts, risk analysts, CTOs, CEOs, CFOs, PAs, EAs. Despite the grown-up titles, the business cards I'd laid out on my coffee table seemed to stare up at me with the expectancy of a classroom of school children.

I picked up my phone and panic-called Cordelia.

'How am I qualified to help them when I can't even help myself?' I asked.

'Seriously? I haven't even had my morning latte and you're throwing that conundrum at me?'

'I don't know what to do. I don't know where to start. I don't—'

She interrupted me with a sharp sigh. 'Take a deep breath and calm down.'

I breathed in obediently.

'Now, what exactly are you worried about?'

'How am I supposed to match them? Where do I start?

Should I be using psychological profiling? Astrology? *Cosmopolitan's* latest compatibility quiz?'

'Or what? Adding up the letters in his name and hers like we did at school?' She laughed. 'Come on, we all know none of that rubbish works.'

I scratched my head. 'Well, according to the most recent studies, psychological profiles are good indicators of compatibility.'

'According to whom? Those who commissioned them, I assume. Look, I think you're overcomplicating things. No need to reinvent the wheel. Why not stick with what's worked for centuries?'

'Which is what exactly?' I asked.

'I don't know, rich men and pretty girls. That seems successful.'

I laughed. 'Yeah, for the divorce lawyers.'

'You have to give people what they want.'

I sighed. 'What if what they want isn't good for them?'

'It rarely is.'

'And what about the men who aren't rich or the girls who aren't so pretty?'

She laughed. 'Leave that to Darwinism.'

I huffed. 'That theory suits you.'

'It suits mankind,' she replied. 'Anyway, I've got to go now. Some of us have proper jobs. But remember you're selling a dream, not reality.'

Following a gentle reminder that the Dior shoe-buying department would never lead the world to peace, I hung up the phone and considered what she had said. If true love was a dream, then what was reality? Disillusioned brides and philandering grooms? Or if Cordelia was right and natural selection would favour the richest men and the prettiest girls, then what would happen to the rest of us? Would we fade to extinction? Nature, it appeared, was already trying to phase out asymmetrical nasal hair.

I knew my doubts shouldn't dissuade me from taking action so I went on to email everyone whose card I'd collected with a light-hearted, 'meet me for a drink, no obligation' kind of invite. Matthew emerged from his room rubbing his eyes, hair upright on his head like he'd slept in a high voltage chamber.

'What is that?' he asked, looking down at the cards on the table. 'Some kind of corporate *snap*? Is this what you've been doing all night?'

I peeled myself off the sofa. 'Cuppa?'

He nodded and picked up a card.

When I walked into the kitchen, the morning rays sliced through the blind, as though desperate to shed some light on the situation.

'Don't match Teresa with Patrick Greene,' he shouted after me.

I switched on the kettle wondering what he was on about.

'Teresa Greene. Trees are green,' he explained when I returned.

I rolled my eyes. 'I hope to find them more than just a socially acceptable name,' I said. I snatched the card from his hand and replaced it with his Dennis the Menace mug. I looked at Dennis then back at Matthew, then back at Dennis. Matthew patted down his hair, but as soon as he removed his hand, it sprang back up.

'So what happens next?' he asked.

'They meet me for a drink and a chat about what they're looking for. Then I match them.'

'And then?'

'Everyone lives happily ever after.'

He nodded his head from side to side as though he were weighing up his left and right brain. 'How are you going to match them?'

'They tell me what they want and I give it to them.'

He scrunched up his nose. 'But most of us don't actually know what we want. We just think we do.'

I sighed. 'I'm not in the mood for one of your Marxist the-media-constructs-our-thoughts lectures.'

He continued. 'Attraction is an entirely biochemical re-action set off by a combination of characteristics to which our genetic programming and social conditioning respond.'

'And what's wrong with that?'

'It's flawed. Look at the divorce rate.'

'We don't marry everyone we fancy.'

'Thankfully.'

I glared at him. 'There's more to love than attraction. We aren't robots driven by neurotransmitters and hormones. We have something called free will. We can think independently from our physical drives and conditioning.'

His full-body laugh caused him to spill tea all over the table. It quickly seeped onto the business cards. I dabbed them with my sleeve but, already, the corners had started to curl.

After Matthew had left for work, I looked back down at the cards and reshuffled them. Then I gazed out of the window at the sky, hoping to be the recipient of some kind of divine inspiration. But, instead, a bird dropping landed on the pane. I watched the greyish gloop slide down the glass, undigested berries lagging behind and I wondered if I too might have bitten off more than I could chew.

That evening, Cordelia had refused to come headhunting for clients again, complaining that her feet hurt, so I'd bribed my other friend Kat, to come instead. We'd settled the negotiation at five rose petal Martinis and a taxi ride home.

'If we sieve through the hookers and the sugar daddies, I'm sure we'll find some decent people here tonight,' Kat observed, scanning the bar. We were at Zuma in Knightsbridge, a favourite with the 'chilled-out jet-set crowd', according to *Harper's* magazine.

I took in the chic minimalist interior and smoothed down my dress, trying to act as though it had been thrown on nonchalantly, rather than the result of three hours of unsatisfactory pontification. Kat leant over the glass bar, her red Gucci dress nipped in at the waist and plunging at the neckline. Three barmen leapt towards her, their attention darting between her Bambi-brown eyes and her perfectly plumped cleavage.

'We need some cocktails,' she declared, pushing her sleek dark bob behind her ears.

Following a flamboyant display of glass juggling, and some kind of cocktail shaker courtship dance, eventually we were presented with two rose petal Martinis. The baby-faced barman grinned victoriously. He leant over the bar and kissed Kat on the lips.

I pulled her back. 'Kat.'

'What?' she asked, grinning.

I shook my head. 'I'd prefer us to focus on the men who've actually gone through puberty.'

She threw a glance over her shoulder and then strode towards a table of businessmen who appeared to be engaged in a serious takeover-bid-type conversation. When she reached the table, her presence diverted their concentration like a resistor in a circuit. Once she'd delivered her opening line, they all laughed and the best-looking one pulled up a chair for her to join them.

Watching from the bar, and sipping my Martini, I wondered where Kat's self-assurance came from. Was it lots of cuddles as a child? Or perhaps, as once discussed during an especially interesting episode of *Dr Phil*, it was a pseudo-esteem masking a deeper insecurity and a need for external validation. Maybe it was simply that big boobs and a pretty face were so well received that the usual fears of rejection and public humiliation weren't there.

Dragging myself away from my appallingly amateur psychoanalysis, I decided that confidence was something I would have to fake, at least until I'd figured out how to source it naturally. I took a gulp of the Martini and then sidestepped towards a group of girls.

They had long legs, dark hair and tanned skin and looked as though they were the result of some kind of accelerated breeding programme between Megan and Stephen whom I'd met the night before. I smiled at the one nearest to me. She sucked on a pink straw protruding from a fussy cocktail and eyed me up suspiciously.

'Are you a journalist?' she asked between sucks.

'No.' I laughed. 'What makes you think that?'

'You look like one.'

I glanced down at my black dress and then back at her. Once I'd worked my way up the seemingly endless legs protruding from tiny leather hot pants, my eyes lingered on her chest, braless and buoyant under a cream silk camisole.

She glared at me. 'What do you want?'

Her features, enhanced to cartoonish proportions, reminded me of a creature from *Avatar*.

'I'm headhunting,' I said.

The rest of the girls' necks swivelled towards me. 'You're a model scout?' one of them asked.

I shook my head.

'Party promoter?'

I shook my head again, suspecting the truth might be a tremendous disappointment. 'I'm looking for single girls who want to meet eligible men.'

When I'd explained my plans to unite lonely hearts across the globe, the girl next to me flicked a mane of hair extensions over her shoulder.

'We only date footballers,' she said.

I stepped back. I'd read about girls like her in gossip magazines. There might have been one on *Dr Phil* too. I was intrigued.

'Why?' I asked.

She stared at me in disbelief, as though I'd just told her I'd never watched *Big Brother*.

'Der, because they earn £150k per week and I'm on £7.99 an hour.'

She went on to proudly list the benefits of her past encounters with Premier League players, which included but was by no means exclusive to: designer clothing, cosmetic surgery, jewellery allowance, provision of luxury accommodation, sports car, private-clinic abortions and a six-figure pay-off at the end. It sounded more like a job than a relationship. I'd also noted that out of the men she'd named, most were married.

'Why do you date the married ones?' I asked, less to highlight the moral issue, which I suspected wasn't a concern, but more to question the real purpose.

She laughed. 'It's not like we expect them to leave their wives.'

'Well what's the point, then?'

'Once you're in with the footballers, sometimes they pass you on to their teammates, the ones who aren't married.'

'They're like matchmakers too,' the only blonde in the group chipped in with a beaming smile.

'Or pimps?' I suggested.

'Hey!' Kat interrupted as she bounded up to me, and began theatrically fanning herself with a handful of business cards. 'Check these out.'

She thrust them in my hand and then opened her bag to reveal dozens more.

'Am I done now?' she asked, glancing over her shoulder. I followed her gaze and saw the underage barman grinning widely, as though his expression had been fixed since Kat's kiss. 'His shift finishes soon. Can I?'

'Okay. Go on then,' I said, checking my watch. 'I suppose I could do with an early night.'

The blonde girl looked at me, then back at the other girls and then back at me. 'Want to come with us?' she asked and the rest of the group nodded vaguely.

Once we were in the taxi, the girl in the hot pants, who I now knew was named Carmen, explained more about the party.

'You only get invited if you're in with the promoters,' she said, checking her make-up in a compact mirror.

'And they only invite girls from agencies,' another girl added.

'What agencies?' I asked.

'You know, for glamour models, promo girls, dancers,' Carmen said.

The blonde girl, who I would later learn was Kerri, smiled. 'They want pretty bubbly girls there.'

'Bubbly?' I asked.

'You know: fun, social.'

I rolled my eyes. 'I don't suppose they invite the wives or girlfriends?'

They laughed.

'So,' I said, 'if you win the hand of a Premier League prince, would you let him come to these parties?'

Suddenly their faces contorted as though I'd suggested one of them don a boiler suit.

When we arrived, I noticed there were no men in the queue, which snaked for a mile around the block, but the girls were huddled together in the line, shivering in the skimpy clothing that was required to gain entry. Boobs were hoisted up, squeezed together or spilling out. Skirts were sprayed on, tops were slashed at the sternum, and legs were elongated with six-inch heels. Every attribute was exploited to secure its maximum market value. Tonight, it was time to cash in their assets.

The men, it was explained to me, were safety tucked up inside, readily paying £500 for a £10 bottle of vodka. I was soon to learn that the mark-up could be justified when the beverage was delivered with a sparkler and a gaggle of nubile girls.

Despite the sleek modern interior, each step down the staircase was like taking a step back in time. Men sat wide-legged at tables, downing drinks, and pulling girls onto their laps as though patrons of a medieval whorehouse. Girls wiggled past the VIP area, until the chosen ones were summoned to straddle their prince's lap.

With rock-hard nipples poking through her camisole,

Carmen was immediately ushered into the VIP area. She blamed the forty-minute queue in ice-cold air, but her friends claimed she'd deliberately tweaked them before catching a footballer's eye.

'It's not fair,' one of them whined. 'My tits are better than hers.'

'And she copied my hair colour,' another one, who I think was called Chastity, said. She went on to explain that the player in question was a reserve they were all targeting. After reading a recent interview, in which he stated he preferred brunettes, she had dyed her hair. The others, except Kerri, had copied. 'Lucky cow,' she added as she watched him pull Carmen onto his lap.

I waved my hand in front of her face. 'Earth to twenty-first-century woman.'

She looked at me and frowned. 'What?'

'Don't you want more than that?'

She looked back at Carmen and the footballer and then laughed. 'More than a rich husband and the perfect life, what more is there?'

'Oh, let me think.' I scratched my head. 'How about independence? Self-respect? To be treated as a human being rather than a collection of body parts?'

She scrunched up her face.

'You know you're not going to look like that for ever, don't you? What are you going to do then? When the VIPs don't want you any more?'

She stepped back and looked at me as though I were one of those crazy people you sidestepped on the street, in case they might bop you over the head or throw you in front of a car or something.

'You're just jealous,' she said, before pulling up her skirt to reveal another inch of tanned thigh.

The loud music thumped through my head and, for a moment, I wondered if she might be right. But when she started jiggling her boobs at a group of men walking past, I turned around, did my best to block out the noise around me, then fought my way back through the crowd.

At the coat check, where the stern-faced assistant was doing a terrible job of pretending to look for my coat, I felt a tap on my shoulder. I turned around to see Kerri, her face framed with soft blonde curls. Under a spotlight, I could see beyond the false eyelashes and thick eyeliner and into her eyes.

'I want more,' she whispered, before handing me her number scribbled on a beer mat.

When I arrived home, I found Matthew, clearly drunk, staggering around the communal hallway, holding a pizza box in the air.

'A gift for you,' he said, laying it down at my feet, 'in exchange for entrance to our humble abode.'

'Forgot your keys again?' I asked, fumbling in my bag for mine.

He nodded.

I opened the door and he lurched forward and, in what looked like one move, landed on the sofa, pizza box still horizontal.

'So how did the matchmunting, I mean, headhating...' He stuffed some pizza into his mouth. 'How did all that go?'

I sighed and slumped on the sofa. 'Vacuous girls and sleazy men.'

He swallowed and wiped his face with his sleeve. 'That's how the clubs make money. Hot chicks and rich dicks.'

'Yeah, I know, but I didn't think I'd have to sell the concept of love, I thought that was a given.'

He offered me some pizza. 'You know the magic wears off after midnight, don't you?'

'Party pooper,' I said, taking the least offensive-looking slice.

A moment later, he sat up, his hair almost springing to attention and pointed his finger in the air.

'That's it. That's what you need to do,' he said.

'What, poop at parties?'

He laughed. 'No, not the poop, just the party.'

I looked down at the cheap meat and greasy cheese that I was about to consume and threw it back into the box, realising that Matthew was right. If I didn't like what was on offer, then it was up to me to provide an alternative.

Chapter 4

THERE WAS A chill in the evening air but I felt hot and dizzy. I opened my coat as I strode alongside the Thames and let the icy breeze whip around my body. With each stride, my temperature dropped.

Having stood side by side for over a century, the giant Edwardian town houses seemed to peer down at me with intrigue. They had undoubtedly witnessed many a young girl hoping to change the world, but tonight, as the commuters bulldozed past me, it was as though they were nudging each other and placing a bet on how long I would last. Lifting my chin up, I reminded myself of the findings from my market research: forty per cent of London's population was single. I continued ahead, the wrought-iron street lamps casting pools of yellow light that seemed to beckon me towards my destination.

When I arrived, the door looked like any other on the street, apart from a shiny brass plaque inscribed with a picture of a bowler hat and a polite reminder that only members were welcome. After weeks of pondering a suitable venue for meetings with clients, I'd concluded that one with a bar would be most appropriate. This unpretentious private members' club, hidden in ancient vaults beneath the Strand seemed to be the perfect match. I pressed the bell, then waited for the receptionist to buzz me in.

A staircase lined with blood-red carpet led me to reception. With each step, it was though I were venturing deeper into the heart of London, leaving behind the hard surface to discover the secret underworld, the pulse that kept it alive. Behind a mirrored desk, in what felt like a dark cave, stood the receptionist, her lips as red as the carpet, her hair as black as the frame behind her. She tapped a nail file on the counter like a bored teenager.

'Yes.' She sighed, the vague glance in my direction quickly redirected to her long scarlet nails.

Once I'd introduced myself, and gone on to explain that every day, and night, for the foreseeable future I would be interviewing prospective clients in the bar, she readjusted her tight black minidress and leant forward with interest, thrusting out her firm tanned boobs in response to the mention of eligible men.

'I look after your cleeants,' she purred in a sultry French accent, punctuated with a sex kitten giggle.

I thanked Brigitte for her help, then followed the throb of the music and the flickering wall lights down the second staircase, tunnelling deeper into the vaults. At the foot of the stairs was a lounge bar, where leather chairs and low tables nestled in shadowy alcoves. A bronze bar stretched across one side of the room, shining and glimmering like an oasis on a desert night. The music pulsed through to the other chambers—a restaurant, and two further bars—like blood from ventricles.

Selecting an alcove near the foot of the staircase, I positioned the chair facing outwards so I could see the clients when they arrived. Tonight I had three consultations: William at six p.m., an accountant who I'd met while dancing 'Gangnam Style' at Apt; at seven p.m. it was Harriet, a risk analyst Kat had found at Zuma; and, finally, Jeremy at eight p.m., a friend of model Mike who I'd met at the champagne bar. I laid my new clipboard on the table and stared at the blank sheet of paper, my heart pounding in time to the quickening tempo of the music.

'Evening,' said the barman after he'd swaggered over to my table, his shirt tight with muscles. 'Looks like you could do with a drink.'

With a gravelly London accent and shaved head, he seemed more 'Guy Ritchie movie' than 'private members' club', but his eyes twinkled with a charm that brought a smile to my face.

'Glass of white, please, whatever you recommend—' I squinted at his name tag '—Brigitte?'

He laughed and then lifted up the tag. 'Must've picked up the wrong one this morning. I'm Steve.'

'Okay, Steve, my wine is in your hands.'

He started flicking through the list and paused somewhere about halfway through. 'White Rioja,' he said, reading from the page. 'It's unpretentious, elegant and full of character.'

I peered at the menu. 'It's also £15 a glass. Do you have something less elegant and more lacking in character?'

He flicked back a few pages. 'The house is approachable and inoffensive and £6 a glass.'

'I'll have a bottle.'

He nodded and then glanced up. I noticed one of his eyelids was twitching. I followed his gaze to see Brigitte wiggling down the staircase, her long, tanned legs balanced on Louboutin heels, her eyes fixed on Steve like a cat stalking a mouse.

'Ellieee, your sex o'clock ees 'ere. I sind eem down?' she said once she'd approached us, her eyes flitting between me and Steve.

'Yes, please,' I replied, picking up my pen and clipboard as though I were about to take notes. Realising my actions were a little premature, I placed them back on the table. 'Please send him down, Brigitte.'

Her gaze was locked on Steve, tracking him as he backed away.

After he'd ducked down behind the bar, presumably to get my wine, she shook her hair and strutted back towards reception. As her tiny toned bottom wiggled up the staircase, I looked down at the red dress I'd borrowed from Kat. It had tracked her curves like a second skin, but on me it seemed ill-fitting, digging in where it shouldn't and gaping where it should dig in. Since learning that I looked like a journalist, whatever that meant, I'd decided to ramp up the glamour a bit. According to Kat, this required a gel-filled bra, uncomfortable shoes and a GHD attack on my hair.

As I took a couple of glugs of the wine Steve had just delivered, moments later, I caught sight of a tall man, wearing a pinstriped suit and grappling with an oversized rucksack. He began carefully navigating the spiral staircase, which seemed somewhat of a challenge due to the dim lighting, his height and the apparent weight of the rucksack. After a few hairy moments, he lost his footing on the final step and did an impromptu leap that sent him into the bar. Attempting to steady himself against the wall, he inadvertently grabbed the frame of a large decorative mirror, which under his weight, swung on its pivot, throwing him again off balance and culminating in an awkward encounter with a couple on a sofa. When the ordeal was eventually over, he straightened his suit jacket, looked up from his polished brogues and scanned the room like a hedgehog about to cross a motorway. I rushed over to greet him and led him back to the table, hoping to avoid further calamity.

'It's lovely to see you again,' I said once we had sat down at the table.

'Likewise,' he said, climbing out from under the gargantuan rucksack. His eyes flickered over my dress, zoomed in on my maxi-boosted cleavage and then settled on the wine list in front of him.

'Let me get you a drink,' I said. 'Would you like a glass of wine?'

He looked startled, as though I'd just offered him a syringe full of heroin.

'Er, yes, why not?' he stammered, one hand still gripping a strap of the rucksack, the other trembling on the table.

Once I'd filled his glass, almost to the top, he wrapped his hands around it. I let him take three big gulps before commencing my questioning. From our initial conversation at Apt, which had been significantly impaired by his flamboyant dance moves, I'd only managed to scribble a few notes down. However, I recalled that at some point, during a prolonged bottom wiggle, he'd told me that he was thirty-four, an accountant, and that he enjoyed playing tennis and growing herbs in his garden.

Halfway through his first glass of wine, he went on to

explain that he had never been married, had no children and reminded me that he enjoyed playing tennis. He was also keen to clarify that the herbs were basil and rocket ('nothing dodgy').

By the time he was on the second glass of wine, his grip loosened on the rucksack and he detailed the exciting career prospects within accountancy. And then explained how, in order for him to fulfil his potential, his hobbies, namely tennis, would have to take a back seat for a while.

By the third glass of wine, he told me he hated his job and that tennis was his life.

By the fourth glass of wine, he told me that one of the herbs was marijuana and that he hadn't had a girlfriend in five years.

'I'm a social outlier,' he said, taking another gulp. 'According to statistics, single men of my age are having sex at least twice a week.'

I laughed. 'Yeah, and men never lie?'

'Why would they, in an anonymous survey?'

'It isn't a numbers game.'

'One would be good.'

'One is all it takes.'

He giggled. 'That's what they said in my sex education classes.'

I smiled. 'So, the one, what would she be like? What are you looking for?'

He sat back in the chair and laced his fingers together. 'I don't know, someone nice.'

I raised my eyebrows. 'Is that all?'

'Hang on,' he said, before ducking down to rummage in his rucksack. When he had resurfaced, he handed his phone to me. 'Here you go. Scroll through.'

I flicked through the images: a girl wearing a tennis skirt and holding a racket, two girls wearing tennis skirts while playing doubles, a girl wearing a flat-fronted tennis skirt and pumps, a girl wearing a pleated tennis skirt, a girl lifting up her tennis skirt and showing her bottom.

'Okay, I get it,' I said, handing the phone back to him. 'You like tennis skirts.'

He looked up and smiled.

'How about a girl who wears a tennis skirt when she plays tennis?'

His grin widened. 'How often does she play?'

I leant back in my chair and sighed. 'Why don't you just buy one of those real-life dolls and dress her up in tennis whites?'

He looked down at the floor. 'I just want a nice girl to spend time with, that's all.'

'Well, forget the tennis skirts and focus on the woman, then.'

He nodded. 'Okay, just tell me what I need to do.'

After he'd left, scaling the staircase like a mountain goat, rucksack now slung casually over his shoulder as though it were a small handbag, I sat back in the chair and thought about the past hour, and how it had taken four glasses of house white for William to open up. I drew a big cross through the earlier notes I'd made, resolving to abandon any formal matching strategy from now on, and to work from my instinct instead.

It wasn't long before I caught sight of my next client, Harriet, slinking down the staircase like a catwalk model. What William had made appear to be a formidable feat, she pulled off with the elegance of a jaguar.

'Ellie?' she asked as she approached.

I gestured for her to take a seat.

She slipped her gently curved hips into the leather chair, then pushed her caramel hair behind her ears and fixed me with fawn-like eyes. She was wearing a simple black pencil skirt and a fitted shirt; there was nothing overtly sexual about her, yet the softness of her skin and the fullness of her lips revealed an intrinsic appeal, leagues above Brigitte's long legs and enthusiast cleavage. There was something else as well and it wasn't just silky skin wrapped around perfect bone structure. There was some kind of aura, a presence she had about her.

'Evening, ma'am.' Steve addressed Harriet as though she were royalty. 'Would you like a glass of the white Rioja?' It seemed he knew better than to offer the house white.

After a quick glance at the wine list, and with gracious diplomacy, Harriet explained that 2005 was a temperamental year for Rioja and that she'd 'prefer a glass of the 2007 Mersault, if possible.'

Steve nodded and then hurried back to the bar, where a stern-faced Brigitte began prodding him on the shoulder.

Harriet had an impressive CV. At twenty-eight, she spoke four languages, had lived in ten different countries and was now working for an American bank in London. She had an interesting family background: her French mother was a professor in neuroscience and her Swiss father was a senior officer in the military. However, the conversation seemed more like a job interview than an open exchange. Unlike William, Harriet only managed a few conservative sips of her award-winning Burgundy.

I decided to get straight to the point. 'So,' I said, leaning forward, 'what kind of men do you like?'

Her cheeks flushed and she picked up her glass and took a sip.

I pointed to a dark-haired man with cute dimples standing at the bar. 'How about him?'

She threw a casual glance over her shoulder, and then looked back at me, shaking her head.

'Why not?'

'Looks like a womaniser.'

I raised my eyebrows. 'What makes you say that?'

She looked over at him again, this time pausing longer. 'He's too good-looking. I don't date men like that.'

'You don't fancy good-looking men?'

She took another sip. 'Successful relationships aren't based on that.'

'What, sexual attraction?'

She shook her head. 'I need someone who fits in with my family, my culture and who matches my intellect.'

'Even if you don't fancy them?'

She took another sip, though this time it was more of a gulp.

I scanned the room once again and noticed a man with a broad smile and blond hair who was sitting on a sofa. 'Okay, what about him?' I pointed.

She turned to look. 'No,' she said, shaking her head.

'Why not?'

She went to put her glass down then lifted it to her mouth again. 'This might sound a little mean.'

'Go on.'

'He's not sophisticated enough.'

'Because?'

'Button-down collar.'

'Okay,' I said, scanning the room, searching for someone who might fit her ideal. I settled on a dark-haired man with intelligent eyes and a Hermes belt. 'Him?'

She looked over, her gaze sizing him up. 'Yes,' she said. 'Yes, someone like him.'

Her glass was half empty when she excused herself for a trip to the Ladies'. I watched her glide across the room, and then have an awkward 'after you, no after you' dance with cute dimples at the bar. I noticed his head swivel, following her as she walked away. However, Mr Hermes belt ignored her as she swept past, seemingly more focused on looking up Brigitte's skirt as she leant over the bar.

When she returned from the toilet, her make-up and composure refreshed, she continued describing her future husband.

'I need a man who can fit in with my life,' she began, her face expressionless. 'He would have an international background, like myself. And a successful career. He'd have to want a large family. And, most importantly, he would need to be from an upper-class family.'

I raised my eyebrows again. 'Why?'

'It's important to have shared values,' she said, staring ahead.

I shrugged my shoulders and pretended to make notes, hoping I hadn't sounded so clinical when I'd listed my requirements to Matthew no less than a month ago.

When she'd finished the last of her wine, she dabbed the sides of her mouth with a napkin and bid me a pleasant evening. I leant forward to kiss her goodbye, but she sidestepped my advances and then offered me her hand to shake instead, as though there had been a gross misunderstanding and she was, in actuality, hiring me to assist her in a business merger.

When I sat back down to yet another refilled glass, I checked my watch and tapped my pen on the table. My next client, Jeremy, was late. Due to my lack of faith in the network coverage in the bar, I nipped upstairs to give him a call. As I approached reception, I saw Brigitte leaning over the desk, boobs squeezed together, bottom in the air as though she were inviting penetration. With a slow deliberate lick of her lips, she pressed a piece of paper into the palm of a man standing in front of her.

'Ahh, Ellieeee. Dis ees Jirimie,' she purred as the man spun round, and flashed me a smile.

'Blatch, Jeremy Blatch,' he said, in the manner of an international spy.

Although a little slick, he was breathtakingly handsome, as though he'd just walked off the set of a Hugo Boss photoshoot. Wearing a grey suit and a white shirt, and with floppy dark blond hair framing dazzling blue eyes, he looked every inch the fantasy Mr Right most women dreamed about.

Suspecting that Brigitte had just passed on her number, and concerned she may try to straddle him if I left it a moment longer, I suggested to Jeremy that we go downstairs to the bar.

'That's a first. I'm usually invited upstairs,' he said with a wink.

I stepped back, surprised to find myself immune to his charms. It seemed my mind had adjusted from its instinctive default of perceiving men as potential boyfriends for myself, to assessing them objectively on behalf of others. Right then, I saw him as prime stock for the single girls of London.

Once settled in the bar, he unbuttoned his jacket. Through his slim-fit white shirt, I noticed the outline of a tight stomach and taut pecs. Oblivious to my X-ray assessment, or politely ignoring it, he ordered a Martini.

'I want to meet someone special,' he said, before I'd had the chance to begin questioning him.

'I'm tired of meeting airheads and bimbos,' he continued, nodding in the direction of Brigitte, who just happened to be wiggling past our table. When she saw Jeremy looking over, she bent down to pick up something from the floor, waving her bottom in the air like a mallard. He looked away, evidently unimpressed.

'No, I'm being unfair,' he continued. 'Some of the girls I've dated have been remarkably clever and successful.' He paused, and then looked a bit strained. 'It's just, I don't know...'

'You haven't found what you're looking for?' I said.

'Yes, you're right. I haven't.' He looked down to stir his Martini.

'I thought it was shaken and not stirred?'

He laughed, looking quite chuffed with the analogy.

Unlike William and Harriet, Jeremy seemed to have no inhibitions when talking about his personal life and relayed his childhood with a mix of passion and nostalgia.

'Life used to be so simple,' he said, having described the farm in Somerset where he grew up. 'When did it get so complicated?'

He downed his Martini, and then went on to explain how he'd play outside all day with his dog, Rusty.

'He never left my side. He didn't care how much I earned or what car I drove.' He threw a glance to the ground. 'And back then neither did I. Now life is all about work.' He picked up his phone. 'And the reason I'm working so hard—' he frowned at the screen '—is so that one day I can have that life back.'

During his second Martini, he went on to explain how his dad went bankrupt when Jeremy was eight years old, and that the family had had to move to London for work. And that they couldn't afford to take Rusty with them.

'I begged my dad to keep him, promised I would find a job to pay for his food.' He gripped the Martini stirrer. 'But he wouldn't listen.'

'What happened to him?'

'It was a cold day that day, so cold.'

'What day?'

'The day my dad shot Rusty with a .38 special.'

My hand few to my mouth. I heard a snap and then saw the Martini-stirrer fall to the table in two pieces.

'That was the moment I vowed never to be poor again,' he said.

After he'd blinked his tears away, we ordered more drinks. Then he explained how, when they'd first moved to London, he'd bunk off school and wash cars and windows to help his mum out with the bills and that by the age of eighteen, he had grown it into a national cleaning company.

'And now, six businesses later, I find myself running a hedge fund,' he said, sinking back into his chair.

'What a story.'

'Yeah, great, isn't it? Now I get to wear this bloody suit every day and pretend to be someone I'm not.' He laughed, though I could tell it was forced. 'And now, I'm embroiled in this ridiculous life. I own a watch that allows me to dive to a depth of three hundred metres. I can turn my Bang and Olufsen sound system on from my desk. I employ some-one to book my flights, wash my underpants, clean my toilets and buy my clothes. I have twelve thousand square foot of property that I hardly use, a forty-foot yacht and a car that can accelerate from zero to sixty in two seconds.' He sighed. 'The women I meet, they don't want me. They want a lifestyle.'

I cocked my head and thought about what he'd said.

He leant forward and picked up the broken stirrer. 'I guess I'm looking for an old-fashioned girl.' He paused. 'I want a big family, and a wife who has the time and patience to nurture our children. Not work all hours or shop all day while some stranger plonks them in front of the TV.' He looked at me, his eyes clouded to the dull blue of his silk tie. 'Are there any women like that left in the world?'

I nodded while the image of Harriet flashed through my mind. I tried to suppress it, after all, nothing on paper would put them together, but there was a strange feeling niggling in my stomach. And I knew it was more than a litre of house white.

Later that night, vivid dreams disturbed my sleep: a party, Harriet shaking hands with faceless men from behind a Venetian mask, William laughing, waving a joint and wearing a tennis skirt, Jeremy dressed as a dog and holding a shotgun and Brigitte, naked, sprawled across the desk at reception. I woke abruptly when I felt myself falling down a never-ending staircase, blood-red carpet spiralling into darkness. I sat up in bed, my heart pounding as I gasped for air. That was when I realised that there was no going back, that I couldn't let them down.

They had put their faith in me, and now all I had to do was the same.

Chapter 5

'GOOD AFTERNOON, MRS RIGBY.' The coiffed estate agent held out his hand.

I fixed my gaze on his tie. I couldn't stand to look at the house in its entirety.

'It's Miss,' I said, staring at yellow stripes on baby-blue silk and trying to ignore the bay windows that seemed to be taunting me in my peripheral vision.

'Yes, of course. Shall we take a look around then?'

My stomach tightened and I wondered if this wasn't the worst idea I'd ever had. Matthew had diagnosed me as 'borderline psychotic' once I'd told him that I'd made an appointment to view the house Robert and I were once going to buy. He said that it was tantamount to kissing the cold corpse of a loved one as a means to say goodbye.

'The front door is all original. Beautiful detail in the stained glass,' the estate agent said, stroking the frame.

I followed him into the hallway and took a sharp breath.

'Magnificent entrance, don't you think, Mrs Rigby? Ten-foot ceilings. Original panelling. Simply stunning.'

I nodded, swallowing hard.

'Expansive lateral space. Great for entertaining.' The estate agent wandered off towards the kitchen.

I looked around at the oak floors and marble fireplaces and I felt a weight pressing on my chest. I thought back to the last time I was in this house: skipping over the threshold with Robert at my side and a three-carat diamond on my finger. Back when my head was buzzing, a confetti-coloured future dancing around my mind. But now, as I stood in the hallway, staring up the grand staircase, I realised that the life I had planned to live in this house—the dinner parties, the children, the love, the laughter, the miniature schnauzer—would never be mine.

'Mrs Rigby,' the estate agent called. 'Come through to the kitchen.'

I walked down the passage, towards the back of the house and into the open-plan kitchen. It was flooded with light and exactly as I remembered: a white gloss handleless heaven. I stared at the granite surfaces, where I'd imagined being creative with the contents of an organic produce box, then at the walls, where I'd envisaged hanging thoughtfully collected paintings from upcoming artists, then finally at the breakfast table where I'd foreseen bustling family mealtimes with cheeky yet cherubic children.

The bi-folding doors were open onto the garden, where mature trees erupted from a lush green lawn. A rope swing was swaying in the breeze, as though the spirits of my imagined offspring had refused to leave. No one could blame them.

'You won't get a better family home in London,' he said,

opening the kitchen drawers so he could then demonstrate the self-closing mechanism. 'Do you and your partner have children, Mrs Rigby?'

Suddenly, I felt flushed, my heart rate quickened. 'Er, not yet,' I stammered, waving the question away.

The agent winked as though somehow he'd mistakenly gleaned that I were about to bear a litter of ankle-biters.

'Wait until you see the nursery,' he said, beaming.

I looked around the room. The sunlight bounced off the white gloss units and into my eyes. Bounce. I rubbed my temples. Bounce. My skin felt hot. Bounce. The light seemed to grow brighter and whiter. Bounce. Bounce. My vision blurred and suddenly sharp pain shot through my head.

'Mrs Rigby? Mrs Rigby? Are you okay?'

I regained consciousness to find the estate agent fanning me with the property pamphlet.

'Mrs Rigby?'

The image on the front moved closer then further away, then closer. I could feel the dizziness returning. Closer, then further away, then closer.

'Can I get you a glass of water, Mrs Rigby?'

I snatched the pamphlet from him and threw it to the ground.

He looked startled. Then he smoothed down his tie and pretended to check his watch. 'Perhaps we should resume the viewing when you're feeling better, Mrs Rigby?'

I glared at him. 'It's Miss,' I said, clambering to my feet. 'Not Mrs.'

'Yes, of course,' he said, holding out his hand. 'Let's chat next week, Miss Rigby.'

I had one last look around, kissing the cold corpse on

the head, then the agent closed the door behind us. He was right. It would make someone else the perfect family home.

'What do you mean there aren't enough champagne glasses?' raged Cordelia, throwing up her arms, as though she were initiating an angry version of the Mexican wave. 'This is outrageous!'

Steve took a step back and blinked. 'I was told that one hundred and fifty people were coming,' he answered in a matter-of-fact voice. 'So there are one hundred and fifty glasses.'

He pointed to the table where they stood, looking all polished and proud.

I raised my hand tentatively. 'There are more people coming than I—'

Cordelia interrupted, still glaring at Steve. 'We have three hundred guests arriving in—' she checked her watch '—oh, fifteen minutes. They're each expecting champagne on arrival so you'd better have this resolved.'

With a hair flick that signalled the conversation was over, she flounced off, the length of her stride impaired by the tightness of her pencil skirt. In repose, she looked like a forties screen siren in her skin-tight black-and-white monochrome outfit, but when she walked, particularly at any speed, she assumed the gait of an elongated penguin.

Kat jumped up and down on the spot, her dark bob lifting and falling like a jellyfish on a mission.

'Champagne cocktails,' she declared on the final bounce, but our vacant expressions clearly signalled a need for further explanation. 'In cocktail glasses?' She peered over the bar. 'Looks like you've got enough of those. We'll need to name it something in theme, like…' She paused and put her finger on her chin 'Cupid's Crush or Sexy Slush.'

Steve smirked. 'Sexy Slush?'

'I don't think Cupid has a crush,' I added, immediately aware that it was in no way constructive.

'Have you got any rose petals?' Kat suggested 'Or lychees? I'll call Mario at Zuma. He knows exactly what to do with a lychee.'

Steve scrunched up his face. 'One hundred and fifty cocktails in fifty minutes—they'll get what they get.'

'Let me help.' Kat jumped up onto the bar, flipped her legs over and landed, quite acrobatically, on the other side. Brigitte popped up as though she had been hiding there all along.

'I weel 'elp Steve,' Brigitte said, lunging towards him, boobs bursting out of a flimsy halter-necked top.

When I suggested to Brigitte that, given she was the receptionist, she might be best placed greeting the guests at reception, she spun around, rising on her heels. Her green eyes narrowed to slits and she hissed something in French that Cordelia later translated to 'stupid pouting horse'.

By eight p.m., aside from three hundred luminous pink cocktails lined up like a Texan beauty pageant, the bar was a vision of understated elegance. Cushions lay strewn across the sofas, while freshly plucked flowers leant against crystal vases like models draped over yachts. To the haunting sounds of Bar Grooves as it echoed through the vaults, shadows moved across the walls like the ghosts of parties past.

In the bronze gilt mirror suspended on the wall, a girl looked back at me, the optimism of her orange dress almost enough to distract from the apprehension in her eyes.

'You look gorgeous,' Steve said after I'd caught him watching me.

My shoes pinched, my bra was too tight and it was an effort to hold in my tummy. *Funny how looking good means feeling bad*, I thought as I picked up one of the overdressed cocktails. Only after I'd fought my way through the tacky paraphernalia, and mastered the curly straw, did I feel the warmth of the alcohol burn in my stomach and spread through my veins.

By the time my muscles had started to relax and my breathing had slowed, excited voices began to trickle down the staircase and groups of girls flooded into the bar like migrating salmon. Modelling this season's Gucci and Dior, they strode into the room with the veneer of a Miss World procession. Pilates-sculpted muscles were vacuum-packed in spa-fresh skin, and finished with St Tropez tans. Hair shone the L'Oreal spectrum of shades from deep chestnut to champagne blonde. Nature's flaws were concealed by MAC, nature's blessings were enhanced by shimmer.

A girl with a Heidi Klum body walked down the staircase and straight towards me. 'Where are the men?' she asked, scanning the room like an assassin.

I checked my watch. It was eight-ten p.m. 'They'll be here soon,' I said.

She glared at me as though she expected me to produce one from my pocket. I ushered her towards the cocktails.

'Would you like one?' I asked.

She took a glass, holding it away from her as though it might explode at any moment.

'It's a Cherry Plucker,' I said, trying to match the enthusiasm with which Kat and Steve had christened it.

Using the umbrella as a probe, she examined the contents

with the precision of a pathologist, eventually retrieving a freakishly large cherry, which she held aloft, as though she had located the tumour that had turned an otherwise good cocktail bad. She handed me the glass, but retained the cherry presumably to send it for further testing. With a cocktail in each hand, I took a large gulp of each and then smiled, feeling like a politician at a press conference, making a point out of eating a GM vegetable. As the sugary syrup lined my throat, I looked up to see two men strutting down the staircase side by side, all cheekbones and jawlines. It was Mike and Stephen whom we'd met at the champagne bar.

Throwing the cherry to the ground, Heidi Klum, along with what Steve had described as the 'Stepford-Wives-in-waiting', moved towards them like starved piranhas. I took another sip from each cocktail and wondered when it was that the hunters had become the hunted.

Next down the staircase was a pair of pneumatic blondes, teetering and tottering with almost contrived instability. Their bottoms were lifted by five-inch heels and their pretty faces were eclipsed by giant yellow hair. Almond-shaped nipples poked through white vests, and mahogany-stained legs protruded from bottom-skimming skirts. At a glance, they could have been twins. *Like dogs and their owners*, I thought as I walked towards them, *it's funny how friends grow to look the same.*

'Hiya. I'm Stacey.' The prettiest one introduced herself. 'And this is Lacey.' She pointed at her friend.

'Where are the men?' Lacey asked, scouring the room, her pupils constricted like those of a lioness.

'There are two in there,' I said, pointing to the crowd that I suspected contained Mike and Stephen. Stacey laughed, but Lacey just looked confused. I checked my watch again: it was eight-twenty p.m. 'They'll be here soon,' I said, before walking away.

I found Kat at the bar, laughing and leaning towards Steve. His attentions were alternating between the cocktail production line and her cleavage, which had a cherry wedged in it.

'Do they require a garnish now?' I asked, pulling the cherry out.

She laughed. 'Lighten up, stresshead.'

I pulled myself onto a bar stool. 'Where are the men?'

We both turned to Steve as though he were the spokesperson for the entire male species.

'Men don't arrive to parties on time,' he said, pushing another cherry into Kat's cleavage.

'But the girls have made the effort to be here,' I said, pulling the cherry out and lobbing it towards the bin. I missed.

Steve frowned and then picked another one from the overfilled jar in front of him. 'Desperate,' he said, handing it to Kat.

'It's a singles party. There's no need to play hard to get,' she said before popping it in her mouth.

'That's the only way to play,' he replied, screwing the lid on the jar.

It was just before nine p.m. when the rest of the men started to arrive. The beat of the music quickened as Omega watches, Dunhill cufflinks, Church's shoes and Dax-waxed hair piled into the bar. Musky cologne overpowered the fading vanilla notes and the air grew thick and heady.

While the women had claimed the sofas, the men commandeered the bar, jostling for position and ordering rounds as though their spend was directly proportional to their self-worth. Once the pecking order had been established, the dominant males leant back expansively while the girls eyed up the contents of their ice buckets.

Last into the pit were two men wearing Diesel jeans and Paul Smith jackets, their hair styled as though they'd arrived via a wind tunnel. Cordelia informed me they were entrepreneurs, the co-founders of a well-known online business, which had recently floated on the Stock Exchange. Stacey and Lacey tottered over at their fastest speed, but two brunettes got there first, targeting the men with what looked like a well-rehearsed pincer movement. Their smiles were demure, but their eyes betrayed an excited recognition.

'Do they already know each other?' I asked Cordelia.

She let out a dramatic sigh. 'They were listed as *The Times'* most eligible bachelors last week. Everyone knows them. Ellie, you *have* to sharpen up.'

As the night progressed, the assets stretched: American Express pre-authorised inflated bar bills and the girls hammed up their sexiness. While the men with the biggest budgets gained territory around the bar, it was the girls wearing the least clothes who secured the most champagne, only to be usurped by those who were grinding against pillars or pretending to be lesbians.

'Is that really it?' I asked Cordelia, while the men gawped at Stacey and Lacey

Cordelia laughed. 'If you wave a sausage in front of a dog's nose, it won't be able to think about anything else.'

I rolled my eyes. 'Come on, men are more sophisticated than that, aren't they?'

'Yes, of course,' she replied. 'When there are no sausages, they can be delightful company.'

'But if there are sausages everywhere they go, then surely

the urge would abate, and they'd suffer from some kind of aversion, like sausage fatigue?'

'Sausage fatigue?' she said, flicking a sheet of golden hair over her shoulder. 'You mean because there is an endless supply of boobs and bums on offer, men will get desensitised?'

I nodded.

'They already are,' she said, pointing at Stacey who was now pretending to bite Lacey's nipples through her top. 'Those two will have to get their internal organs out in a few years to even warrant a second glance.'

With that she shuffled off, seemingly oblivious to the fact that her skirt was working against her.

When Stacey and Lacey's show was over, I noticed Kat tailing three tall muscular men as they strutted round the room like silverback gorillas. After I'd caught her eye, she rushed towards me.

'They're RAF pilots!' she squealed, flapping her arms excitedly.

I rolled my eyes, recalling the million times she had described her 'ultimate fantasy'.

'He's an injured pilot ran aground in a field and you're a virginal milkmaid who comes to his aid,' I said in a dull monotone.

She fanned her flushed chest. 'Well, thinking about it, it would be unlikely that there would only be one pilot in the aircraft. Maybe it would be more plausible with three?'

I shook my head and watched her stride across the room, sticking out her boobs and hitching up her skirt.

As the night drew on, the walls of the cave grew damp and sticky. Styled hair softened, sweat glowed through face powder and natural scent overpowered the synthetic. Masks slipped and inhibitions gave way to instinct.

This wasn't an orgy. This wasn't a bunch of teenagers on holiday in Kavos. These were professional people, who, earlier on, had been sharing awkward exchanges about the economy and current affairs. Now they were writhing on leather sofas: tongues locked, limbs entwined, hands up skirts, down tops, under shirts, down trousers. The candles, once flickering gently, were now burning violently, wax dripping down their shafts.

Perched on a sofa in the only uninhabited alcove, I looked on, watching an equities trader dry humping a pretty florist at the bar. He really reminded me of something. Now what was it?

'Randy dog,' a man's voice said, directed at me.

Yes, that's it, I thought, before looking up to see a broad smile beaming down at me. We both turned back to see the subject's bottom bobbing up and down with increasing momentum.

'He's with me, I'm sorry to say,' he said, still grinning.

I smirked. 'Can you put him on a leash, then?'

He laughed. He sat down next to me, fixing me with the most beautiful brown eyes I had ever seen. 'I'm Nick,' he said. 'Mind if I join you?'

I shuffled up the sofa, eyeing him suspiciously.

'So you're the brains behind all this, then?' he asked.

I nodded. 'Although there's not much brain activity happening here tonight.'

He looked around the room and smiled. 'What were you expecting?'

'I don't know…a little more self-restraint.'

He laughed. 'If you put kids in a candy shop—' he gestured in the direction of a man, whose hand was emerging from a short denim skirt '—they get sticky fingers.'

I tutted, then rolled my eyes while he continued to laugh at his own joke.

'And you?' I asked. 'Haven't you found a florist to dry hump or a sticky place to put your fingers?'

He shook his head. 'There's only one girl who caught my eye.'

'And?'

'She seems to have a bit of an attitude problem.'

A smile edged out from the corners of my mouth.

'I knew you'd crack eventually,' he said, his hand skimming mine as he reached for his drink. Suddenly, a tingle shot up my arm and a flash of white light ripped through the bar. I looked up, my eyes squinting against the neon beams, as though abruptly awoken from a dream. The music stopped and voices hushed.

'Time, everyone,' Steve announced. 'Bar's closing.'

The light shone down on us, and when Nick looked at me, it was with such intensity that I suddenly felt as though every pore, every blemish and every scar that I'd hoped to conceal were exposed. A surge of panic raced through my nerves and I jumped up from my seat, mumbling something incoherent about needing to help tidy up. Then I walked away without looking back.

Absent from the comforting canopy of candlelight, the crudeness of reality was unveiled. The guests clambered to their feet and wiped their lipstick-smudged faces as though desperate to reclaim some dignity. From a hidden alcove, I watched everyone leave. My eyes tracked Nick as he sauntered up the stairs, my stomach churning when I noticed a leggy brunette tottering after him. When he smiled at her, the smile that I'd secretly hoped he'd reserved for me, the electricity tripped and the room was plunged back into darkness.

By the time Steve had flipped the fuse, the bar had emptied out. I dropped back down on my seat. Only a few hours earlier, before the guests arrived, the atmosphere had seemed charged and full of anticipation, but now the flowers had wilted, with their stems slumped and petals curled. The candles had withered down to useless stumps, droplets of wax eating away at the polished veneer. Beside them stood smeared glasses containing fluids mixed and merged. Beneath the tables, trampled cherries bled into the carpet.

'Imagine all the shagging that's going on tonight, thanks to you!' Kat said as we shared a taxi home.

'There might be a little baby being made as we speak,' Cordelia joked.

I huffed. 'That's not how it's supposed to work. I was hoping for blossoming love not rampant sex.'

'Don't the two go hand in hand?' Kat answered.

'I'd settle for rampant sex,' Cordelia chipped in.

'Rampant rabbit for me tonight,' Kat said before curling her bottom lip. 'Not quite RAF pilot. But—' she paused, retrieving a damp piece of paper from her cleavage '—I got their numbers!'

'So, what about *you*, Ellie?' Cordelia asked. 'That guy you were chatting to—what happened there? He looked gutted when you walked off.'

'Yes, he was cute but—'

'He had a cute butt, I saw.'

'Kat, stop it,' Cordelia interrupted and looked back at me. 'But what?'

'But I don't have time for a relationship at the moment. I'm concentrating on other things.'

'That's utter bollocks!' Cordelia shouted, waving her arms around. 'You haven't had a relationship since...' She paused, placing her hands back on her lap.

'You can mention it, you know. I'm not going to break down into a gibbering wreck. Since I got dumped by my fiancé, you meant to say?'

'No. Since your lucky escape from that twat. *That's* what I meant to say. You know it wasn't your fault.'

'Look, I really don't want to talk about it again. It's in the past.'

'You never want to talk about it. And it's not in the past if it's stopping you from meeting someone new.'

'I'm fine. I just want to focus on—'

'Whatever!' She rolled her eyes. 'Great strategy. You'll never get hurt again if you never have a relationship again. Brilliant idea!' She folded her arms and looked away from me.

'Okay, that's enough, ladies!' Kat interrupted. 'You can have one of my pilots if you like?' She turned to me with a silly grin.

'I'd make sure she washed the milkmaid outfit before borrowing that though,' Cordelia said, unfolding her arms and offering me her olive branch smile.

I leant forward and put my arms around them both. 'Stop worrying about me, you two. I'm fine.'

Initiating a drunken group hug was a bit of a challenge in the back of a fast-moving taxi, especially as the driver took a sharp corner onto my road at our most vulnerable moment. Kat went flying, bottom over boobs and onto the taxi floor, Cordelia managed to retain her composure for a few seconds and grabbed my arm to steady me, but as the driver slammed on the breaks outside my flat, it was too late. I knew I was going down and that she was coming with me. Flying out of our seats, I landed across Kat, my face cushioned by her inbuilt airbags, but Cordelia continued to slide around the taxi before finally settling between Kat's legs, her mouth open against black satin knickers, hands gripping her lace-topped stockings. It was like a particularly creative scene from Girls Gone Wild.

The taxi driver did a double take in the rear-view mirror.

'All right, ladies?' he said, turning around and looking a little alarmed, but clearly refusing to acknowledge any responsibility in the matter.

'Yes, we're fine, thank you,' Cordelia replied, her recovery marginally thwarted by the penguin ensemble.

When we were vertical again and safely out on the street, I leant in to pay the driver. He looked at me, his eyebrows knitted together, with an unsettling empathy in his eyes.

'You're a nice-looking girl,' he said, peering down my top. 'You'll find a man, don't worry.'

I rolled my eyes and Kat slammed the door.

'There goes your tip,' Cordelia said as she waddled after us.

Lying in bed that night, wedged uncomfortably between a fidgeting Cordelia and a snoring Kat, I realised how much the dating game had changed. Before I met Robert, I'd never had to look for a man. They'd always seemed in plentiful supply and ever eager for a date. However, from my observations that night, it seemed that now the men had all the power. And it appeared it was us women who had handed it to them. With a cherry on top.

I wondered if Matthew was right. Had men been socially conditioned by the recent wave of engineered sex bombs—sporting glued-on hair, mutilated boobs and creosoted legs—so that a normal girl didn't stand a chance any more?

One who wasn't prepared to strut around with her bottom in the air, proclaiming a love of anal and threesomes?

My temples throbbed at the injustice of it all. As I pulled the pillow over my head to drown out Kat's snores, I remembered the brunette trotting after Nick, her ridiculously short skirt riding up over her bottom. I felt a rage burning inside. It was as though my blood had been on a low simmer but tonight the heat had been ramped up a notch.

Chapter 6

HE SLAMMED HIS business card on the table 'This is me. Google me. *Now* can we talk about what I'm looking for?'

'Er, hang on,' I interrupted, picking up his card. 'Richard Stud. Consultant gynaecologist.'

I looked up to see him shifting uncomfortably in his seat.

'Is that *really* your name?' I asked, assuming he was having me on.

He let out an irritated sigh. 'Yes. It is. It's not like my parents gave me any choice in the matter.'

'Okay. Sorry. It's just—'

'I know. A gynaecologist called Dick Stud. I've heard it all before. There's also dermatologist called Mr Cream, so you can use that one for your dinner party anecdotes too if you like.'

'Sorry, I didn't mean to offend. Honestly, I thought it was a joke. Anyway, I've had to live with the name Eleanor Rigby, so I know where you're coming from.'

'What's wrong with that?'

'It's a Beatles' song.'

He shrugged his shoulders.

'About a desperately lonely woman who died a spinster? Anyway, moving on from my issues, let's talk about yours. Apart from bottom groping in wine bars, what do you like to do in your spare time?'

Two days prior, I'd received a call from a man with a familiar Irish accent. The man explained that he had been headhunted in a bar a few weeks back and wanted to book an appointment to see me. It was only when he arrived that I'd recognised him as the bottom-groper from the queue at Apt. I suppose I could have argued the accuracy of his use of the term 'headhunted', or his suitability as a client in general, but something stopped me. When I'd first met him, his jet-black hair and white teeth made him look like one of those cheesy Just for Men adverts. But this time— albeit through the haze of a cherry-plucker hangover—with his bright blue eyes and floppy hair, he reminded me, a bit, of Rob Lowe.

Behind him, the lounge bar gleamed as though it had been the subject of an extreme makeover. In the twenty-four hours since the party, the carpet had been shampooed, the sofas scrubbed and the surfaces polished. Fresh flowers replaced the old, new candles replaced withered stumps and the shadows seemed to have crept back into the crevices. Aside from a few resistant stains, all traces of the night had been erased.

During the prerequisite discussion about his family and career background, I sensed we were both losing interest.

'Okay,' I said, improvising a drum roll on the table. 'Now you get to tell me what you're looking for.'

He smiled. 'You're going to love this.'

'Go on,' I said, before taking a sip of coffee.

'I have absolutely no idea. That's my answer. I honestly don't have a clue what I'm looking for. I just want someone nice.'

I smiled. 'That's great. Open-minded is the best way to be when dating,' I said, though not entirely convincing myself. 'So you don't have a type at all?'

He shuffled in his seat again. 'I used to have a type, but not any more. I love all girls: tall, short, slim, curvy, blondes, brunettes, white, black. I suppose the main issue would be settling with just one.' He laughed.

I frowned.

'That was a joke,' he said. 'I'd be more than happy with one. The *right* one.'

'Okay, so how do we find the right one?'

His eyebrows met in a semi-frown. 'I don't have any trouble attracting girls, or finding girls I'm attracted to. But—' he leant back in his seat and looked up to the ceiling '—I go off them.'

'You go off them?'

He nodded.

'Can you explain?'

He scratched his nose. 'It's quite difficult to explain when I don't really understand it myself.'

'Try.'

'Okay, well, when I meet a girl I like, I fall in love easily,' he explained, still scratching his nose. 'It's a bit like a favourite T-shirt. I'll wear it all the time and then one day I'll look at it and hate it. And then throw it out.'

'Because you've found a new favourite T-shirt?'

'Not necessarily. Sometimes. Other times, I'll just wear other T-shirts until I find a new favourite one.'

Steve appeared at our table. 'You can never have enough T-shirts,' he said, nodding at Dr Stud, who then laughed. 'Any more drinks?'

'Thanks for the insightful input, Steve, another coffee for me. Still haven't quite metabolised those cocktails.'

'You're better off with water: rehydrate and flush out that acetaldehyde,' Dr Stud suggested, before turning towards Steve. 'I'll have a beer, please, mate. And I like *your* T-shirt.'

He nodded at Brigitte who was squeezed into a tiny red dress and pouting next to the bar. I turned around. I hadn't noticed her until now, yet Dr Stud, who'd had his back to the bar, had somehow managed to assess her attractiveness and ascertain that she was something to do with Steve.

'The male sixth sense,' I said after I'd shared my thoughts with him. 'The ability to determine cup size and sexual availability without turning your head.'

He laughed. 'And the female equivalent? The ability to calculate total net worth with a casual glance.'

I smirked. 'So do you think what you earn is important to women?'

He laughed, but this time it sounded forced and irritated. 'Of course. You wouldn't believe the number of women I've pulled just by telling them I'm a doctor.'

'But that's not because of how much you earn.'

'No?'

'No, it's more of a profession fetish. You know, a sort of white-coat-hyper-competent-House-meets-George-Clooney-in-*ER* combined with I've-married-a-doctor-didn't-I-do-well type thing.'

He leant back and laughed. 'I thought we weren't discussing your issues?'

My cheeks flushed. 'Sorry, please continue.'

'And I think,' he continued, still half smiling from my outburst, 'that's half the reason I get fed up with the girls I date. It's as though they're too stupid to plan their own lives, so instead they're waiting for me to do it for them. It's pathetic really.'

I opened my mouth to say something, but he continued.

'I've got this friend who quit being a doctor the day she married. She studied for seven years and then only worked for one. What's that all about? Seriously, what's the point of putting women through university if they're just going to give it up when they get married?'

'But that's only one girl,' I said.

He didn't respond, but simply took a sip of the beer Steve had just brought over.

'So I think what you're saying is that you want to date an independent woman?' I asked, picking up my pen, poised to take notes.

'That's what most girls think they are. But they're not.'

'Okay, okay,' I interrupted, now feeling the need to defend my team. 'Let's rewind a bit. The night we met. In the queue for Apt.'

'Yes.'

'You were pretty offensive.'

He raised his eyebrows.

'Grabbing bottoms and making reference to anal sex is likely to put off the intelligent, independent women. We want to be wined, dined and cherished. Not objectified and manhandled.'

He smirked. 'Manhandled? Do people still say that?'

I frowned. 'Don't deflect.'

'I was hardly Benny Hill chasing you around the club to

clown music. Honk, honk.' He pretended to squeeze a pair of imaginary boobs.

'It was still disrespectful.'

'You disrespected yourself, wearing that miniskirt.'

I laughed. 'It was a dress actually and it wasn't that short.'

'It was tight around your bottom. And, yes, it was short.'

'So you're saying I was asking for it?'

He shook his head. 'Of course not. But—'

'Yes, go on, please.'

'You wanted men to notice. Or you wouldn't have worn it.'

'Is it a crime to want to look nice?'

'Nice or sexy?'

I rolled my eyes.

'Okay. So this is how it goes.' He sat forward in his chair and stared at me. 'I work my arse off in a job which gives me a good salary and lifestyle. I then use this to wine and dine a woman who feels she is entitled to it just for being her wonderful, beautiful, miniskirted self. And then, if I behave correctly—i.e. spend enough money, shower her with enough compliments, pander to her neuroses—then I am allowed sex. I'm supposed to pretend it is the best sex I have ever had and never want it with anyone else again. From then onward, I am expected to continue this ridiculous charade until she has borne her desired number of children and we are old and withered. Unless I get fed up with her unending list of demands, and leave her, or have an affair, in which case I will be back at square one, only with half my income gone.'

When he had finished, he sat back in his chair and took, what seemed to be, a triumphant sip of beer.

'So, is that what you think marriage is?' I asked, raising my eyebrows. 'A woman taking and a man giving.'

He looked to the ceiling. 'More like, a woman demanding and a man giving up.'

I looked up at the ceiling too, hoping to find some inspiration there. 'Do you think there's another way?'

He looked back down towards me. 'That's why I'm here.'

After he'd left, I wrote up my notes, concluding with 'No extreme feminists' written in capitals and underlined twice. I thought about what he'd said. No matter how much I wanted to disagree, I couldn't deny he had a point. On one hand, women had fought enamelled tooth and acrylic nail to be treated equally in the workplace and in society, but, on the other hand, when it came to dating, it seemed as though we were driven by some primal urge to be protected. We wanted men to take control and to look after us. We wanted to be perceived as sex goddesses but not as sexual objects. Obsessing over our looks yet not wanting to be defined by them.

'The reason we will never be true feminists,' I recalled Kat explaining after she'd unveiled her new double Ds, 'is because we care too much about what men think. Until we stop caring, women will always compete with each other and will always be seeking approval from men.'

'But men should love us for who we are,' I'd answered.

'To get a man to love us for who we are, we first have to attract their attention. We have to stand out from the competition or we will be overlooked.'

She'd also had a point, well, two actually, and they had both been staring defensively back at me.

I dragged my mind back to the present and noticed Brigitte loitering by the bar, her eyes tracking Steve like she was the Mona Lisa. I let out a deep sigh. In the past few weeks, since vowing to become the world's best matchmaker, I'd pored over almost every dating and relationship guide ever written and every psychology paper published. Yet I still hadn't found the answers. Were they written on an ancient rock in a temple in the desert? Guarded by ghosts of loves lost? Were the answers on the wind? In our hearts? Who had them? Did Oprah know? Dr Phil's wife always seemed pleased to see him, so maybe he knew?

With only a few minutes before my next consultation, I decided to postpone my philosophical ponderings and picked up my phone to check my emails. My stomach flipped when I saw his name:

To: Ellie
From: Nick
Subject: Spiritual guidance
Hi Ellie,
It was a pleasure to meet you at the party, though I feel further discussion is required re: your attitude problem.
I suggest working on your yin–yang balance over dim sum on Saturday?
Nick x
P.S. I won't bring the randy dog.

My hands were trembling. *My God, get a grip.* I was acting like one of those girls I despised: the type to get all excited at the prospect of a boy liking them as though that's all they live for. The ones who couldn't hold a conversation because their eyes were glued to their phone just in case he texted. This wasn't who I was. I was an independent laydee now. Instead of throwing my hands up Beyoncé-style, I quickly emailed him back.

To: Nick
From: Ellie
Subject: Re: Therapy?
Hi Nick,
Thanks for the offer but I find public eating venues a further source of frustration. Particularly those that necessitate the incompetent use of chopsticks. Perhaps you should invite the girl you left with? She might enjoy a discussion about how clothing inhibits her qi.
Ellie x
P.S. Randy dog needs a trip to the vet's.

I paused and then removed the kiss, then added it again. Removed. Added. Sent.

Looking up, I saw Brigitte directing a petite woman across the room towards my table. Size-zero thin with rich auburn hair, and wearing a black polo neck and a short tartan skirt, she looked as fragile as a porcelain doll. I was surprised she hadn't been blown away by a gust of the wintry wind that had been howling through the streets that morning.

'Oh! My! Gaaad! I so can't believe I'm doing this! This is crazy!' she shrieked at Brigitte with an unmistakable New York twang, complemented with wild gesticulations. It was like watching a badly dubbed movie. Brigitte stepped back and the others looked on, their expressions united in disbelief.

There's no way that voice should be coming from that

person, I thought, as she introduced herself as Cassandra and then slipped her tiny frame into the chair in front of me.

'Oh, my God! It's so good to meet you!' she said as her lips stretched across a mouth crammed with shiny white teeth.

After a few minutes, my eardrums had adjusted to the volume and my brain had just about managed to process all the information she had fired at me. After explaining every detail of her start-up internet business and zipping through each of her thirty-six years of life, she moved on to list her current hobbies. When she'd wrapped up the outdoor pursuits category with sailing, rock climbing, skiing, caving, tennis and hang-gliding, I let out a deep sigh and then ordered us each a large glass of wine.

I took a gulp before broaching the topic of men.

'I'm so not fussy!' she squealed at full volume. 'Just as long as he can keep up with me! Ya know!' She erupted into a raucous laugh.

I nodded and took another gulp of wine.

'I'm divorced,' she continued, and then almost downed hers. 'So I'm not fussed by the whole baggage thing.'

I offered a sympathetic smile.

'Oh, don't worry. I'm totally over it!' she squealed, grabbing another glass of wine out of Steve's hand as he walked past. 'He's such a cliché, ran off with his secretary.'

Immediately I visualised the mismatched couple sprinting away from Cassandra.

'Now he's moved the little slut into my house. And he's hidden all our money offshore, somewhere so my lawyer can't find it. It's pathetic. He's pathetic.'

'That doesn't seem fair,' I said cautiously.

'Don't feel sorry for me,' she replied. 'Save it for her.

Now *she* has to look at his droopy ass, scrub the skid marks from his underwear and pretend his weird puffing-into-the-vagina cunnilingus is mind-blowing.'

I laughed, albeit a little awkwardly.

'Now,' she said, downing the rest of her wine. 'It's time I had some fun.'

As soon as we were done, like a tornado she swept out as quickly as she'd arrived. I picked up my pen and notepad and began scribbling down my thoughts. Just as I flagged a potential pleated tennis-skirt match with William, a thin wisp of air wafted down the staircase. I glanced up to see a woman looking down at me with eager eyes.

'Ellie?' she asked.

I nodded.

'Sorry, I'm a bit early,' she said, while attempting to remove several layers of clothing and an oversized scarf. 'Joanna.'

Forty minutes early, I realised, as I watched her drape a coat, two cardigans and said scarf over the back of her chair.

She was tall, about five feet ten inches, and probably a size fourteen. When she sat down, almost apologetically, she looked as though she'd been allocated the wrong body. As though there'd been some terrible mix-up with her genetic coding. And while she was waiting for the mistake to be rectified and the smaller size to be delivered, it seemed she'd resolved to tolerate the cumbersome costume.

Her face was attractive: fine bone structure, a snub nose and a friendly smile. But her skin looked pale and grey, like the 'before' image for a miracle face cream. Her ash-blonde hair was the type that a stylist might diagnose as unruly and a shade that could have been described as flat or dull, or even lifeless.

As she spoke, I imagined a team of 'professionals' buzzing around her, suggesting highlights to lift the dull tones, low lights to add warmth and a treatment to add shine. When my daydream had concluded with Joanna leaving a salon with an armful of products and a puzzled expression, I waved Steve over and ordered two glasses of wine.

She took tiny sips as though not wishing to exceed the prescribed dose and then began to explain why she was here.

'And they married in my church,' she added after she'd described how her boyfriend of seven years had recently left her for a girl ten years her junior.

'You own a church?' I asked.

She shook her head, and took another slightly larger sip of wine. 'No. Our church. The one we'd planned to marry in.'

'Oh.'

'And now she's pregnant,' she said, looking into her glass as though it might be a crystal ball. 'She stole my life. Stole my dreams.'

We went on to discuss her job as a HR manager and her hobbies: dining out, country walks, city breaks and occasionally visiting galleries. While she was describing a recent Dali exhibition she had enjoyed, she stopped abruptly and gripped the stem of her glass. She looked up at me. Her brow was creased and her eyes were teary.

'Do you think you can help me?' she asked.

I looked back at her, at her stooped shoulders, at the rolls of skin spilling over her waistband, at her too-short trousers, at the leg stubble sprouting over pop socks, at the fingernails bitten to the nail beds and I wondered if she had given up, given up the fight she'd decided she could no longer win. But when my gaze moved up into her dove-grey eyes, beyond the mournful glaze, there was something that I recognised, something I couldn't ignore.

'Yes, of course,' I replied, before downing the rest of my drink.

Once she'd left, I pulled on my hat and coat, climbed the stairs out of the club and rejoined civilisation. By now, the sky was black and the wind had whipped itself into a frenzy, sending litter flying through the air. Fighting its force, I held on to my hat and marched forwards, watching discarded paper coffee cups rolling past me along the pavement. Redundant of purpose, they were like displaced souls in a world where it was easier to manufacture the new than to recycle the old.

At the station, I joined the bottleneck of passengers, everyone jostling towards their platform, anxious to get home to a place where they have a face and a name.

My phone buzzed.

'Ellieee.'

'Hi, Brigitte.'

'Der ees a guy for you.'

'Who is it?'

'I poot eem through.'

'Hello, Ellie. Hope this is a good time.' It was William.

'Yes, perfect timing actually, I think I might have found the girl for you.'

He made a funny excited noise, somewhere between a laugh and a cough. 'That's great. I'm so pleased.'

'I hope you like her, her name is Cassandra, she's American, full of energy.'

'She sounds wonderful. Does she play tennis?'

Beep, beep. There was a call waiting.

'Hang on a minute, William, I have another call.'

'Hello?'

'Hi, is that Ellie?'

'Yes, speaking.'

'Hey, it's Nate, we met at the Royal Exchange?'

After a few days of keeping me guessing, Cordelia had revealed that Nate and Josh were the co-stars of a popular primetime show in America. Once she'd said it, I'd immediately checked out their relationship history on Google.

'Nate, yes. Hi. How are you?'

'Great, thank you. Listen, the reason I am calling is I'd like you to set me up on some dates in London. Do you have time to talk now?'

Beep, beep.

'Yes, sure. Hang on one second I have another call.'

I pressed Hold.

'Thanks for holding. Yes, she loves tennis, has a varied selection of pleated skirts, one of which she wore when I met her. She loves herbs—'

'Ellie. Is that you?' Another voice came down the line. My stomach flipped. My hands started trembling.

'Yes. It is I,' I said, most oddly, in the manner of a Shakespearean actor.

'It's Nick.'

'I know,' I replied.

'Well, I appreciate your offering of a girl with a love of herbs and a varied selection of pleated skirts, but I was hoping I could take you out instead?'

'Sorry, I can't. I'm too busy,' I said, my face flushing. 'I'm independent. Hang on. Hold for a second.'

'William?'

'Yes.'

Thank God. 'You'll love Cassandra. I'll call you tomorrow with all the details. Have a good evening.'

'Thank you, Ellie. Thanks so much.'

I clicked Hold again.

'Nate?'

'No. It is I, Nick,' he said.

'Argh, stupid retarded phone. Hold on.'

I clicked again. 'Nate?'

'Yes.'

Phew.

'Is it a bad time? I can call again tomorrow.'

'No, no, it's fine. So you were saying you would like some dates?'

'Yes. I had a good feeling about you when we met. My judgement's all messed up, so I'm going to leave the decision in your hands. I'll put you in touch with my sister, she lives in London. She can tell you everything there is to know about me. Okay?'

'Well, I'd rather it came from you—'

'Awesome. I've already transferred your payment. She'll call you tomorrow,' he added before hanging up.

I clicked Hold. 'Nick?'

The line was dead.

Either I'd inadvertently hung up or he'd given up. When I looked up, the platform had emptied out. I stood alone while the train I'd rushed to board pulled away from the station.

Chapter 7

UP SINCE DAWN, I sat cross-legged on the lounge floor, surrounded by paper: notes on clients, notes on feedback for clients, notes on feedback for their dates, notes on matches, notes on who was dating, notes on who wasn't dating and notes on who should be dating. In only two weeks, I'd already matched over a hundred couples and I was beginning to lose track. Sharon with Mark; David with Claire. Or was it Mark and Claire? Hadn't Mark already dated Claire? Or was that the other Claire?

'There are too many Claires.' I sighed, running my hands through my hair.

'Yes that's the problem with the world,' Matthew chipped in as he emerged from his room. 'Too many Claires and just not enough time.'

'That's really not helpful,' I replied.

'What's not helpful is you sitting here ruminating about matches and getting no sleep.' He clapped his hands as though he expected me to jump on my hind legs or roll over.

'What?'

He clapped his hands again. 'Come on. Let's go.'

I frowned. 'Where?'

He threw a coat at me. 'Chop, chop. We haven't got all day.'

Following the vague explanation that he was planning to 'cheer me up', Matthew bundled me into the driving seat of my car and himself into the passenger seat.

'Drive!' he said, smacking his hand on the dashboard.

When I'd reminded him that we were in fact civilians in a Nissan Micra, rather than FBI agents commandeering a New York taxi, he relented and typed a postcode into my satnav.

'Purley Way, Croydon?' I asked, after we'd joined the dual carriageway.

He nodded with a conviction that implied an out-of-town retail park, rather than a soulmate, might be harbouring the key to my future happiness.

Just as the blue Ikea towers came into view, the satnav announced that we had arrived at our destination.

I shook my head in an effort to enhance comprehension.

While I was attempting a reverse parking manoeuvre, Matthew produced an Ikea brochure from his man bag.

'White gloss handleless heaven,' he announced, presenting a double-page spread featuring a white contemporary kitchen. 'It's on me.'

I frowned, wondering why he was acting like The Milkybar Kid for Swedish furniture.

He grinned. 'This quarter, I am the delighted, yet baffled recipient of a bonus, which appears to have been calculated via an entirely flawed methodology, and seemingly indirectly proportional to my productivity at work.'

I scrunched up my face, as my bumper crunched into a post. 'How much did you get?'

He shrugged his shoulders. 'Fifty grand.'

My jaw dropped. 'Bloody hell.'

He laughed. 'I absolutely *didn't* earn every penny.'

I pulled up the handbrake. 'Wow.'

He waved the brochure in my face. 'Check out this bad boy. It has an integrated coffee machine.'

I shook my head. 'Absolutely no way. It's your money. For you to spend. On *yourself.*'

'Oh, come on. I'm loaded now. Let's splurge.' He jumped out of the car, ran round to my side and opened the door.

I smiled, letting him take my hand. 'In that case, can I have an ice-maker too?'

He nodded, still grinning.

'I'm joking!' I said, slapping him on the arm. 'Seriously, I'm not letting you pay for a kitchen.' I grabbed the catalogue and stared at the images. Glossy units seemed to multiply on the page. Like an army of shiny white Daleks lining up for battle. I started to feel dizzy again. My temples began to throb.

I hurled the catalogue into the bin as we passed. 'I appreciate the sentiment, I really do, but we both know a kitchen's not going to make me happy.'

He squeezed my hand. 'Maybe not,' he said, still leading me towards the entrance. 'But Ikea meatballs might.'

Seated in the canteen, we stared at the trays in front of us.

'It's a wonder the chef hasn't been awarded a Michelin star,' Matthew said, spearing a meatball onto his fork. 'What with his unfaltering commitment to quality and creative experimentation with horse meat.'

I sat opposite him, slumped into my chair, barely mustering a smile.

He sighed. 'Okay. So, how many have you got?'

'Meatballs?'

'No, Claires.'

'Ten, I think.'

He stuffed a forkful into his mouth with one hand and tapped on his phone with the other. 'And how many clients?'

'Two hundred and something.'

He chewed then tapped on his phone again. 'According to this website, Claire is the 555th most popular name.'

I huffed. 'How is this helping anyone?'

'Well, statistically, from your sample size, you shouldn't have any Claires at all.'

'And?'

'Well, maybe people named Claire are more likely to be single? Maybe men don't like the name.'

I snatched the phone out of his hand and looked at the screen. 'These are stats from the US. And, besides, your hypothesis is totally flawed.'

'Stereotypes,' he said, stabbing another meatball. 'I bet if you look at your figures, you'll find loads of different trends. And when you've got a big enough sample size you'll be able to pinpoint the most eligible criteria in a man and a woman. Height, age, colouring, education and even name.'

'Yeah, hold the headlines. Women want men who are tall, dark, handsome and preferably not called Marvin.'

He popped the meatball into his mouth and shrugged his shoulders.

'Look, I have more important things to be doing right now than engaging in another we-live-in-a-brainwashed-society debate.' I held my head in my hands. 'I've promised all these people I'll help them.' I lifted my head and stared at the mountain of meatballs. 'Two hundred and something promises. So far, not one has been fulfilled.'

He leant across the table and scooped some mash from my plate. 'You need help.'

I stared at him. 'I hope you mean practical and not psychological.'

He smirked, his expression softening. 'Promise me you won't make any more promises until you've found someone to help you?'

Five minutes later, my phone rang and just as Matthew forked the final meatball off my plate, I'd ended the call with yet another firm promise.

Matthew wiped his mouth with a napkin and glared at me.

'It was a journalist,' I said, pointing to some gravy he'd missed on his chin.

He frowned.

'From *Glamour* magazine.'

Still frowning.

'I couldn't say no.'

He was scowling now.

'It's free publicity in a leading women's magazine.'

His expression softened.

'She needs three eligible bachelors for a feature.'

His eyebrows lifted.

'By tomorrow.'

He jumped out of his seat, grinning. Then flexed his non-existent muscles, coiffed his product-free weekend bouffant and struck a pose against a pillar in the restaurant. 'One down, two to go.'

'You're hardly a bachelor,' I said. 'You've had a girl-friend for two years.'

'About that,' he said, eyeing a previously undiscovered meatball nestled between my plate and the tray. He popped it into his mouth then chewed slowly and swallowed. 'There's something I need to tell you.'

I stared at him, trying to read his expression. The chewing wasn't helping.

He swallowed, then cleared his throat. 'We got engaged at the weekend.'

I stared at him some more, wondering if this was the prelude to one of his jokes. 'What? You and Lucy?'

He smirked. 'No, me and Demetri, my secret Brazilian lover. Of course me and Lucy.'

I looked at Matthew, then down at the empty plate, then back at Matthew. 'Why didn't you tell me?'

'I just did.'

'You know what I mean.'

He scrunched up his mouth and shifted in his seat.

I rolled my eyes and explained, once again, that I was okay and not about to break down at the very mention of anything wedding related, and that perhaps, after ten years of friendship, an afterthought, over meatballs in the Ikea canteen was not the most desirable way to be informed of a close friend's future nuptials.

He looked sufficiently sheepish so I leant forward and gave him a hug. 'Congratulations,' I said, squeezing him tight.

He pulled back and stared at me for a moment, as if to check I was okay and not about to run amok with my meatball fork, stabbing happy couples who were browsing furniture.

'Come on,' he said, taking my hand, 'let's get these Claires on some dates.'

Back at the flat after Matthew and I had paired off all my unmatched Claires and other clients as best we could, it was time to make my way into town for another appointment. I squeezed into a navy shift dress which was borderline in terms of snugness on a skinny day, but after a plateful of meatballs seemed to defy Hooke's law of elasticity. I sucked in my tummy and grabbed my bag.

The moment the door to the flat clicked shut behind me, something felt different. Although disgruntled by his means of communication, Matthew's happy news had put a spring in my step. I took a deep breath. The chill in the air had lifted, the frost on the grass had melted and tulips poked their heads out from the soil as though they had awoken from a deep sleep. But it wasn't until I looked up to see the sun edging out from behind the clouds, and felt its warmth on my skin, that I realised just how long the winter had been.

On the way to the train station, I began phoning the eligible bachelors I'd recently acquired to ask if they might like to take part in a 'once in a lifetime opportunity' to reach an audience of over one million women. Sadly, most of them didn't share my enthusiasm for international media exposure while labelled as a lonely single and politely declined. But by the time I'd arrived at the bar, and after I'd reiterated that *Glamour* was the title of the publication and not the nature of the shoot, Mike and Stephen had been persuaded. Also, a barrister called John was a maybe depending on his schedule.

Later on at the club, and nestled comfortably in my favourite leather chair with a glass of wine, I was preparing to meet Alistair, an architect who had sent an online enquiry, when a text message somehow squeezed its way through the walls of the vaults to appear on my phone.

Fancy 'crashing' at mine again tonight? x

Kat's text included a photo, which was taking its time to download. Baffled, I shook my head and then looked up to see Brigitte wiggling towards me, her boobs bobbing up and down in a too-tight V-neck jumper.

'Ellieee. There ees a man to see you,' she said, stopping and placing her hands on her hips as though she'd reached the end of a catwalk. 'I sind 'im down?'

I nodded, then, preoccupied with my search for magazine fodder, began to assess all the groups of businessmen in the bar. The journalist had asked for eligible men, which she'd defined as good-looking and wealthy. In fact, she may have said wealthy before good-looking. Either way, the purpose of the feature, as she'd gone on to explain, was to highlight the struggles such men have finding women who can see beyond their looks and wealth. I suspected it wasn't in my best interests to point out that an airbrushed photograph, alongside an article discussing their net worth, might not be the best way.

The appearance of a pair of shoes coming down the staircase broke my trance. In other contexts, when meeting someone new, it was a face-on affair and the whole person came into focus at once. But, because the lounge bar was underground, I met most of my clients feet first, which, although a little strange, afforded me time to assess areas often otherwise neglected.

After the black leather brogues came expensive-looking charcoal-grey trousers. I took a sip of my wine. Nice thighs. Smart belt. Fitted blue shirt. Great chest, lovely muscles.

The room suddenly felt hot and stuffy. My face flushed and my breathing quickened. His face came into view. *Oh, shit. Shit, shit, shit.* It was Nick.

Striding towards me with his gorgeous smile at full capacity, he held his hands up. 'I'm Alistair,' he confessed.

While emitting a machine-gun-like laugh, I proceeded to spill half my glass of wine down my chin and dress.

'It's the only way I could get to see you,' he explained, looking on sympathetically as I dabbed my chin with a napkin. 'What with you being so busy and independent.'

I smiled inwardly and then moved my phone away from the puddle of wine on the table.

'Can I sit down?'

'Yes, sorry, sure,' I said, glancing at the screen which had just lit up.

'So how long have we got? How long would it take you to discover Alistair's deep and dark inner soul?'

'I've got another consultation in an hour,' I said, noticing that Kat's photo download was complete. I squinted my eyes at the image.

'Great, that means I have your undivided attention until then,' he said, following my gaze. His eyes widened. 'Is that a milkmaid?'

Lurching forward to reach the phone, I accidentally knocked it on the floor. Nick swooped down to grab it and then stared at the screen. He looked back at me, his mouth open.

'I don't think that message was meant for me.'

He smirked. 'Isn't that your friend from the party the other night? The one who was chasing those pilots around?'

'I'm surprised you can recognise her from that angle.'

He looked back down at the screen and turned it sideways, then upside down. 'She's got distinctive eyes,' he said, before handing it back to me.

Our giggles hushed when Steve approached the table. 'Did I miss something?' he asked.

'No nothing, just a funny text, that's all,' I muttered.

Steve handed me a glass of wine. 'Thought you might want another, seeing as you're wearing the last one.'

I looked back down at my dress, which was now sporting an interesting across-the-boob wine stain.

'And your boyfriend?' He turned to Nick. 'What can I get you, mate?'

'He's not my boyfriend,' I said.

'Not *yet*,' said Nick. 'A whiskey for me, please.'

Following what appeared to be some kind of fraternal nod of approval, Steve left and I looked across at Nick. His expression fell somewhere between delighted and constipated.

'So then, *Alistair*.' I picked up my pen and notepad. 'Describe your perfect woman.'

He smirked. 'A milkmaid with no knickers and inhuman flexibility.'

I rolled my eyes.

'Or,' he added, leaning forward, 'if you don't have one of those, how about a stunningly beautiful, independent yet busy blonde, wearing an impossibly tight navy dress with an ominous stain?'

I pretended to take notes, hoping my face didn't look as hot as it felt.

He leant forward. 'I mean you. Just to be clear.'

He reached for my hand. Before he made contact, I pulled away and picked up my glass. Following a long awkward sip of wine, my phone vibrated as another text appeared.

It was a long-winded message from John, the barrister, describing his entire week's work schedule and explaining that it wasn't compatible with the photo shoot tomorrow.

'He must be lying,' Nick said after I'd shown him the text. 'Men never offer that much detail unless they're lying.'

I sat back in my chair and rapped my fingers on the table. 'Doesn't it take one to know one, though?' I asked, eyebrows raised.

'No.'

I leant forward and looked into his eyes. 'You could be lying. How can I trust you?'

'Because, Your Honour, as I clearly stated, men offer excessive detail when they're lying and mine was a one word answer.'

'Hmm, so I'll have to let you off on a technicality,' I said, leaning back again. 'But I'm watching you.'

I pointed to my eyes and then back at him.

He took a glug of whiskey. 'So what makes you so suspicious of men?'

I laughed. 'I could ask the same of you. You're the one who said John was lying. Anyway, back to the photo shoot, the day's nearly over and I only have two bachelors.'

He sighed. 'Do you realise that so far you've deflected every personal question I've asked?'

'Have I?' I asked, immediately aware that I had just proved him right.

'Okay.' He finished his whiskey and placed the glass on the table. 'Here's the deal: I'll do that bloody magazine shoot tomorrow if you'll promise to answer one question.'

'Deal,' I said, reaching across the table to shake his hand. As soon as we touched, I suddenly felt panicked so I pulled my hand back.

'What's the question?' I asked.

He looked me in the eye. 'Is there someone?'

'What do you mean?'

'I mean, is there someone?'

I giggled. 'Is that some kind of cryptic philosophical question?'

'It's a simple question. Are you with someone?'

I shook my head. 'No.'

'You're single?'

'That's two questions.'

He smirked. 'No, it's not. It's the same question.'

'Yes. I'm single. And no, there isn't anyone.'

'Okay,' he said, standing up. 'That's all I needed to know.' His smile beamed down at me and, when he touched my shoulder gently, the panic suddenly returned. 'You're off the hook. For now,' he added before walking way.

As he walked towards the stairs, Brigitte leant against the banister, her legs and lips slightly parted, her pupils narrowed to slits.

'*Au revoir*, Alistair,' she purred, but he ignored her then threw a glance back over his shoulder towards me.

When he was out of sight, Brigitte shook her black hair and strutted over.

'Der ees a woman to see you. I sind 'er down,' she said, before redirecting her attention to Steve who was loitering behind the bar.

While I waited, I wondered what exactly it was that Nick thought he liked about me. Had my GHD'd hair triggered neuronal connections linked to images of super-sexy models in marketing campaigns? Or maybe he'd received a string of subliminal messages from the media which programmed him to be especially responsive to navy blue? Or was it more instinctual? My waist-to-hip ratio? The distance between my eyes? The width of my smile? Maybe it was Freudian and I reminded him of his mother. Or perhaps it was my smell, an unconscious indication that our immune systems were compatible.

It couldn't really be my personality. He hadn't felt the full force of that yet. So it had to be something else. There were plenty of other girls he could have chosen. And I hadn't exactly been receptive. Maybe he just liked a challenge or had some masochistic urge to be punished. But, whatever the reason was, I decided it was unlikely to be more than a string of assumptions extrapolated from first impressions and resolved to regard it with caution.

My thoughts were interrupted by a middle-aged lady sitting down in front of me and placing her hands on her lap as though she had just joined a bus queue. It took a few moments to register that she was thirty years older than I was expecting her to be.

'Emily?' I asked.

'No, don't be silly, dear. I'm Susan, Emily's *mother*.' She opened her Margaret Thatcher handbag. '*This* is Emily.'

She placed a photo on the table. It was of a fresh-faced brunette, wearing a summer dress and eating an ice cream on a pebbled beach. Her nose looked slightly burned, I noticed.

'She's pretty,' I said, unsure as to what she expected.

'She is very pretty, dear. Never had any problem with suitors. Plenty of boys sniffing around.'

'Does she know you're here?' I asked, suspecting that her mother had taken it upon herself to find poor Emily a husband.

'No, of course not, dear,' she said, waving my question away. 'Can I get a cup of tea, dear? I'm parched.'

I suppressed a giggle and tried to think of who she reminded me of as I waved Steve over.

'Mrs Doubtfire,' Steve whispered in my ear after he'd taken her order of 'Lady Grey, in a pot, two tea bags, splash of cold water.'

Yes, there was definitely something Robin-Williams-in-drag about her, but perhaps with a little bit of Angela Lansbury thrown in.

Emily's mother was quick to the get to the point. 'Emily needs a good man. The problem with her is she chooses the wrong ones. And she sleeps with them too. That's her mistake. He's not going to buy the donkey if he can get the ride for free, is he?'

I frowned at the bizarre analogy.

'And she could do with losing a few pounds.' She pointed to Emily's thighs in the photo. 'She's got my hips, poor love. She has to be careful. Men don't want to marry a little Oompa Loompa, do they now? That's what I tell her. But she doesn't listen.'

'You tell her she's an Oompa Loompa?' I asked, unsurprised as to why poor Emily might be packing on the pounds.

She shook her head. 'And look how short that skirt is?' She pointed back at Emily's thighs. 'She complains about the men she meets. But you know what I say?'

'Go on.'

'If you don't like the fish you're catching, then change the bait.'

'I thought Oprah said that?'

Suddenly Steve was standing next to us with a pot of tea. Emily's mum looked him up and down.

'You seem a nice young man,' she said, snatching the teapot from him. 'But Emily can do better than a barman. Are there any biscuits?'

'It's more of a wine bar,' I replied, noticing that Steve had skedaddled.

'If they sell tea, they should have biscuits. Some nice Bourbons would go down a treat. But probably best for you they don't, though. That dress is a little tight already, isn't it, dear? And that awful stain. Soak it in vinegar water to-night. That'll lift it.'

I forced a smile and she continued.

'What Emily needs is a wise woman like you to send her on the right path. With a job like this, you must have all the answers, dear. It's too late for me. Martin left me years ago and now it's just me and Gerald.' She took another sip of tea.

'Gerald?'

'Yes, dear, Gerald, the old boy, flea-ridden furball, love him with all my heart. But I want more for Emily. So how much do you charge? I've got some savings for a rainy day.'

'Let me have a chat with Emily first and I'll only charge if she's willing to give it a go.'

'That's sweet of you, dear. But you will persist with her, won't you? She's stubborn as a mule that one.'

Wonder where she gets it from? I thought as I watched her marching up the stairs, knocking people out of the way with her handbag.

When I arrived home, I found two Post-it notes from Matthew stuck to the fridge. The first was a list of URLs for recruitment websites along with a stern reminder that I 'needed help'. The second informed me that he had moved out to live with Lucy and her parents because he felt uncomfortable living with another woman now they were engaged. His upbeat recompense was that I could help myself to any of his food in the fridge. Uninspired by his offering of half a tin of baked beans and some stale bread, I rummaged in the freezer drawer for my emergency microwavable meal. While I consumed the contents, the appearance of which differed vastly from the image on the packet, I thought about Matthew and how much I would miss him. I knew that the only thing constant in life was change, yet, knowing it did little to ease the pain. I'd taken it for granted that Matthew would always be there, with his untameable hair and unsolicited opinions. I looked down at the congealed macaroni cheese and let out a deep sigh. Matthew had his life to live now, his handleless kitchen to design, his children to raise, his schnauzer to walk. But it felt as though I had been left here waiting, abandoned, in the holding pen that was singledom.

I threw the rest of the meal in the bin, grabbed a half-empty bottle of Pinot Grigio from the fridge, filled a glass to the brim, then sat down to type the first web address into my laptop.

It only took a few minutes to set up a profile, but I paused when I came to the job description box. I was tempted to type: 'Flatmate, confidant and matchmaker required; must have unruly quiff and quirky sense of humour.' However, I knew Eros would be disappointed if, after all his effort in summoning me, he discovered I was prioritising my personal life. I needed to focus. I'd received a hundred new enquiries that day alone, I had another party to organise and I still hadn't finished matching all the Claires. I took another gulp of wine and began to type:

'Matchmaker wanted.'

I paused again as I considered what to write.

'Must care about people, be a self-starter and willing to work antisocial hours. No qualifications necessary.'

I filled in the rest of the details with an overwhelming sense of relief that help would soon be on its way. Then, just as I was about to shut down my laptop, an email slipped into my inbox.

To: Ellie
From: Jeremy
Subject: New addition
Attachment: RustyJunior.jpeg
Hi Ellie
Harriet and I wanted to say hello from the Scottish Highlands and introduce you to our new family member!
Love and thanks
J + H
xxx

Family member? It had only been a few weeks! I opened the image, half expecting to find a black-market baby propped up in an infant hiking sling. However, instead it was of Jeremy at the top of a mountain, grinning against the wind, his arm wrapped protectively around Harriet. Between them, nestling snugly was a large and excited-looking puppy, all paws and ears and with his tongue hanging out. The puppy's eyes shone with contentment, the kind that is only experienced by those who are truly capable of living in the moment.

A tear weaved its way down my cheek. Maybe I didn't have all the answers. Maybe there were no answers. Maybe a string of extrapolated assumptions was all we needed to begin. And, as with the mountain Jeremy and Harriet had climbed, it wasn't the research, equipment or clothing that took them to the top, it was the motivation and will to get there.

Chapter 8

To: Ellie
From: Mandi
Subject: Cupid's apprentice
Dearest Ellie,
I was so excited to read your ad for a matchmaker and (without wanting to sound big-headed!) I believe I was made for this role and this role was made for me. (Isn't that a song?)
I'm sure you'll receive hundreds of applications, so, instead of waffling on about my interest in dating and relationships and having transferable skills from my current sales role, I would like to take a more unorthodox (and I hope you don't think unprofessional) approach and get directly to the point.
Pretty, pretty please (with lashings of pink icing, and some of those sugary silver balls on top) give me the opportunity to meet with you. I promise you won't be disappointed!

I have attached my CV and a photo of me hosting my annual 'Cupid party' for single friends.
Yours hopefully!
Mandi
xxx
P.S. I'm free tonight.

I SHIELDED MY phone from the low rays of the setting sun and opened the image. I could just about make out what looked to be a real-life Disney character: white-blonde hair, Colgate smile and teeny-tiny pink Cupid outfit complete with bow and arrow. I smiled, lifted my face to the sun and let the warmth soak in, knowing it would soon be lost to the concrete horizon.

By the time I arrived at the club, the amber sky had turned inky blue and my phone sprung to life, Cassandra's number flashing on the screen. The accompanying ringtone seemed louder than usual, as though it had adjusted its volume to reflect the caller. It was the seventh time she'd called that day and I'd meant to return her call along with William's four missed calls, as they had obviously been on a date and had something to tell me. But, for some reason, I'd been putting it off.

I let Cassandra's call go to voicemail, and called William first, suspecting his version of events would be kinder to my eardrums.

'Hi, how are you?'

'Hello, Ellie. Sorry. Can you hold on a moment?' His voice was hushed, and his words were followed by some rustling, and the sound of footsteps on a tiled floor. 'Right, that's better, ouch, ow.'

'Are you okay?'

'Not really. I'm in the hospital.'

The phone nearly slipped from my grasp. 'Oh, God, what happened?'

'It's all a tad embarrassing really.' He cleared his throat. 'Nothing serious though. I broke something.'

'Broke something?'

'Yes. Something personal.'

'Something personal?' *What*, I thought, *like his watch*?

'Something private.'

'Something private?'

He sighed. 'Please don't make me say it.'

I heard more groans and then fortunately, for both of us, the penny finally dropped.

'Oh, God. Oh, dear. Poor you. Will *it* be okay?'

'The doctors say I need to rest it.'

I imagined a willy with a thermometer lying on a sofa.

'Is there anything I can do to help?' I asked. 'Or Cassandra, perhaps she could help?'

'Well, she's the one who got me into this fine mess in the first place.' He laughed. 'Ow, laughing is not a good idea.'

After William, evidently growing more at ease with the topic, had gone on to explain the entire treatment plan, which included a pioneering programme of rehabilitative physiotherapy, I became desperate to steer the conversation away from the anatomical fragility of the male member.

'So, apart from the…the incident, the date went well?'

'Yes,' he replied. 'I suppose.'

'You suppose?'

'She was nice.'

Of all the words to describe Cassandra, *nice* was not one that immediately sprang to mind.

'But,' he went on, 'she's probably a bit too much for me.'

Ah, I thought, *here comes the truth*. I checked my watch. I only had a few minutes to spare. 'Try to sum up your thoughts in one sentence.'

He took a deep breath. 'She was lovely-looking: slim, elegant, well dressed. Great skirt. It was pleated. And quite short, rather like a tennis—'

'One sentence, William,' I interrupted.

'Oh, yes, okay. Right.'

'Did you like her personality?'

'She was a little loud.' He paused. 'But she made me laugh and she was clever too.' He paused again. 'I think I'm going to need a few more sentences.'

I laughed. 'Okay.'

'And she drank a lot.'

'That's quite normal though.'

'No, I mean, she drank *a lot*. She'd drained her glass before I'd even picked mine up. Then she got this wild look in her eye.'

'Wild?'

'When we left the bar, she dragged me into a cab—' he interrupted himself with a nervous laugh '—and then back at her flat it was as though she were…how do I put this?'

'Just say it.'

He coughed. 'Ouch.' I heard some more rustling, and then he cleared his throat. 'Okay, if you must know, it felt as though she were auditioning for a triple X-rated *Cirque du Soleil*.'

I took the phone away from my ear and looked at it for a moment, while my mind conjured imagery for contemporary clown porn. 'Did you tell her to stop?'

He paused again. 'I did, eventually.'

'What do you mean "eventually"?'

'I think it was at the point she launched herself at me from a sex swing while brandishing a dildo. And then again, when she clamped my nipples. And once again when she inserted some kind of plugging device up my bottom.'

I giggled, though this time more from panic than amusement.

'Any protest just seemed to encourage her. If I'm honest, hospital was a welcome relief.'

Concerned I might be liable for William's future therapy sessions, I ended the call with a promise to note his preference for missionary twice a week and 'a special treat' at the weekend. Then, I shook my head to try to lose the disturbing image of Cassandra flying through the air, to the soundtrack of *Alegría* while aiming a dildo at William's bottom.

A gale had begun to whip up outside, so I moved into the club, before dialling her number.

'Oh. My. God. Ellie!' she bellowed as the wind funnelled down the stairs behind me. Struggling to turn the volume down, I accidentally hit the loudspeaker button. 'I didn't even know that a penis could break. Did you? Have you ever broken one?'

Her voice boomed across reception like a misjudged soundcheck. A group of men waiting to be seated stopped talking and looked over.

'No, but I'm sure it happens all the time,' I replied, pressing buttons until I was confident the loudspeaker function had been disabled. The men nodded, while Brigitte smiled with what looked to be a kind of satisfied recollection. *Maybe it did happen all the time?* I thought. *Perhaps I should add it to my list of things to do before I'm thirty.*

'I didn't do anything, it just sort of slipped out, you know. When I landed back down on his lap he started screaming.'

'Landed?'

'He was writhing all over the place like I'd torn it off or something. A real drama queen. So, I called a taxi to take him to hospital.'

'You didn't go with him?'

'No. Is he okay?'

'Yes, he's fine. He just needs to rest it.'

She laughed. 'Rest it? Does it get its own hospital bed and gown?'

'Cassandra.'

'Sorry, but it is funny.'

When her extended belly laugh had concluded, she explained that, although William was a lovely guy, she'd prefer a man more 'up for the job' next time.

Then was, I realised, the time when a professional matchmaker was supposed to offer insightful feedback. I moved to the corner of reception to talk more privately, although I was aware that ship had already sailed.

'Could I offer you some advice?'

'Go on, then,' she replied.

'Maybe tone it down a bit next time.'

'Tone what down?'

The men were still loitering around the reception desk clearly in no hurry to be seated.

'Perhaps save the sex toys for your second date,' I said in a hushed voice.

'What? I can't hear you. Speak up!'

I expanded my point slowly and clearly. The words *anal* and *plug* bounced back at me from the acoustics of the reception walls. The men's concealed sniggers were quickly drowned out by Cassandra's laughter cackling down the phone.

'Don't be such a prude. You English, seriously. That was only my starter pack. I've got the proper stuff in the dungeon.'

'What?'

'I'm joking.'

I sighed. 'Listen, whipping out a dildo on the first night will put most men off. And the men who *are* into it probably wouldn't stick around for a relationship.'

'*C'est la vie.* They obviously aren't the right men for me, then. I'll wait for one who loves me for who I am. Next!'

When I'd ended the call, with a promise to add 'open-minded' to Cassandra's list of wants in a man, I went to call Matthew, wondering what his take would be on the scenario. However the moment I went to dial his number, I stopped myself. He wasn't back at our flat with a bottle of wine, waiting for me. Instead hc was with his fiancée, no doubt designing their new kitchen or searching online for a schnauzer puppy. I slipped my phone back into my bag and continued down towards the bar, a heavy weight in my step.

Through the crowd, I noticed a pretty blonde on a stool at the bar. She waved at me and I walked over.

'Claire?'

She nodded.

'Sorry I'm late, having one of those days,' I explained, pulling up a stool next to her.

'I heard,' she replied in a Californian accent. 'I walked past you at reception. Did she really plug his ass?'

I nodded and she laughed.

After Steve had poured us each a glass of wine, she explained why Nate had suggested I meet her.

'He's my twin brother,' she began, flashing teeth identical to his. 'I know him better than he knows himself. But—' she took a sip of wine '— this whole process is pointless. He's wasting your time. No one will measure up.'

'To what?'

'To whom, you mean. To Rebecca, his first love.'

I remembered the name Rebecca from my Google search on Nate's relationship history. Claire went on to explain that Nate and Rebecca had been inseparable since high school. She dragged her nails along the brass edge of the bar.

'She was like a sister to me,' she said, just as one of them snapped off. 'But then Nate fucked it all up.'

I frowned. 'How?'

She examined the nail tip and then threw it on the floor. 'Sleeping around.'

She went on to explain that when Nate's acting career took off, fans started throwing themselves at him and that he was too weak to resist.

'And, of course, after a few years, when the bright lights had faded and the groupies had lost their appeal, he realised that a quiet family life was exactly what he wanted. And Rebecca was the one he wanted it with.'

'And now she's with someone else?'

'Yes, married, baby on the way.' She looked down. 'But…'

'But what?'

'She still loves him.'

'Oh.'

'But, she'd never take him back. She'd sooner stay in a loveless marriage than forgive him for what he did.'

'How do you know it's loveless?' I asked, thinking of the baby about to be born into this.

'She loves Nate. She always has. But she knows he's no good.'

'He's your brother.'

'Once a cheater, always a cheater.'

'You really believe that?'

She nodded. 'Anyway, despite all this, it seems he's determined for you to match him, so you may as well go through the motions. But I'm telling you, no one will be good enough, so best of luck.'

As she marched up the stairs and out of the bar, I wondered how a pretty girl, with the 555th most popular name in America, had lost her faith in men.

Still perched on the stool after the bar had emptied out, I noticed a stream of light shining down from the ceiling. I looked up to see a skylight I hadn't noticed before, tunnelled through the walls of the vaults. Outside, dusk had come and gone, yet a light shone through, brighter than the glow of the street lamps and whiter than the sliver of moon.

Through the gleam, a girl bounced down the stairs, grinning and waving. Just as in her photo, her ice-white smile sparkled and her bright blonde hair shimmered as though she'd been doused in fairy dust. Wearing a hot-pink pencil skirt and a tight white shirt, her corporate-Cupid ensemble was completed with a pink handbag from which she retrieved a heart-shaped notebook.

'I'm so excited,' Mandi said as she sat down, 'so, please excuse me if I talk too fast. I do that when I'm nervous. And excited. I'm so excited. I said that already, didn't I? Sorry. Do you mind if I take notes?'

She gripped a sparkly pink pen, which had a glittery heart, bouncing on the end. Unsure as to what questions an employer should ask a potential matchmaker, I went with the first that sprang to mind.

'What is love?' I asked, immediately fearing she might misinterpret the question as a prompt to the lyrics of Haddaway's one-hit wonder.

She grinned, put down her pen, looked up to the skylight and then back down at me.

Half an hour later, after she had regurgitated her extensive knowledge on the topic of love, which appeared to be drawn from an array of Jennifer Aniston movies, Celine Dion lyrics and a broad spectrum of fairy tales, she eventually arrived at a conclusion.

'Celine's so wise, almost like a guru.' She clasped her hands together. 'She said that love was a single soul inhabiting two bodies. Isn't that just magical, she's amazing, isn't she?'

'I thought Aristotle said that?'

She frowned and then made a note in her book.

Next, with that day's revelations still fresh in my mind, I decided to try her with some real-life case studies. But before I'd fully considered how to form the sentence, the words blurted out.

'Have you ever broken a penis?'

She cocked her head and stared at me for a moment. 'No, but I'm sure it's quite a common occurrence.'

I smiled, trying to maintain a professional poise.

Following my cue, she flashed her shiny teeth and laughed. 'Ah ha, that was brilliant. You were testing me, to see how I would deal with the more challenging scenarios. Brilliant. Did I do okay? I think I did. I wouldn't want to be presumptuous though. I hope I passed. Did I pass?'

I nodded.

'This is so exciting. I'm so good at dealing with issues like this. I don't mean broken penises. Or is it *peni*? Like cacti? Well, I probably would be, if required. When I was a Girl Guide, I was brilliant at first aid, won an extra badge for my slings. Not that a penis would need a sling. Or would it? But that's not the point, is it? What I meant was, I'm really good at dealing with personal issues like this. Like that—I love it. I'm rambling, I know, I'm just so excited, I love helping people, that's what I meant to say. I'm talking too much, I know. I do that when I'm excited. I know, I said that. Sorry. Do you have any more questions? Please.'

I went on to describe the Nate-Rebecca scenario.

'Well, that *is* a tricky one,' she said and then took a deep breath. 'On one hand, I can totally see how poor Rebecca might feel. I mean, all those girls, she must have been heartbroken. And she has every reason to worry that he might not change his ways. And she has a baby on the way. The baby needs a stable home. Deserves love, deserves its mum to be happy. But if Nate really has changed and, you know, grown up and all that, and realised that she is the love of his life, and if she still loves him, well then they should get back together.' She took another deep breath. 'But he can't just swan back in her life and expect it all to go in his favour. He must earn her love and trust back and that starts by him changing his life before he even tries to get her back, to prove that he is serious. Don't you think? Oh, I really hope they can work it out. It would be so sad if they couldn't work it out, wouldn't it? Can I help them, if I get the job, can I help Nate and Rebecca, please?'

I quickly processed my thoughts. An experienced recruiter would have most likely responded with words such as 'consider' and 'application' with a promise to get back to her the following week, but I couldn't see any reason to delay. I'd already made up my mind.

'Welcome to the world of dating,' I said, and stood up to shake her hand. She leapt forward, bypassing my hand and flung her arms around my neck.

'Thank you! Thank you! You won't regret this.' She jumped up and down and started clapping like a seal. 'This is so exciting! I'm so excited. I said that already, didn't I? Sorry. When do I start? Can I start tomorrow?'

The beam from the skylight seemed to follow her path as she bounced up the stairs and out of the club.

Just as I was packing up my notes, preparing to go home, Brigitte slinked towards me.

'Ellieee your nixt cleeant ees 'ere.'

'But I don't have any more appointments tonight.'

'I sind 'er down,' she said, clearly perceiving it as my problem to solve.

I grabbed my phone and scrolled through the calendar to look for any missed appointments, when in breezed a leggy blonde. Her hair was swept up into a high ponytail, which was swinging like a palomino's tail. Encased in a tight charcoal-grey dress, her thoroughbred body was toned to perfection: one of the lucky few whose liver appeared to enjoy destroying unwanted fat cells, as though it were partaking in some kind of blood sport.

She swerved past the few remaining men in the bar as though accidentally touching one might result in the transmission of an incurable disease. Then she strode towards me with her hand outstretched.

'Hi,' she said, and then sat down opposite me, locking me with a cold fixed glare. Her face was as striking as her figure: sharp cheekbones and staggering turquoise eyes. She should have been beautiful, but there was something that didn't quite work, a certain hardness that I couldn't define.

I flicked through my calendar. 'I'm sorry, but I don't re-call scheduling an appointment with you.'

'I'm Victoria,' she said as though it would explain ev-erything. 'A friend of Harriet's.'

I raised one eyebrow. Well, I intended to raise one but, having never fully mastered this quizzical gesture, I most likely raised both, resulting in an expression of surprise rather than intelligent scepticism as intended.

She continued, unfazed by my bizarre facial contortions. 'I sent an enquiry via your website but you didn't get back to me, so I thought I'd come along to see if anyone was ac-tually working at your agency.'

'That's weird,' I replied. 'When did you send it?'

'Oh, I can't remember, at least an hour ago.'

I suppressed an eye roll. 'Well, you certainly would have had a response by—'

'Whatever,' she said and lifted her hand as though stop-ping traffic. 'We're wasting time, let's get on with it.'

I sat back down and heaved my bag onto the seat next to me.

'Garçon, champagne. J'ai soif,' she said, snapping her fingers at Steve, who couldn't look less French if he tried.

While he took an uncharacteristically long time to bring our drinks, we spoke—well, to be accurate, she spoke—about what she was looking for in a man. He had to be tall, good-looking, successful, wealthy, never married, no chil-dren (yet) and good family values.

'So you want children?' I asked, just as the champagne arrived. Steve placed her glass down on the table with a sinister grin.

'About time.' She glared at him then looked back at me. 'Well, I want to leave a legacy.' She took a sip and pulled a face. 'With my looks and intelligence, I have a duty to breed, don't you think?'

I hoped she was joking, but her earnest expression revealed otherwise.

'Not to the detriment of my career or social life, of course. I'll have a nanny, a live-in au pair or something. And a cleaner. I'm not into any of that domestic stuff. Hideous. Anyway, how about Jeremy? I could see myself with him.'

'Jeremy?'

'Yes Je-re-my,' she repeated as though I were a moron. 'Harriet's ex.'

'Harriet's ex?'

'Yes Harriet's ex,' she continued impatiently. 'Are you unwell?'

'No, I'm fine, thank you for your concern, just a little confused. As far as I'm aware, Harriet and Jeremy are dating. Besides, I don't think you two are suited at all.'

'Harriet dumped him last night, so he *is* available, actually. That's why I decided to come by before you matched him with anyone else.' She glared at me, her eyes opaque like ice on a lake. 'Or if you can't manage him, I'd like one of these?'

She slammed down a magazine opened at the centre-spread feature.

'We're too rich to get married.' I read out the title and looked down at the men. It was the magazine feature I'd roped Nick into.

'But not that one.' She pointed at the photo of Nick, his arm casually slung over a leather sofa in an uncharacteristically arrogant pose.

I need someone who understands my lifestyle, or so Nick had said, as I gathered from the captioned quote above his head.

'Shit. He's never going to forgive me for this,' I muttered.

'Sorry?' she interrupted. 'Are you paying attention? This feature is about your dating service, is it not?'

'Yes, it is. But it was supposed to be about eligible men who struggled to find nice girls to date. Not about how rich they were.' I stared at the page and then cringed at the hyperbolic descriptions of Nick's property portfolio and extensive wine collection.

'Whatever. Please pay attention. If I am going to hire you as my matchmaker, you will have to sharpen up.'

After handing me a pre-counted cash payment, she explained that she would be in touch tomorrow regarding her date with Jeremy. Then she flounced off, almost mowing Brigitte down as they passed each other on the staircase.

Steve was giggling when I walked over to pay for the champagne.

'I've only put one glass on the bill,' he said. 'I think the other one might have been contaminated.'

I smirked and then opened the magazine on the bar. 'What do you think about this?'

He scanned the page and his laughter faded.

'Wasn't that the guy you were with the other day?'

I nodded.

He continued reading and shook his head. 'Not good, sweet cheeks. Not good.'

I sighed, looking up to the skylight. All I could see was black.

'But, on the plus side, if he can forgive you for that, he could forgive you for anything.'

His throaty laugh echoed in my ears as I made my way home, fighting against the wind as it funnelled through the empty streets.

Chapter 9

WILLING A MESSAGE to arrive from Nick, my eyes flitted between the screen of my laptop and my phone. It had been two weeks since the magazine feature. Two weeks of unsettled weather, storms gathering and then passing in the blink of an eye. Just as the sun looked as though it might prevail, clouds would sweep across, like a damp blanket over a fire. And with each day, my hope was fading.

Lying on the sofa, laptop balanced on my legs, I gazed through the window, up at the sky. I watched the sun trying to burn through a wispy cloud and I imagined the email I had been willing to arrive for the past two weeks. If I concentrated hard enough, maybe by the time I looked back down at the screen it would be there at the top of the list.

The email would begin with a brief yet plausible justification for the two-week delay, then, with wit and charm, Nick might go on to explain how entertained he was by the feature, how hilarious he found it and perhaps suggest a drink that evening to dissect it properly. Later that evening, at an intimate wine bar, most likely one with a terrace overlooking the Thames, we would sip Provencal rosé from crystal glasses. Of course the weather would now be glorious. I could wear my new Warehouse dress and we might share some canapés, perhaps little crostini with an exotic terrine or some kind of tapenade. We would laugh and joke until the sun set, painting the sky pinky orange, and then, as he took my hand in his, he would gaze deep into my eyes to see his future reflected back at him. At that moment, he would be certain that, after years of searching, finally he had found 'the one'. Many more blissful nights would follow and, in no time at all, possibly three months, he would ask me to move in.

I kept staring out of the window, my mind continuing to wander, as I imagined living with Nick in his Hampstead pad. We could take strolls on the heath. And get a dog, one of those cute little scruffy ones. Perhaps redecorate and buy a new bed; a rococo carved wooden one painted white. I had always liked the shabby chic look. However, I reminded myself, it would be sensible that we invest in durable furniture that would also work with the interior of the town house we would buy when we were married. Providing Nick proposed within a year, then the wedding would be the following summer, after which we would start trying for a family. I would be thirty then. That's a good age. Not the originally targeted twenty-eight, when I'd planned to have my first child, but close enough. Nick would be a great dad. We'd probably have girls. Alternatively, one girl and one boy. Names? Maia and Patrick. Or Joseph. Yes, I like those.

For two more hours I waited for the email or call—either would work in this scenario—which would begin it all. My future happiness was hanging by a thread. But, infuriatingly, it was now ten a.m. and again nothing. Frustrated by this annoying delay on my path to fulfilment, and noticing yet another ominous-looking cloud drifting towards the sun, I decided to type an email.

To: Nick
From: Ellie
Subject: Sorry
Still talking to me? x

I called Matthew in a panic.

'No, that's pathetic. Delete it immediately,' he instructed. 'Hide your phone and laptop if necessary. What *has* got into you?'

'Don't you get all judgemental now, just because you're *engaged*.'

'I'm not being judgemental. You're being mental. Anyway, I thought you were off men?'

'So did I.'

He sighed, another one of his what-did-I-do-to-deserve-a-friend-like-you sighs. 'And you said *no* when he asked you out.'

'I did.'

'It's a classic case of wanting what you can't have,' Cordelia explained after Matthew had insisted I conference her in. 'When he wanted you, you didn't want him. Now you know he probably hates you, you want him. Now it's safe for you to want him with no danger of him wanting you back. You see, you're still avoiding getting hurt.'

'Or she's just being a twat,' Matthew chipped in.

'Are those my only two options?'

'Look, if he likes you, he'll get over your humongous fuck-up and call. You'll just have to wait and see,' Matthew said, before excusing himself from the conversation.

'Just don't try and sabotage it if he does, okay?' Cordelia added.

'What, like you did with Harry?'

'I dumped him. That's not sabotage. That was a well thought out and thoroughly considered decision.'

'You'll be back together next week.'

'Won't.'

'Will.'

'Won't.' She huffed. 'In fact, I wanted to ask you to set me up on some dates. This time I want someone who doesn't think employment is an infringement of their human rights.'

I hung up the phone, having promised to present Cordelia with a more ambitious, slightly slimmer version of Harry by the end of the week. Then I noticed yet another missed call from Emily's mother. Having left Emily a series of overenthusiastic voicemails, I suspected she was now screening my calls or maybe even in the midst of filing an injunction against me. However, I decided to give her one final try, but this time from my landline, withholding my number, in the manner of an amateur stalker.

'Hullo.'

'Emily?'

'Yes. Who is this?'

'My name's Ellie, I've left you a few voicemail messages about my dating service—'

'My mother put you up to this didn't she?'

'Well, yes, but—'

'That bloody woman! Why can't she just keep her giant nose out of my business?'

'I'm sure she means well.'

'Listen. Thanks for the call, but I'm really not that desperate that I need to use a dating agency. Okay? No offence.'

'You'd be surprised who uses the service, though. In fact, I set it up because I was single—'

'You sound old though,' she said, cutting me off again. 'No offence.'

'I'm twenty-eight.'

'That's quite old to still be single though, isn't it?'

'You're only three years away from twenty-eight.'

'Four actually, I'm only twenty-four. Twenty-five next month.'

I laughed, remembering how I felt at her age. With all the time in the world, the possibilities were endless. Life was an exciting journey, to be embraced with wild abandon, safe in the belief that everything would work out okay in the end.

'All right, I'll leave you in peace. But if you ever want to meet up for a chat, save my number.'

'Yeah, whatever. If I ever get that desperate, shoot me. No offence.'

Once I'd hung up the phone, I scrolled through Mandi's emails, which seemed to be dominating my inbox. Most of them, it appeared, were regarding the party she'd insisted we bring forward two weeks to mark her arrival.

'I love parties!' she'd said the day after I'd hired her. 'I'm so brilliant at parties! We should make it a ball. A masquerade ball. Yes! It simply has to be a ball. This is so exciting! This will be the best ball ever! Let's do it next week!'

After deleting twenty of her emails with the subject title 'Decorations', I moved on to Victoria's daily email, demanding a match within the next hour. I quickly sent her Dr Stud's profile, along with a photo of him leaning against the side of a yacht. It was a perfect scene: his sculpted muscles glistened in the sun, his jet-black hair flopped over ocean-blue eyes. His smile was as broad as the horizon and his teeth were as polished as the deck. She replied immediately.

'No. Too short. Have you heard back from Jeremy yet?'

When I'd worked my way through the remaining matches, including a last-minute decision to send the newly single Cordelia on a date with Dr Stud, I lay my head against the arm of the sofa. While I'd been working, thick clouds had crept in and smothered the sun, one after the other, layer after layer. I pulled up the sash. The air hung heavy outside, dense and motionless. My skin felt sweaty and my head throbbed, and it felt as though every promise I'd made was in there, banging away with a tiny hammer. When more emails piled into my inbox, to the point where I thought my laptop might actually topple over, I wondered if now might be the time to recruit another matchmaker.

Five minutes later, double-strength coffee in hand, I began scrolling through the CVs. Straight away I stumbled upon one from a girl named Thea. Her personal statement was concise if a little aggressive and the attached financial projections I thought unnecessary, however, overall she seemed to be an ideal candidate to offset Mandi's wayward exuberance. Immediately, I texted her to ask if she was available that night.

That evening, as the moon shone down like a spotlight in the sky, I stepped out of the taxi and onto the red carpet. Mandi, as though having been set the task of finding a castle to house all the princesses in the world, had picked the Hurlingham Club as the venue for our masquerade ball. The cool air sent shivers down my spine as I lifted up the hem of my silver dress and then climbed the flagstone staircase, making my way into the grand entrance hall.

When I walked through the arched doorway, I felt like I'd stepped into Mandi's fairy tale. Palm trees, glistening with fairy lights, lined the vast corridor that led to a twenty-foot atrium, which was lit up like a desert sky. Against the backdrop of red velvet and gold gilt, Mandi, wearing a full-length white satin gown, rushed over with an excited totter. Her soft blonde curls tumbled over her shoulders. An enormous white sparkling mask adorned her face. With her hourglass figure and flawless complexion, she looked like a real life Masquerade Barbie.

'I'm so glad you're here. Isn't this amazing?' She twirled around on the spot. 'I hope you don't mind, but I asked the props company to add these to the order.' She pointed proudly at the deep red satin sashes that hung from the ceilings. 'And a few other extras.' Elaborate candles, plush-looking cushions piled on velvet chaise longues and—wait—weren't they *marble* statues?

'What about our budget?' My dazed head grappled with the sums.

'I know. It was a bit extravagant, but our clients deserve it, don't they? Don't you think? It looks so amazing. I'm so excited for them. And besides, we can't put a price on romance, can we?'

'I thought that's exactly what you did.' A sharp tone interjected and we both turned around. 'Put a price on romance, I thought that's what this business was all about.'

A tall and slim woman was standing behind us. Mandi looked at her, then at me and then back at her.

'I'm Thea. Which one of you is Ellie?'

'I am.' I stepped forward and held out my hand.

With her tanned skin, mane of mahogany hair and slinky black dress, Thea looked like the wicked yet beautiful queen come to tempt Mandi with an apple. She locked onto me with her dark, almost black eyes, as we took a seat on one of the overdressed sofas.

'I hope this is a serious business and not just a couple of silly girls matchmaking,' she said after she pulled a be-jewelled cushion out from under her, and studied it with curiosity.

'Yes, of course,' I replied.

'Good. Because that's why I'm here. I think we could build this into an incredibly successful business.'

'This isn't Wall Street.' I laughed. 'It's a dating agency. But I admire your spirit.'

She sat forward in her seat and stared at me. 'The dating industry is currently worth in excess of a hundred million in the UK alone. Globally over two billion. Projected to be over four billion in five years' time.'

I looked around, wondering if somehow we'd been transported to an episode of *Dragons' Den*.

'That's great. But is it okay if I ask you a few questions first?'

'Sure.'

I pulled a notepad and pen from my bag. 'So,' I began, feeling a little disconcerted by the intensity of her stare. 'What appealed to you about the role?'

She laughed. 'I'm not going to pretend that I've always wanted to be a matchmaker, that it's my dream profession, or that I think love conquers all. I'd be a liar.'

Mandi wedged herself between us on the sofa and glared at her. 'So what do you think love is, then, Thea?'

Thea turned to Mandi. 'It varies with context, but generally speaking, I believe that romantic love is a social construct, a cultural concept engineered to control and manipulate society. François de La Rochefoucauld said that some people wouldn't have fallen in love if they had not heard there was such a thing, but, in my opinion, no one would have fallen in love if they hadn't been taught to expect eternal fulfillment upon meeting their soulmate.' She ran her finger along the gold piping of the chaise longue. 'It's a bit like Muslim fundamentalists believing they'll get seventy-two virgins if they strap explosives to their chest and jump on the Northern Line.'

Mandi's mouth opened and her eyes widened, as though we were debating the tooth fairy's very existence. 'You can't be a matchmaker if you don't believe in love. That's like being, I don't know, a musician who's deaf. It just wouldn't work.'

Thea rolled her eyes. 'Ever heard of Beethoven?'

Mandi clasped her hands together. 'Oh, I love that movie.'

Thea rolled her eyes again and pulled a cigarette out of her bag. 'Mind if I smoke?' she asked, already in the process of lighting it.

Straight away, I imagined blazing red sashes, a palm tree inferno, an invalid insurance policy and a crippling restoration fee.

'Being a realist—' Thea went on.

'Pessimist,' Mandi muttered.

'Being a realist—' she glared at Mandi '—I see love for what it is, which means I can help people on a practical level. Help them put a strategy into place for finding a partner. Despite the challenges.'

'What do you think the challenges are?' I asked, watching her ash drop onto the tabletop.

'We all say we're too busy. It's too hard to meet people. That's just a cover. The real issue is our expectations. The truth is we don't deserve to be happy. Wc aren't entitled to love. We have to earn it and fight to keep it. And even then most of the time it shits all over us.'

She inhaled deeply and puffed out the smoke in perfect concentric circles. Mandi started wheezing.

'And from what authority do you speak?' I asked, immediately realising that my inner Shakespearean actor had made a reappearance.

Unfazed by my random change of tone, she looked up at the ceiling and then back at me. 'My father was a Russian oligarch and my mother an Italian model. I learned more about relationships from their bullshit marriage than I ever did from my PhD in Psychology. Any more questions?'

Mandi leant forward. 'Have you ever broken a penis?'

'No,' she said, stubbing out her cigarette on the floor. 'But I would have liked to.'

I stood up with a smile and shook her hand. 'Welcome to the team.'

Mandi's wheezing escalated. She swallowed hard and then, with watering eyes and a red face, retrieved a pink glitter mask from her bag and offered it to Thea.

'This is for you,' she said.

Thea turned her nose up, as though she had been handed a snotty tissue. 'I brought my own, thanks.'

She pulled a black-feathered mask from her bag.

After they'd flown off in different directions, like the white and the black swan, I heard the throb of Buddha Bar music filtering through the atrium. It merged with the excited chatter of the guests as they funnelled through the corridor. After dismissing my mask as 'too boring', Mandi had replaced it with something that resembled a stuffed flamingo, the weight of which kept dragging it down my nose. Each time I pushed it back up, it slipped down again, but if I tipped my head back, I could just about see through the pink plumage.

I felt a tap on the mask. 'Is Ellie under there?'

I pulled it off and saw Jeremy looking back at me. He was wearing a black dinner jacket and a white shirt. His hair was swept back from his face. I half expected him to leap behind a pillar and start shooting Russian spies.

He looked down at my mask. 'Wow, that's a bit carnival.'

I laughed. 'I think it might actually be a recycled carnival float. I keep imagining little Brazilian people jumping up and down on it.'

He laughed, but his eyes didn't crease.

'So, how are you?'

'I'm okay.' He looked down at the floor. 'I got here early to have a quick chat. Do you have time?'

Glancing around the room, I saw Mandi introducing guests and Thea studying what looked like a price list at the bar.

I looked back at Jeremy. 'Sure. What's up?'

He blinked a few times and then looked back down at the floor. 'Harriet and I split up.'

A tear tracked down his cheek.

I offered him the mask. 'You can have this if you want?'

He laughed. 'I'd rather be seen bawling my eyes out in public than wear *that*.'

I led him to a chaise longue. After moving the many cushions aside, we sat down. Jeremy frowned as he tossed the remaining cushion, a red velvet bolster with gold tassels, to the floor. 'I love her, Ellie.'

'I know,' I said. 'What happened?'

His fist clenched. 'Her father.'

I raised my eyebrows.

'We went to stay with her family last weekend. At their country "estate".' He made silly inverted comma hand gestures around the word.

'And? What were they like?'

'Her mum was lovely. Quiet, but nice. But her dad. What a wanker. He treated me like I was some sort of backwards kid Harriet had brought home to show the family.'

I tried not to smile. It seemed inappropriate.

'And every time I spoke, he interrupted me or disagreed with what I had said.'

'The dads are always hard to win over. You must know that. Harriet is his little princess.'

'Yeah, well, I wasn't going to be treated like that.'

'No.'

'And then there was an incident with one of his gun dogs and a confit of duck. Which I got the blame for.'

I laughed.

'After that, he suggested I might be more comfortable eating in the parlour with the dogs. Pompous twat. Who does he think he is? And who the fuck says "parlour"?'

I raised my eyebrows.

'Anyway, now he's forbidden her to see me. He said a big-eared farm boy wasn't good enough for his daughter.'

I frowned. 'Your ears aren't big.'

He laughed. 'It's a saying.'

'Oh, right.' I shrugged my shoulders. 'Anyway, I'm sure Harriet's smart enough not to take her father's views as fact.'

'Apparently not,' he said, brushing a strand of hair off his forehead. I noticed a shadow on his knuckles.

'You didn't hit him, did you?' I asked.

'Not the father. The brother.' He rubbed his knuckles. 'A younger, more stupid version.'

I sighed, though inwardly feeling a strange kind of admiration.

'You should see him though: two black eyes and a broken nose. Us farm boys can pack a punch, you know.'

I shook my head. 'Not exactly the sort of impression you're supposed to leave on the potential in-laws.'

'They started it,' he said, his face breaking into a smile. 'Posh twats.'

I leant forward and patted his arm 'Let me speak to Harriet and—'

'Is that *Barbie*?' Jeremy interrupted.

I looked up to see Mandi swishing towards us.

'You must be Jeremy,' she gushed, grabbing his hand. 'There are a million girls asking to be introduced to you. Come and mingle!'

He shrugged his shoulders. 'I'm only here as a wingman.' He waved for his friend to come over.

When a dark-haired version of Jeremy came into focus, I realised it was Mike from the champagne bar. When Mandi noticed him, she looked as though she were about to spontaneously combust.

'Quick, quick,' she squealed, before leading them towards a huddle of blondes.

Only moments earlier when the venue had been empty, the polished floorboards had seemed like a lake at dawn: vast, still, expectant. But in the short time I'd been talking to Jeremy, over three hundred pairs of shoes were now bearing down on them, leaving scuffs and indents as they trampled towards the bar, where champagne flowed like water from a spring. Long dresses swung and shimmered. Black suits met blacker masks. Skin glowed, jewels glittered, eyes locked and bodies followed.

William languished on a chaise longue, his arm draped around a delicate-looking Japanese girl. Shorn of the rucksack and nervous disposition, he looked almost like he belonged amongst the illuminati. Thea and I looked on, sipping champagne.

'What do you make of that, then?' I asked after I'd given her the full story.

'Well, once you've had your cock broken, what's the worst that can happen?' she said, her face deadpan.

I smirked.

'People fear what they don't know and women were an unknown entity to him. But after Cassandra—that was her name right?'

'Yes.'

'After she broke his cock—'

I winced. 'Stop saying "cock". Call it something else.'

'Okay, after she broke his *penis*, and he survived and the world didn't end, he probably realised that he had been worrying for nothing.' Her dark eyes glistened.

Mandi bounced towards us. For a moment, the white of her dress almost blinded me.

'Look at William and Mitzi! That's Mitzi.' She pointed. 'The one next to William. She's Japanese. A jewellery designer—from Japan—she's called Mitzi. I introduced them. Look, he's holding her hand. This is so exciting. I'm so excited.'

William and Mitzi looked over. Mitzi waved and Mandi clapped.

'She plays tennis and everything.'

'And everything?' Thea asked, her eyebrows raised.

'They were *made* for each other! Don't you think? I've matched so many people tonight. I love this job. Come on, Thea, let's go match. It's so much fun.'

'No, thanks, not really my style.'

Mandi wagged her finger at Thea. 'If you're going to be a matchmaker, then you're going to have to match people.'

Thea pulled down her mask, as though Mandi might be contagious. 'I'll work my own way, thank you.'

After Mandi had flounced off, I looked around the room at the newly formed couples. For the first time since I had conceived the idea, I felt a twinge of pride. Granted, it wasn't what I'd initially envisaged, and I wasn't yet convinced I was peddling true love, but it was something. Something, I realised, glancing at William and Mitzi, that had the potential to become so much more.

Suddenly, I felt a prod on my arm. I turned to see a woman with a deeply furrowed brow and accusing eyes.

'Ellie?' she asked.

'Yes,' I replied, removing my mask.

'There are no canapés left.' She waved the party invitation in my face. 'The invitation states canapés included. Look. Cana—'

'Excuse me,' Thea interrupted, swiping the invitation out of her hand. 'She *can* read.' Thea turned back to me. 'Don't worry, Ellie, I'll deal with this.'

Thea turned back to face the woman. 'Sorry, what was your name?'

'Sharon, I'm a friend of Joanna's.'

'Listen, Sharon. You are correct, the invitation does indeed state that canapés are included, but as you'll notice here—' she pointed at the card '—it also states that the event started at seven p.m. It is now ten p.m. Adopting a common-sense approach, one would assume that the canapés would have been offered at the beginning of the event.'

Sharon put her hand up to dispute, but Thea continued.

'However, as a gesture of goodwill and considering that you—' Thea looked her up and down, her gaze lingering on Sharon's wider-than-average girth '—look so *hungry*, we will offer you a burger on the house. And a big plate of fries. Looks like you might want some of those as well. Is that satisfactory?'

Sharon was now holding her tummy self-consciously. 'Actually, don't worry, I'm not that hungry, I just wanted to make the point. Thank you.'

She backed away, as though the Rottweiler had met a panther.

I half smiled at Thea, unsure as to whether I should thank her or fire her. I then spotted Joanna in the crowd, wearing an ill-fitting turquoise cocktail dress. It seemed as though she was still waiting for the correctly sized body and had decided to make do with the outdated wardrobe for the old one in the meantime.

I approached her for a chat.

'Sorry about Sharon,' she said. 'She's the only single friend I have and I didn't want to come on my own.'

'No problem,' I lied. 'Seen any men you like so far?'

'I haven't had the chance to have a proper look around but, yes, there are a few good-looking men.'

'A few?'

She pointed at Jeremy, who was leaning on the bar, lining up tequila shots. 'What about that one?'

'No, I don't think so,' I said, wondering if she was under the misguided impression that she looked like Harriet.

'Or that one?' She pointed at one of the two remaining pilots.

'Joanna, he's twenty-seven years old. I really don't think so.'

'Or him?' This time it was Mike.

'No, no, no.'

She folded her arms. 'Well, you suggest someone, then?'

I pointed out Greg, a forty-two-year-old divorced chiropractor with two kids, a kind heart and sweet face. He would be good for her.

'Eeeew no,' she said and screwed up her face. 'He's minging.'

I wanted to shake her, perhaps a little more rigorously than acceptable and say: *Joanna, he's not minging, he's average. You are also average.*

Instead, I said: 'He's a nice guy, you should give him a chance.'

But she shook her head like a child refusing an offering of steamed broccoli when she'd been expecting ice cream.

'What about *him*? Look, he's smiling at me.'

Following her gaze, my throat closed up, my heart pounded and, before I had given it permission, my face had broken into a silly grin. When he reached us, I looked up into his beautiful brown eyes and basked in his forgiving smile.

'Hello, you,' he said.

I took a quick sip of champagne, careful not to spill any down my dress. 'I'm so sorry about the magazine debacle.'

His grin widened. 'Aside from full-scale public humiliation and a standing ovation at work, it was nothing really, water off a duck's back.' He moved closer. 'So you weren't tempted by my extensive wine collection, then?'

'I'm Joanna,' she interjected, holding out her hand.

'Nick,' he replied without taking his eyes from mine.

'Ellie's not single. Well, she might be, but she's not here as *a* single. She's working. I'm single.'

'I'm taken,' he said.

'Oh, right. Well, why are you here, then?' she asked.

'The DJ. Love his work.'

S Club 7's 'Don't Stop Movin' bellowed through the speakers.

We laughed, but Joanna frowned. Fortunately, Mandi, who'd been watching the scene, swept Joanna away towards Greg the chiropractor.

'S Club 7?' I asked Nick when we were alone.

'You're not exactly in a position to comment, after all, it *is* being played at your event.'

I held my hands up, though not in time to the song. 'The DJ insisted we give the crowd what they want.' I pointed to the dance floor, which was a mess of writhing limbs.

I turned back to Nick. 'So, about your wine collection? Apparently Bordeaux is the wife and Burgundy is the mistress. Could you commit to one?'

'I'm a Bordeaux man through and through,' he said, slipping his arm around my waist and then kissing me gently on the lips. The tingle shot from my mouth to my toes.

Suddenly, adopting the awkward gait of a baby giraffe, I pulled away, and then looked at my watch as though I had somewhere to be. He moved towards me and took my hand.

'Better leave you to get back to work, but I'll see you for

dinner on Saturday?' he asked, eyes fixed on mine. 'Anything you don't eat?'

'Olives,' I answered, aware that I had just agreed to a date.

'Damn, that rules out the all-you-can-eat olive buffet, then.'

I giggled and then watched him walk away, realising that Kat was right. He did have a cute butt.

Dragging my eyes and thoughts back to the party, I noticed Jeremy slumped at the bar, clearly feeling the effects of his tequila binge. Then my gaze shifted to a girl beside him and her familiar high ponytail. It was Victoria. I hadn't even noticed her arrive, but there she was, her ample chest bursting out of a blood-red Dolce & Gabbana tube dress. I realised that this wasn't going to end well at all.

I walked towards them and Victoria's eyes tore through me like a laser through flesh.

'Jeremy, can I have a word?' I asked.

'Um, excuse me, Ellie. I would prefer it if you didn't interrupt, we were having a conversation.'

She turned away from me, shoving her sharp elbow into my ribs.

'It won't take a second,' I said, grabbing Jeremy by the arm and then leading him back to the sofa, which swallowed him up like a Venus flytrap.

'What are you doing?' I asked.

He picked up a cushion and studied it intently. 'Are these things multiplying?' he slurred and then tossed it at William and Mitzi on the neighbouring sofa. Then he threw another. Then another. 'Don't do it, she'll break your heart!' he shouted as they shielded themselves from the onslaught.

'You know this could ruin things with Harriet,' I said, removing the fourth cushion from his grasp.

'What, cushion throwing?'

'No. Victoria.'

'Who?'

'Her. The one in red. With the tits.'

'Oh, yes.' He nodded vaguely.

'She's Harriet's friend, you know?'

'It's already ruined. There's no going back.' He collapsed back down on the sofa. 'She's made herself clear.'

'You're drunk. Just don't do anything stupid, okay?'

I looked into his eyes, hoping to reach through the tequila glaze, but before I could say anything else, Victoria strutted over, wedged her bottom between us, and thrust her bouncy boobs in his face.

There wasn't much else I could do. The rest was up to him.

'She's a piece of work,' sneered Thea.

'We have to stop her!' Mandi shrieked. 'Jeremy loves Harriet not *her*. And what about their puppy? Rusty Junior, he needs a stable home.' Mandi's arms flapped wildly as Victoria leant forward to kiss Jeremy. 'Ellie, *do* something!'

I shook my head. 'David Attenborough can't stop a lion from killing a baby antelope. Sometimes we just have to let these things play out,' I said, though more to convince myself than anyone else.

Thea pulled Mandi's mask down as if to shield her from the scene.

'I hope he throws up in her mouth,' she said before leading Mandi away.

Chapter 10

'HOW COULD HE do this to me?' Harriet asked between snotty, rather undignified sobs. 'Two weeks after we split. And he just goes out and sleeps with, shags—' her voice was getting louder '—pokes, bangs—' louder still '—sticks his cock in another woman, like I meant nothing to him. How could he?'

I took the phone away from my ear and stared at it. This wasn't the Harriet I had previously met, who was so poised, elegant and controlled.

'Right, let's rewind a bit,' I said, wondering if the lion had actually killed the antelope. 'Have you spoken to Jeremy?'

'No and I never will again.'

'So how do you know he slept with Victoria?'

'*She* told me. This morning, she called. She said she thought it best I know.'

'Best you know?'

'Yes.'

'What did she say?'

'That you set it all up at the party last night—said they would be a great match.'

'Oh, really.'

After an accusation had been made, the defence always seemed less plausible than the lie itself. It was as though the one who got in first had the advantage. I went on to explain what really happened, but Harriet dismissed it.

'Don't worry. I'm not angry with you,' she said. 'If he loved me then he wouldn't have done it.'

'If you loved him, you wouldn't have ended it.'

She sniffed, but did not reply.

'So why did you?'

'It doesn't matter why. None of it matters any more.'

Her sobs rapidly escalated and then suddenly the line went dead.

I imagined Harriet with her eyes red and swollen, her caramel-coloured hair stuck to her face, her cheeks wet with salty tears, and I felt restless. I tapped my fingers on the table with one hand and held a pen in my mouth with the other, my bare toes kneading the rug below. I would call it burnt-orange chenille, but Matthew insisted it was baby-poo shagpile. Could the truth ever be real or was it just a product of our flawed perception?

When my jaw clamped down on my pen and snapped it in two, I decided to call Victoria. It went straight to voice-mail, the haughty tone of her message incensing me further.

'Victoria, it's Ellie. If you wish to continue using the service, meet me at the club. Four p.m.'

Then, I lobbed the broken pen in the bin and dialled Jeremy's number, satisfied that it was still early enough to punish his hangover.

'Morning, Ellie,' came the muffled voice down the line.

'How's the head?'

'It hurts.'

'Self-inflicted pain doesn't warrant sympathy,' I replied sharply.

'Ouch.'

'So?'

'So, what?'

'So, Victoria?' I was getting impatient.

There was silence on the other end of the line.

'What happened?'

'Nothing,' he replied eventually.

'Oh, come on. The truth please.'

'That is the truth.'

'Victoria told Harriet you slept together.'

'What?'

'Harriet is devastated.'

'I didn't sleep with her. Why would she say that?'

Because she's an evil-girl-hating-relationship-thwarting-man-stealing-big-breasted bitchpants? 'I don't know why, Jeremy, I'm not a mind reader.'

'I shouldn't have left with her. I'm never drinking again.'

'You left with her?'

'As far as I'm aware, "Thou shalt not share a taxi" isn't listed as one of the Ten Commandments.'

I forced a laugh. 'And then?'

'She prised her way into my flat,' he conceded.

'What, with a monkey wrench?'

'You know what I mean.'

'And then?'

'And then nothing.'

'Nothing?'

'Have you ever considered a career in the military?'

'Don't answer a question with a question,' I snapped.

'For the last time. Noth-ing. Happ-ened.'

'So you put the kettle on and shared a nice pot of tea?'

'Not exactly.'

'So what exactly?'

He sighed. 'Promise me you won't tell Harriet.'

'I promise.'

'It's all a bit vague. I was drunk.'

'I noticed.'

'Before I say anything else, you have to believe me, nothing happened.'

'Okay, I believe you.'

Ten minutes later, Jeremy had relayed a confusing encounter involving a surprise erection, a distressed Rusty Junior and a threatened photograph posting on Facebook.

'I still don't understand how she got a photo of your, er, thing?'

'She unlocked the toilet door. With her hair clip or something. I'd been in there for ages, trying to wee with this ridiculous hard-on.'

'And then she just took a photo?'

'First the dog burst in, barking and growling at it, as though it were an intruder. Then she followed with her phone and then flash.'

'She definitely got a photo?'

'I think so. She said if I didn't call her today, she would post it online.'

I scratched my head.

'How am I going to explain this to Harriet when I don't even understand it myself. I mean, it was huge. The biggest it's ever been. It's only just started to go down now.'

'Okay, Jeremy, too much information.'

The conversation ended with Jeremy vowing to win Harriet back and adamant that honesty was the only precursor to forgiveness.

I stood up and paced around the flat. Framed by Ikea pine, my reflection stared back at me. I moved in for a closer look. My hair was beyond what could pass for tousled, there were two deep creases between my brows. My skin looked grey and my eyes opaque. My thoughts moved onto Nick and our date tomorrow night. Strange scenarios started running through my mind as I wondered if last night, he too had been sporting a freakishly large hard-on in the presence of a sexpot with perfect breasts. Or, if he had remained loyal to me in thought and action since we'd met? I was beginning to understand that the idealism of love and the brutality of truth were not compatible, yet there seemed to be an irresistible urge to merge the two. To force them together like a bad Hollywood plot.

Pulling my hair up into a ponytail, hoping it might give me cheekbones like Victoria, I sucked in my tummy and stuck out my chest. Uninspired by the result, I attempted a few half-hearted sit-ups, a couple of bottom-lifting exercises and then gave up, moving back to the coffee table where my laptop whirred and groaned, as though it were complaining that it lacked the capacity to receive any more information. I opened my inbox to find it was full of emails about last night's ball.

'There was a girl. She was wearing a dress. I didn't get her number, do you know her?'

I forwarded it to Mandi.

'I didn't meet anyone I liked, can I have a refund?'

I forwarded that to Thea.

'I lost my mask, do you have it?'

No, but there's a pink one I could give you.

Moving down the list with ruthless efficiency, my flow was interrupted by a ray of light reflectcd on the screen. I blinked and, when I opened my eyes, an email from Mandi had arrived, the copy pink and bold, flashing hearts framing the text.

To: Ellie
From: Mandi
Subject: Scary Thea
Hi Ellie,
Hope you're having a wonderful day! I am on such a high after last night. I'm so excited about the people I've matched. I really think, for many of them, it was love at first sight! Anyway, I'll update you at our meeting tomorrow, but, for now, I just wanted to mention that I think Thea scared some of the guests last night. Just wanted to share my thoughts with you. No secrets with me. I'm as open as a book! Open mind, open heart.
Spread the love!
Mandi
xxxxxxxxxxxxx

The light faded, a black cloud moved across the sun and another email arrived in quick succession.

To: Ellie
From: Thea
Subject: Fairy annoying
The business has real potential. But Mandi is doing my head in—I can't work with her.
Thea

I puffed out my cheeks and rapped my fingers on the table. It had been naive of me to think they would work well together. After all, they were more Tom and Jerry than Richard and Judy, but individually they both had clear strengths. A bit like the contradiction within my own mind, I decided, given that I was still idealistic but now from my experiences also part cynic.

'If I can resolve their differences then perhaps I could resolve my own,' I explained to Matthew after I called him for advice.

'Have you been reading those self-help books again?'

'Here I am, trying to better myself and resolve my inner conflict, and all you do is take the piss.'

'That's what I do, remember.'

'Fair point. So, any advice?'

'Champagne silk.'

'What's that supposed to mean?'

'Sorry, picking a tie.'

'A tie?'

'For the wedding.'

'Oh, right. Were you going to send me a Post-it note?'

'Yes, already sent. So, back to fairy and scary.'

I laughed. 'What should I do?'

'Let them fight it out.'

'Really?'

'Two extreme views generally settle in the centre somewhere eventually.'

'Yeah, that's worked really well in the Middle East.'

'Trust me, scary will soften and fairy will harden.'

'Do you know how dodgy that sounds?'

He sighed. 'Call Cordelia.'

'I have—she's not answering.'

'To the left.'

'What?'

'There's a guy between my legs with a tape measure. Can I call you back?'

When the line went dead, I stared at the laptop screen until an email from Cordelia arrived, I stared at the screen for a little longer, until I had plucked up the courage to open it.

To: Ellie
From: Cordelia
Subject: Dr Stud?
Dr Dud more like. Worst date of my life. You are in serious trouble.
C x

Usually offering three kisses, she had trimmed it down to one. The last time that happened was when she thought I'd slept with her boyfriend. Not good. It seemed bad matchmaking was a crime equal to a betrayal of the worst kind. The sooner I got the hang of it, the better for all concerned.

Cordelia finally returned my call just as I was walking to the club.

'His hands were everywhere,' she explained. 'Despite the fact that we'd been in a public place and I'd remained fully clothed, it still felt as though he'd given me a full internal examination by the end of the evening.'

'And what is his problem with women: "They belong in the kitchen or, if they're naughty, sometimes in the basement"?'

'He was joking.'

'Was he?'

'He has an off-the-wall sense of humour.'

'Based on his deep-seated beliefs that women are infe-rior and only there to entertain and serve him.'

'I think you're overreacting. He's very sweet when you get to know him.'

'No thanks. Anyway, Harry and I have been talking.' She paused. 'And...I've decided to move to Spain.'

Following a lengthy debate about whether, given her fam-ily history of melanoma, it would be wise for her to move so many degrees closer to the equator, I shrugged my shoul-ders and conceded. We settled on the promise of quarterly visits and weekly phone calls.

After I'd hung up the phone, I marched towards the club. The Edwardian town houses flashed past in my peripheral vision, estate agent signs tied to their railings. The resi-dents of London seemed as transient as the clouds in the sky. Someone had added an 'i' between 'To' and 'Let' on one of the signs and I wondered how many smiles it would evoke, before it was wiped off or washed away.

Before heaving open the door to the club, I checked my phone and saw a text from Kat:

We've been reposted to Iraq. Leaving tomorrow! Good-bye drinks tonight? xxx

We? Since when did such couple-centred terminology, commonly reserved for announcing pregnancy, expand to encompass that of military command?

Deserter x

I texted back, adopting a Cordelia-style 'withdrawal of kisses when offended' approach. How could she leave me at this critical juncture? And what was with these sudden life-changing decisions? Were we all simultaneously experienc-ing some kind of early onset midlife crisis? I'd abandoned a respectable career to pursue international recognition as a professional matchmaker. Cordelia had quit her equally respectable job to live with her inconsistent boyfriend at his mum's beach flat in Spain. And now, Kat, chasing her military-clad toy boy into the melee of a war against, well, we're not quite sure so let's call it 'terror'. At least Matthew was behaving like a normal person: marrying his adorable fiancée at an appropriate age. But, for all I knew, he could have been typing an email that very moment, explaining that instead, he was moving to Bangkok to live as a ladyboy and that the tailor had been measuring him for a champagne silk minidress.

Victoria strutted down the staircase, wearing camel-coloured Joseph trousers and a tight cashmere jumper, her ponytail swinging almost smugly. She looked like the cat that got the cream, or had stolen someone else's cream. In fact, the expression in her eyes seemed a bit catty. Catty, catty cream-stealing bitchpants.

'Whatever is this about?' she asked nonchalantly as she slipped her narrow hips into the chair in front of me.

By now, I had worked myself into a silent rage, certain I was about to right the wrongs of centuries of women. Today Victoria was going to pay. Retribution was nigh.

'You know full well what this is about. Your behaviour is unacceptable,' I said, gripping the glass of wine in front of me, fighting the urge to tip it over her. 'So, unless you have a good explanation, I have no choice but to terminate our working relationship.'

'Our working relationship?' She sat back in her chair and let out a nasal laugh. 'If you're referring to Jeremy, it takes two to tango.'

'From what I saw you were tangoing all over Jeremy.'

My fingers twitched on the glass stem. 'You're supposed to be Harriet's friend.'

'They had broken up.'

'That's not the point. It's an unspoken rule never to touch your friend's ex as a matter of respect. Surely you know that?'

'Not in my rule book.'

'What—*The Bitches' Guide to Man-Catching*?'

Her face dropped, but I decided that now I'd started, I may as well finish.

'When I first met you, you were rude, obnoxious and offensive. Since then my opinion has only deteriorated. You deliberately set out to seduce Jeremy, for what reason I do not know, but without consideration for anyone's feelings but your own. And there are two exceptionally nice people who have been hurt in the process.'

Her face began to crumple.

I kept on. 'But despite your best efforts, Jeremy didn't want you. Did he? He wants Harriet. He loves Harriet. Not you.'

Her lip quivered and her eyes welled with tears, but I wasn't done.

'Hand it over,' I said.

She looked down.

'Hand me your phone. I want to see the photo.'

She looked up, her eyes flooded with tears, and then pushed her phone across the table.

I flicked through the images, which seemed exclusively of Victoria in an array of designer outfits, and against an array of spectacular backdrops. When I came to the photo of Jeremy and his manhood, I had never seen anything quite like it. Just as I was about to hit delete, hoping the image hadn't had sufficient time to fully imprint on my memory, I noticed something odd in the background. I zoomed in. I saw a terrified-looking puppy holding something in his mouth. Something silver, which looked like a blister pack of tablets. I zoomed in some more. The letters 'V' and 'a' were just about visible next to the dog's pink gums.

'Ah ha,' I said, looking back up at Victoria, 'now it all makes sense.'

About to extend my tirade, to include police reports and a possible prison sentence, I stopped when her shoulders began to heave and her bottom lip quivered.

'I'm so sorry,' she said, tears rolling down her cheeks. 'I'm so, so sorry.'

Her head fell into her hands. When she lifted it back up again, it was as though her bitchy mask had been washed away to reveal a little lost girl, one whose kitten I'd just murdered.

I handed her some tissues. 'I didn't mean to be so harsh.'

'I deserved it,' she said between sobs, her body shuddering as she gasped to breathe.

Once Steve had noticed what was going on, he nodded for us to go into a private room next to the bar. I helped her up and, with my arm around her, I led her into the room and towards an armchair, but when Steve closed the door behind us, she collapsed to the ground and then curled up into a ball on the floor. She sobbed uncontrollably while I sat next to her, holding her hand.

'I'm so sorry,' she said repeatedly.

When Steve reappeared with the cup of tea I'd ordered, he also lay down two tumblers of cognac.

'Thought you might want something stronger,' he said.

A faint smile appeared on her red blotchy face. She drank both in quick succession, so we ordered some more.

'I'm a horrible person,' she said.

'No, you're not.'

'I never used to be horrible.' She looked down at her nails and picked at a chip in her nail polish. 'Believe it or not, I used to be a bit like your Barbie of a consultant. The one who was at the party. Candi?'

'Mandi.'

'Yes, that's it. Mandi. But now I've become one of those women I used to loathe.' She continued to chip away. 'Just like the one who ruined my life.'

'Who was that?'

'Long story,' she said, peeling off the final piece of polish.

'I've got time.'

Three hours passed and we hadn't moved from the floor. The two armchairs remained empty. When he brought in the final round of drinks, Steve explained how he'd discovered the chairs in a skip outside. The original tapestry had been covered with an offensive synthetic fabric and the antique wood had been painted over. He said it had taken months to restore them.

When I stood up to leave, the room started spinning and it felt as though the armchairs were orbiting me.

'Got to go to leaving Kat's party,' I burbled, while steadying myself against the wall.

Victoria frowned, trying to process my words. 'Someone's leaving your friend?'

'No, she's leaving. We're celebrating. No, I mean...' The room seemed to flip on its axis. 'Everyone's leaving.' I steadied myself against the wall again. 'They're all leaving. Cordelia, Kat, Matthew...'

Victoria stared at me. She was struggling to focus.

'Want me to come with you?' she asked, raising her arm in the air for me to lift her.

I tried to pull her up. 'Sure,' I said. 'So long as you don't drug her boyfriend.'

Chapter 11

THE SUNLIGHT SLICED through a gap in the curtains and down my optic nerve like a dagger through the brain. I turned away, rubbed my eyes and noticed something moving under the duvet beside me. My mind raced, or as much as it could given its degree of hungover sluggishness. From the curves of the mound, and a glimpse of silky blonde hair poking out the top, I could tell it wasn't a man. I scanned the room, squinting against the sunlight and noticed a crumpled pile of clothes: camel trousers, cashmere jumper. Victoria?

I patted myself down to check my state of dress and was relieved to find my largest T-shirt over the previous day's underwear. *No embarrassing, I'm-not-really-a-lesbian explanations required today then*, I thought. My ankle began to itch. I pulled back the duvet to see neon pink leg warmers around each ankle complete with matching wristbands. As my mind struggled to reconcile my bizarre attire, images of the previous night flooded my mind. Kat's leaving drinks, of course. Initially, it came back in freeze-frames, random images filling my mind: mojitos, an eighties club, tequila. Spearmint Rhino? Finally, the freeze-frames merged to replay the entire embarrassing movie in excruciating slow motion.

If this was a true recollection of events rather than a cocktail-induced false memory, I told myself, *then there would be a troop of lap dancers sleeping in the lounge.* Also wearing legwarmers. I crept out of bed, pushed the door ajar and peered through the crack.

The scene looked like the aftermath of one of Robert's movies. Four alarmingly orange girls were asleep across my floor and sofa. They were wearing various degrees of lap-dancing attire, and in addition, as suspected, they were all indeed sporting leg warmers.

Victoria stirred and poked her head out from under the duvet. 'Ouch,' she said, pushing the hair away from her eyes.

'Morning,' I said, closing the door. 'I would offer you a cup of coffee, but I wouldn't want to wake the...'

I pointed back towards the lounge.

'I was hoping that was a bad dream.' She hoisted herself up out of bed, revealing a flash of neon green. She looked down and frowned.

Later that morning, after I'd sent the dancers away, explaining that despite the previous evening's promises, I hadn't yet raised enough funds to support a comprehensive exotic-dancers-to-internationally-recognised-matchmakers transition programme, but that we would keep them posted on developments. Victoria and I decided to get some fresh air and wandered to the local bistro for brunch.

'What was I thinking?' I asked, rubbing my temples, a full English breakfast laid out before me.

'You were quite funny really,' Victoria said, stabbing a large sausage. 'Rallying around trying to rescue the dancers as though they'd been enslaved in some kind of depraved street brothel.'

'Oh, dear.'

'Most of them told you to piss off.' She laughed. 'But that didn't deter you. And when you'd incited a four-woman mutiny, you commandeered the microphone and launched into some sort of women's lib speech about objectification and subjugation.'

'In leg warmers?'

'Yes, you insisted that fancy dress would help your cause, citing the widespread press coverage secured by Fathers For Justice.'

'Why didn't someone stop me?'

'I tried. But you were having none of it. Of course, you were thrown out, but not before threatening to sue the bouncer for infringement of your civil liberties, pleading the Fifth Amendment.'

'What?'

'Yes, and despite the fact that you were quoting some incomprehensible American TV law, he actually looked quite intimidated at one point. That was until you tripped over and vomited in the gutter.'

I laughed. 'So did you leave with me?'

'Not exactly.' She took a bite of sausage. 'I was thrown out too.'

'Because of me?'

'Not quite.'

I raised my eyebrows. 'For what, then?'

'An altercation.'

'A what?'

'I hit someone.'

'Who?'

'The pilot.'

'Kat's boyfriend?'

She nodded.

'You hit him?'

'It was more of a tap over the head. With the Moët.'

'You *bottled* Kat's boyfriend?'

She shook her head. 'The glass was thick, it didn't smash. Just a heavy clunk really. He deserved it.'

Once we'd cleared our plates, I checked my watch and took a final glug of coffee.

'I've got to head off now,' I said, grabbing my bag. 'I'm meeting Thea and Mandi.'

She looked disappointed. 'On a Saturday?'

'Yep, clients to match.'

'Well, don't worry about matching me,' she said, tightening her ponytail. 'I think I need some time to work things out.'

I stood up from the table. 'I'll call you tomorrow for a chat, anyway.'

'Thanks,' she said and I walked away. 'Oh, and good luck tonight,' she shouted after me.

I stopped and checked the contents of my bag. Inside was make-up, mini GHDs and a dress, which on reflection, seemed more cabaret than canapé. However, it would have to do.

When I arrived at the club, I found Thea and Mandi sitting at opposite ends of a table in the bar. Mandi, grinning widely, was sporting *Charlie's Angels* flicks and a fuchsia pink dress. Her pink notepad and pen were placed neatly in front of her. Thea, wearing tight black trousers and a crisp white shirt, had a cigarette dangling from her glossy red lips. As usual she was acting as though she were exempt from the smoking ban, or more likely she knew that none of the staff would be brave enough to challenge her.

'You look awful,' Thea said, before taking a drag.

I slumped in the chair.

Mandi waved at Steve. 'Stevie Wevie. We have a hang-over situation.'

'Stevie Wevie?' Thea mimicked with a droll smile.

Steve arrived with a coffee and a glass of water, quicker than the speed of light. 'There you go, Ellie.'

Ellie? He'd never called me that before, usually 'gorgeous' or 'sweet cheeks' but never my name. I looked up to thank him, but he was staring at Mandi with a goofy smile fixed on his face.

'Okay, girls, we have a lot of work to get through,' I said.

Mandi immediately produced a giant pink lever-arch file from her Mary Poppins bag. She sat up straight and smoothed down her dress.

'Right,' Mandi said, 'I've collated feedback from each of the event attendees and I've written a report.'

She handed out personalised copies. Mine had glittery butterfly stickers fluttering along the page borders.

'Someone has a lot of time on their hands,' Thea scoffed, picking at the sparkly hearts adorning hers.

'As you can see, from a total of three hundred attend-ees, there were twenty-three couples that got together. That means fifty-six out of three hundred people met someone they liked; an average conversion rate of nineteen per cent. Which isn't bad. But, of course, the best outcome would be actual long-term relationships rather than just first dates, so I will present updated results every month hereafter.

As you can see in the latter part of the report, I have taken feedback from all attendees regarding measures we could take to increase our success. I've listed areas for improvement on the final ten pages.'

She pointed proudly to various charts and tables.

I raised my eyebrows and leafed through her report.

'Wow, Mandi, this is excellent. Obviously we don't yet have the funds to build an online networking platform similar to Facebook—number twenty-four on your suggestions for improvement—but there are some brilliant ideas here.'

'Ahem.' Thea coughed several times until she had mine and Mandi's full attention, then she lifted her cigarette to her mouth and inhaled deeply, careful not to smear her lipstick.

'That's all great, Mandi. But what about the revenue and profits? We are a business after all.' With that, she whipped out a folder of her own. 'This is the P & L for the event. That's Profit and Loss, if you don't know.' She looked pointedly at Mandi. 'As you can see, in the column entitled variable costs, the biggest expenditure was decorations: £1,254 on red sashes, £3,200 on chaise longues and £1,456 on *cushions*.'

Already having performed rough calculations in my head, I knew we'd gone way over budget, but it was partly my fault. Leaving Mandi unsupervised to arrange a party was like sending an excitable child to Hamleys with a suitcase full of cash.

'How did we spend £1,456 on cushions? Is that even possible?' Thea asked no one in particular.

Mandi slumped in her seat. Just moments ago, she'd been like an excited schoolgirl rushing home with a painting for Mummy, only for it to be snatched away from her and thrown in a puddle by her mean sister.

'The lady said the more cushions I hired, then the cheaper each one would be.'

Thea rolled her eyes. 'Look, if we're working together, then the money you spend is money I can't earn. Get it? And in case there is any confusion, I am here to make money.'

'Right,' I interrupted, deciding the best solution to this debate was to change the subject. 'Here are your clients, Thea.'

I pulled a folder of carefully selected profiles from my bag and handed them to her, feeling as though I were handing my children over to a strict nanny. She flicked through quickly and nodded as she turned the pages, as though she had the solution for each one within seconds.

She paused on the last profile. 'A gynaecologist called Dick Stud?'

'Don't tease him about his name, he's quite sensitive about it.'

'So what's his problem? Your notes say that he's offensive to women.'

'Oh, no, nothing really, he's a great guy once you get to know him. He's just a bit, you know, inappropriate sometimes. I've tried but I don't seem to be getting through to him.'

'On it,' Thea said, a look of determination in her eyes. 'I'll whip him into shape.'

'Don't say that to him though,' I said. 'You'll just be inviting trouble.'

She smirked.

'And you, Mandi?' I turned to her. 'Any feedback I should be aware of?'

She took a deep breath. 'Yes, yes, yes. I've been dying to tell you. It's so exciting!'

'Go on, then,' Thea said.

'William and Mitzi. They're totally in love. Since the party, they've literally been inseparable. I know it's only been two days but I'm really excited for them. This weekend they're going to Paris. How romantic. How exciting! I really have high hopes for those two. I already said that, didn't I? Isn't it great though? I'm so happy for them. They met at the ball and now they're in love. It's like a fairy tale.'

'What? Boy meets girl at a party? Call Spielberg now,' Thea said, stubbing out her cigarette.

Mandi's smile faded and she looked back down at her notes. 'But that Nate, you know, the actor?' She mouthed the words as though saying them aloud in a public place might breach the Data Protection Act. 'I'm a bit stuck with him. Every match I send him he rejects. Not tall enough, too tall, not blonde enough, too blonde. What shall I do?'

'Keep trying,' I said.

Her bottom lip curled. 'Can't I try to get in touch with Rebecca, his ex? I really think he still loves her. Remember. You promised I could help them if I got the job. Remember?'

'Have you spoken to him about it?'

'Yes.'

'And what did he say?'

'He said no.'

'Well, then, we can't go against his wishes.'

Mandi scrunched up her tiny nose and twitched it like a rabbit. 'Hmm. Okay.'

'Anything else?' I asked, following a casual glance at my watch.

'Yes, yes, yes!' Mandi began, springing back to life.

'Now for the really exciting news.' She clasped her hands together and flashed her perfect teeth. 'Harriet and Jeremy!'

'Did you speak to them?' I asked.

'Yes, sorry, Ellie, I didn't mean to encroach on your clients, but Harriet called me. She said she called you first, but a security guard at Spearmint Rhino answered the phone, so she assumed she had the wrong number. Anyway she told me all about what had happened with Jeremy and—'

'Have they worked things out?' I asked.

'Yes.' She wriggled in her seat. 'Yes, they did, I've been bursting to tell you. It's so romantic.'

'So what happened?'

'Well, to give you the short version—'

'Yes please,' Thea said, looking as though she'd lost the will to live.

'Jeremy was so determined to win Harriet back, guess what he did?'

'Jumped out of a plane with a box of chocolates?' Thea suggested.

'No, try again,' Mandi replied.

'Chopped off his ear?'

'Ew, no. Who would do that? Anyway, you'll never guess. So I'm going to tell you. He only turned up on her doorstep with his guitar. And, then, serenaded her with the most beautiful song. He'd composed it all by himself. Isn't that the most romantic thing ever?'

Thea put two fingers in her mouth and pretended to gag.

'Harriet said it was so heartfelt. Although, she did mention that the dog humping Jeremy's leg throughout the performance might have killed the moment a little.' Mandi rummaged in her bag. 'Anyway, here it is. I wrote it down.'

Thea rolled her eyes.

She smoothed out a crumpled piece of paper and stood up, lifting her arm in the air as though she were about to perform a soliloquy at Shakespeare's Globe.

'Harriet Harriet, I love you so

Harriet Harriet, I can't let you go

Can't let you walk out of my li-ife

I want to marry you and be your wi-ife.'

'No. Be *my* wife. You've written it down wrong,' Thea said, eyes rolling continuously now, like a dazed cartoon character.

'Oh, yes, that didn't make sense, did it?' Mandi said, sitting back down. 'Anyway, how wonderful is that? They're getting married. Our first wedding!'

She clapped loudly and looked around the room as though she expected everyone to join in. But Thea and I just sat there staring blankly at her.

'I'll give it a week,' Thea said, lighting another cigarette.

The meeting finished shortly afterwards. Mandi was eager to leave in order to help Harriet with wedding plans and Thea was already flicking through the list of clients awaiting her instruction. I sat staring ahead, thinking about Jeremy and Harriet. I wondered whether I should intervene to make sure they weren't acting too hastily, or if instead, I should just leave them to it. Was the role of a soon-to-be-internationally-renowned matchmaker simply to cast the arrow and then move on?

A timid voice interrupted my thoughts. 'Hello, Ellie.'

I looked up at the expectant face peering down at me.

'Oh, hi, Joanna, please take a seat. How are you?'

'Good. Thanks for agreeing to see me.' Her body landed in the chair like a heavy bag of shopping. 'I'm sure you have better things to be doing on a Saturday night.'

'I have a date actually. In an hour.'

'Oh, I'm so sorry. I can come back another time.' She stood up to leave.

'No, no, no. It's not a problem. Actually, it's a great distraction from first date nerves.'

She smiled. 'Well, it's good to know the matchmaker is as human as the rest of us.'

I laughed. 'Oh, you don't know the half of it.'

She sat on her hands and shuffled from side to side. 'So, the reason I wanted to meet up, as I said on the phone, was because I haven't had a date yet and I'm wondering why not.'

There was an uncomfortable delay between her question and my answer. In my mind, I was swinging between a Mandi response and a Thea response. Mandi would have undoubtedly explained that Mr Right was out there waiting for her and that she should be patient and never give up hope. Thea, on the other hand, would have most likely rolled her eyes and given her a frank deconstruction of the current singles market.

I hoped to settle somewhere between the two. 'Do you remember the men you pointed out at the ball?'

'Yes. I do.'

'And did you see the girls there?'

'Not really, maybe a few.'

'What did you think of them?'

She looked baffled. 'I was mainly looking at the men.'

I scratched my nose. 'What I'm trying to say is that the girls were stunning.'

She frowned.

'That's your competition. The girls who are after the same men as you are unbelievably gorgeous.'

Her gaze dropped. 'But it's not all about looks, is it?'

'It's not. But many of those girls are intelligent and interesting too, just the same as you. And younger.'

Her smile faded.

'As I see it, you have one of two choices.'

She raised her eyebrows.

'Either you compromise on your criteria or you—' I paused to consider how to say it '—make more of an effort with your appearance.'

Her shocked expression led me to think that perhaps my time for consideration could have been longer. 'I've never had complaints before.'

I sighed, imagining a world where men told women the truth: 'It's not you, it's me,' might become: 'Yes, it is you. You have a long bottom and your voice sounds like fingernails down a blackboard.' Perhaps that would be better. With such rules in place, we could readily inform men that they smelled of pickled onions and/or had a furry neck.

I thought for a moment before speaking again.

'Okay, so imagine you want the dream career. What would you do about it?'

'What relevance does this have?'

'You wouldn't just turn up at an interview in your old jeans, no preparation and say you should just take me as I am because I've never had any complaints before.'

'No, of course not. But this is entirely different.'

'It's not. The competition out there is enormous. The kind of man you want is what most women want. So you have to compete with them.'

'But what about the men? Don't they want a nice girl?'

'There are plenty of lovely men out there. However, the

men you pointed out at the ball were the same three men that all the other girls were after.'

She nodded slowly. 'But I didn't fancy anyone else.'

'Did you give anyone a chance?'

She huffed. 'And what about you? The man you were talking to, is he the date tonight?'

I nodded.

She flicked her wrist. 'But you're naturally gorgeous anyway, so I suppose you don't have to worry about the competition.'

I stared at her for a moment before an idea came to me. I jumped up from my seat.

'Come with me,' I said, then hauled my bag from under the table and led her to the Ladies'. 'I've got to get ready anyway, so I'm going to do a quick demonstration.'

After retrieving my make-up remover and cotton pads from my bag, I wiped off the make-up that I had applied liberally that morning in attempt to conceal my hangover. Bare and exposed in the strip lighting, my skin looked dull and grey, with an alarming green tinge. I turned her towards the mirror and pointed at my face in the reflection.

'There you go. See.'

She looked on quizzically while I scraped back my hair to reveal my badly touched-up roots and sticky-out ears. To complete my deconstruction, I unzipped my dress, exposing pasty skin and greying Marks and Spencer underwear.

Our reflections stared back at us: two rather unremarkable peas in a pod. Without make-up or styled hair, we both looked like just average women, not sexy or glamorous, not even close to fresh-faced girl next door. I wondered how she had the confidence to live her life that exposed.

'See?' I said. 'Everything being equal, why would a man

look at me like this, compared to the girls at the ball? He wouldn't look twice. But most of the other girls would look just like us, stripped down.'

She looked on, saying nothing.

'The annoying thing is,' I said as I rummaged in my make-up bag and began the routine application. 'I know it's unfair— ' I applied serum, line plumper and moisturiser '—we shouldn't have to do this—' then primer, a corrector to offset the bags '—media conditioning…idealised beauty—' I added eyeshadow base and powder '—unattainable ideals—' then eyeshadow on my lids and then brows '—we should reject them—' then eyeliner and three coats of mascara '—take a stand—' then blusher and lip gloss '—and boy-cott the industry.' I pulled a black Wonderbra from my bag, followed by its matching thong. 'But,' I said, hoisting my bra on, 'we've come to expect—' I wiggled into my dress '—this is how we should look—' I squeezed my feet into my size-too-small stilettos '—and it would take a brave woman—' I adjusted my neckline, appreciating the bra's sterling effort '—to go on a date without it.'

Joanna looked on in silence as I singed loose curls into my hair. 'And that,' I said, replacing the lost shine with a gloss spray, followed by two squirts of synthesised phero-mones, packaged by Yves Saint Laurent, 'is the secret to natural beauty.

'Now come with me,' I said, and then led her out of the Ladies' back to the bar.

Steve wolf-whistled when he met us on the stairs. 'Look-ing good,' he said without even registering Joanna's pres-ence.

When we walked through the club, the men stared. They were not quite the looks that Victoria or Harriet may warrant, but looks of approval and interest nonetheless. When we parted company at the entrance to the club, I expected a flurry of 'thank yous', as though I had opened her eyes to the world and it all made sense, but instead she looked me up and down.

'Thanks,' she said. 'But all that gloss—' she pulled open the door '—it's really not me.' She walked out onto the street, arm raised to hail a taxi. 'Hope the date goes well though.'

When I arrived at the restaurant, I scanned across a sea of glossy heads to locate the bar. Thinking I'd seen it, I strode ahead, tummy in, shoulders back, towards…the kitchen.

'Madam. Can we help you?' an anxious-looking waiter asked, as though I were trying to penetrate the MI5 head office. A hand grabbed mine and I turned to see Nick smiling. I looked into his beguiling brown eyes and blushed.

'I've got us seats at the bar,' he said, leading me away from the relieved waiter. 'But if you'd rather sit in the kitchen, then I'm sure that can be arranged.'

After a pre-dinner gin and tonic, my hangover became a long and distant memory and Nick and I chatted as though we only had this one night to share each other's stories. When he spoke, I couldn't help but stare. His smile seemed reassuringly familiar, yet his eyes betrayed a mysterious glint, as though there was a deep hidden cave in his soul, filled with treasure, that he were inviting me to open.

'Your table is ready,' The *maître d'* informed us and then led us through to the dining area.

'Right,' I said gripping the menu. 'I have to warn you, I'm hungover so that means I'm hungry.'

'The way you wolfed down those nuts at the bar, I was a

little concerned. Thought you might have worms or something.'

'Maybe a dead one from the tequila bottle.'

He winced. 'Sounds like quite a night.'

By the time I'd given him a censored version of events,
he was belly laughing.

'That's why they don't allow women in strip clubs,' he
said. 'How did you get in, anyway?'

'Pretended we were journalists. The doorman was of
the understanding I was writing a feature entitled "Female
Empowerment Through Erotic Dancing".'

He smirked. 'So is this a regular thing you like to do?'

'What, go to strip clubs and incite feminist anarchy?'

He laughed.

'It was Kat's leaving do. Her boyfriend thought it would
be something they might enjoy together. Because she's bisexual now.'

He raised his eyebrows. 'You don't sound too convinced.'

'Well, during the twenty years I've known her, and depending on the boy in question, she's been a Jehovah's
Witness, a Hell's Angel, a militant fundamentalist for the
Animal Liberation Front, a professional air guitarist, a uni-
cyclist, a naturist and, most recently, a gangster rapper. So
adding the relatively unremarkable bisexual to the list, well,
quite frankly, I'm surprised it hasn't happened sooner.'

He topped up his glass. 'Looking forward to meeting
her, she sounds hilarious.'

He wants to meet my friends? I visualised Mandi sitting next to us, clapping wildly, wedding bells in her eyes.

By the time the food arrived, we were on our second
bottle of wine and our conversation, initially filled with

intelligent and witty exchanges, had degenerated into outrageous flirting and stupid jokes.

'What did the Californian roll say to the Nigiri roll?' I said, confident I was about to trigger a bout of uncontrolled laughter. 'Roll over.'

He frowned and then laughed. 'That's not even a joke. What is that? It doesn't make sense!'

'No, that's not what I meant,' I said, scratching my head. 'It was the sashimi. The sashimi said it to the, er, to the Californian roll.'

He continued to look perplexed.

'Oh, I can't remember the sodding joke. It's really funny though.'

'I'm sure it is,' he said, taking my hand, and leaning forward, his eyes drawing me in. 'You know, if you weren't such a greedy guts—' he paused '—and if your jokes weren't so, so terrible—' another pause '—not to mention being barred from Spearmint Rhino—' He squeezed my hand. 'Well, without all that, you could have very nearly been my perfect woman.'

I sat back and looked at him. 'Only the perfect can demand perfection,' I said, flicking some sticky rice in his direction.

Later that night when we walked along the bank of the Thames, hand in hand, I looked up at the cloudless sky and imagined Eros busily mapping out a glittering future for us in the stars. The moment Nick's lips met mine, sparks shot through my veins and into my heart, like a defibrillator, bringing me back to life.

PART TWO

Chapter 12

'BLONDE HAIR, BLUE EYES and big tits,' he said to Thea.

In the past three years we had matched thousands of singles, and although we were still a long way from finding the answers I'd hoped, Thea had at least learned to temper her eye rolls. And right now, her expression was fixed at something that could have even been described as earnest.

'Would you consider green eyes?' she asked.

'No,' he said, pushing up his sleeves to reveal a diamond-encrusted Rolex. 'I dated someone with green eyes once. It didn't work out.'

I continued typing on my keyboard on the table next to them, in the lounge bar, and brushed the hair away from my face to sneak a sideways glance at him, although I already knew what to expect.

He wore a shiny grey suit, the garish end of Gucci. His watch was obnoxiously bling like a bank balance on his wrist. His hair: blond, highlighted. Tan: deep, natural. Eyes:

blue, sparkling. Smile: cheeky, lopsided. Teeth: even, white.
Age: I'd guess, thirty-seven. Height: around five feet seven
inches, unfortunate considering his other physical attributes. Body language: overtly male, legs splayed, hand
near crotch, shoulders wide. Eye contact: good. Champagne
choice: predictably expensive. I'd met enough men like him
to make a quick assessment, although this one seemed to
be on the more depressing end of the spectrum.

I looked over at Thea, watching how her dark hair hid
her face as she leant over a notepad and began writing. He
sat opposite her, his hands miming two large beach balls.

'Like this,' he said, a self-satisfied smile sweeping across
his face. 'Are you looking?'

Thea raised her head and the curtain lifted. I could tell
she was fighting to suppress an emotion. I supposed it was
either amusement or fury, but I couldn't quite tell.

'Yes, got it,' she replied. 'Please continue.'

'And I like nipples that point upwards.'

'Upwards-pointing nipples,' she said, scribbling away.

'And I prefer pink to brown.'

'Preferably pink.' She paused and looked up, eyes narrowed. 'Is that a deal-breaker? The pink nipples?'

He weighed his head from side to side and I pictured a
tiny cluster of brain cells rolling around inside his skull.
'Yes. Definitely pink. I'm not fussed which shade.'

'There are shades?'

'Of course, from light pink, like the colour of your nail
varnish, to a dark pink, a bit like your lipstick.'

'Wow, you learn something every day.'

'I'm surprised you didn't know that.'

'Surprised?'

'Yes, you being a—'

'Matchmaker?'

'No, being a woman. You must have seen hundreds of your friends' nipples.'

'My friends don't have hundreds of nipples.'

'You know what I mean.'

'Oh, you mean all those topless pillow fights we have?' He nodded and winked.

She locked him with Medusa eyes. 'Right, now your turn.'

'What else do you need to know?'

She ripped out a sheet of paper from her notepad and slid it across the table along with a pen. 'Draw an outline of your penis for me, please.'

'An outline?' he asked.

I wondered if he had selected the wrong word for clarification.

'Yes, sketch the outline and then add in any unusual features.' Her expression remained fixed at a plausible serious.

He picked up the pen. 'Does it have to be to scale?'

'Preferably. Or else you can indicate the measurements.'

With an expression of intense concentration and with a tight grip on the pencil, soon his sketch was complete. Then after a further five minutes of shading and corrections, he held the sheet of paper aloft for Thea to see.

'Obviously we'll have to verify this with a photo,' she said, taking it from him and studying it.

He leant back in his seat. 'Will you want that signed by my bank manager?'

'Ex-girlfriend will do. But if your bank manager is happy to do it…'

Moments later, after he'd left and the buzz of his phone

was fading into the distance, Thea turned to me with a tight smile.

'Another Prince Charming,' she said, handing me the sketch. 'Good sport though.'

I looked at the drawing, winced and then quickly folded it away. It appeared his ego wasn't the only thing that was inflated.

'So, what were you scribbling down?' I asked. 'Potential matches?'

She shook her head. 'Shopping list.'

I sighed. 'Thea.'

'What?'

'He's a client. You're supposed to be focused on helping him.'

'I am.'

'Go on, then.'

She laughed. 'Well, under all the bravado, there's probably a lost little boy who just wants to be loved.'

'Thea. Stop it,' I said, although I couldn't help but share her reluctance.

'Know any stupid girls with big tits who want a rich guy?'

My mind flicked through its archives, searching for someone who might be able to tolerate him. Or even like him. Then I had a thought. 'Hmm,' I said, nodding slowly, 'but she's not stupid. She's quite intelligent actually. Her name's Kerri.'

'We don't care about her name. What's her cup size?'

'FF.'

'Nipples?'

'Hang on.' I picked up my phone and typed her name

into Google images, then handed the phone to Thea. 'There you go, pink nipples.'

Thea sniffed. 'Of course, a glamour model. She looks so...what's the word?' She drummed her fingers on the table. 'Yes, that's it. *Intelligent.*'

I rolled my eyes, something I appeared to have acquired from Thea. 'You okay to arrange the introduction?'

'Sure,' she said, stuffing her notebook back into her bag. 'Living the dream.'

The lounge bar hadn't changed much since the first day I'd walked down the staircase three years ago, but something of the magic had been lost. I remembered how the fast-beating pulse of music initially drew me in, the allure of the hidden cave and its impenetrable stone barrier. The pull of the spiral staircase had been like a whirlpool sucking me in, filling me with fear, excitement and anticipation. But, by now I had sat in every seat, uncovered every cushion, felt every undulation of the floor, tracked every crack in the plaster, sampled every drink on the menu. It felt more like an old friend than a new lover.

It wasn't as though essential maintenance hadn't been carried out: there'd been a lick of paint here, a new painting there. But even the antique chairs had lost their allure, their saggy centres and gnarled legs betraying their age. There had been talk of replacing them with new Philippe Starck–type designs: fine leather stretched over taut springs, but nothing, as yet, had quite measured up.

As for the bar itself, the faces behind it had changed more frequently than the flowers displayed upon it, yet Steve and Brigitte remained as permanent as the blood-red carpet, soaking up the years with only a slight tread to mark their endurance. Despite endless rebuffs, it seemed Brigitte hadn't quite given up hope that the initial bout of casual sex with Steve would someday lead to something more.

She wiggled down the staircase, holding hands with a little boy whose head was about the same height as the bottom of her miniskirt.

'*Il est très mignon,*' she said with a convincing smile.

Behind her was Harriet. '*Il est très épuisant,*' she said, her expression more befitting someone who had trekked across a desert and just stumbled upon the first watering hole. 'Henry. *Attends!*'

The disjointed stagger with which Harriet descended the staircase was barely comparable to the elegant slink that I'd witnessed the first time we met. She sat down in front of me, her hair dishevelled and her eyes disorientated. Behind us, Brigitte swung Henry around in her arms with a contrived giggle and intermittent glances in Steve's direction, as though she hoped it might provoke a desire for fatherhood. That was until Henry presented her with a snotty tissue from his pocket, at which point she dropped him to the ground as though he were brandishing a venomous spider.

It had been almost two years since I'd last seen Harriet at Henry's christening. Essentially, nothing had changed. She still had the bone structure of a porcelain figurine, the wide eyes of a fawn, hair to rival an Arabian racehorse, and still, despite several biscuit smudges, the intrinsic chic of a Frenchwoman. But something was missing and it was more than the exhaustion that accompanies the voracious demands of a two-year-old.

'Oh, I don't know.' She sighed, pushing her hair back from her face. 'It's just not how I imagined it would be.'

I poured her a coffee. She looked at it, picked it up and

then put it back down. 'I don't think I'm cut out for motherhood.'

I looked down to see Henry trying to post his snotty tissue into my bag and I wondered if any of us were.

'I love Henry to bits, but being with him all the time, it's so…well, at first it was the lack of sleep, the endless rotation of feeding, burping, changing. I thought when that was over it would be okay. Then it was the food throwing, the kamikaze toddling and adamant refusal to nap. Now, it's the blatant disobedience.' She turned around. 'Henry, come back with that!'

He toddled off with a wad of papers from my bag.

She sighed. 'Whenever I have a chance to do something and, you know, have one minute to myself then I'm needed. For something. My time is not my own any more. He takes all of it. I don't have time for anything.'

'Time for what?'

'Time to do anything. Time to write an email, time to make a phone call, time to read a book, time to watch the news, time to eat, time to sleep, time to have a conversation—'

'Mummy!' Henry shouted.

She pulled the hair tightly away from her face. 'Time to think. Time to breathe.'

'Mummy! Ephenant!'

Henry ran towards us, waving a piece of paper. Steve was closing in on him, looking alarmed. I swung around, saw what it was and then snatched it from his grasp.

Henry's face turned a deep purple, his eyes filled with rage. 'Ephenant! Ephenant!'

Without breaking eye contact with me, Harriet reached into her bag and handed him a custard cream. Henry's expression of inconsolable despair instantly morphed into one of sheer delight.

'Is that an elephant?' Harriet asked. 'He loves elephants.'

'Not really,' I said, stuffing the penis sketch back into my bag. 'More of an impressionist's interpretation of one.'

She shrugged her shoulders and then lifted her coffee cup.

'So do you have anyone to help you look after Henry?'

'"Help? You need help? You have one child. My mother brought up six of us by herself. And she baked her own bread." That's what he says.'

'Jeremy?'

She nodded. 'He thinks I'm a useless mother.'

'He said that?'

'Not in so many words.'

'Life's too short to bake bread.'

'That's what I said.' She swirled the coffee in her cup. 'But whatever I do is never enough. I just feel like a massive failure.'

I looked at Henry who was now hanging upside down from the bar, seemingly finding the experience hilarious. 'But he looks so happy.'

'Yes, when he's not screaming the house down.'

'Isn't that normal though, the terrible twos?'

Finally, she took a sip of coffee but then pulled a face, as though the bitterness was overpowering. 'I hid in the cupboard the other day.'

I frowned.

'Jeremy found me there when he came home early. He was furious.'

'He was home early?'

'Yes, I know, that's more of a shock than me hiding from

my child. He left a board meeting to take Rusty to the vet's. Again. That bloody dog is a liability.'

I tried not to laugh.

'In the space of six months he's eaten four pairs of Henry's shoes, one pair of wellington boots, a plastic bunch of grapes and a rubber giraffe called Sophie.'

'But he's okay, though?'

She nodded. 'He's just fine. Everyone's just fine.'

'And you?'

'Me, well, every day is the same. And with every day, I get further away from who I was, and closer towards who I am becoming. My fate, my destiny, which apparently involves baking bread.'

'Or hiding in cupboards?'

She smiled.

'And Jeremy?'

'He's never there. Unless Rusty needs him, of course. And even when he is home, his mind isn't. It's "the fund this", "the fund that".'

She looked at me, her eyes dull and opaque as though there were a mist clouding the lens and suffocating the light that once burned so brightly.

'We haven't had sex in eight months.'

I sat back, assuming she would quickly correct the units to weeks. She didn't.

'Oh,' I said, gesturing for Steve to clear the coffee cups and bring over some wine.

'I think he's bored of me,' she went on. 'Well, even if he isn't, I'm bored of me.' Henry clambered onto her lap, smearing more biscuit on her trousers. 'And,' she said, peeling him off, 'I just don't feel sexy any more. The whole giving birth thing—' she wrinkled her nose and nodded downwards '—it's like blowing up a balloon, it never goes back to how it was.'

Steve hovered by the table holding two glasses of wine.

Harriet's face flushed. 'Sorry,' she said, looking up at him. 'Not the sort of conversation you want to overhear.'

He smiled and placed the glasses on the table. 'That's nothing. At least she's not asking you to draw it.'

I waved him away and turned back to Harriet. 'Have you spoken to Jeremy about this?'

She shook her head. 'He's got enough to deal with. You know his fund lost millions, don't you?'

'No, I didn't.'

'It's on the verge of going bankrupt.'

'That's terrible.'

She shrugged her shoulders.

Henry, now standing on her lap, was tugging on her hair clip. '*Arrête ça,*' she said, ripping it from his sticky grasp.

'I hate the fund. I hate his job.' She gulped down her wine and then stared into the glass. 'I lost my family when I married him. And now it feels like I've lost him too.'

'Henry's your family now.'

'And he needs his daddy.'

Henry's face lit up. 'Daddy!' he shouted. 'Daddy!'

'No, darling. We'll be seeing Daddy later. Not now.'

His face crumpled. Harriet handed him another biscuit and then looked up at me. 'What should I do?' she asked.

I scrunched up my mouth and considered what to say. 'You have to talk to him.'

'When? Henry never sleeps. He's like a little Margaret Thatcher, fully functioning on five hours. And even when he does sleep, Jeremy's working.'

'I'll look after the little chap for an evening if that would help?'

Henry scowled, but the light in Harriet's eyes temporarily reignited.

'Would you? Really? It's just Jeremy doesn't trust baby-sitters and we don't have any family here. And I know he'd trust you. Wouldn't you like that, Henry? Stay with the lovely lady?'

He poked his tongue out.

'I'll drop him over on Friday,' she said.

After I'd led Harriet and, following a misunderstanding regarding ownership of the elephant sketch, a now wailing Henry to the door, she turned to me. It was as if she was trying to think of a way to stall, a way to stay longer.

'What are your plans for the rest of the day?' she asked.

I laughed, but it came out as more of a snort. 'My car's been impounded, so I have to collect it from a place called Perivale.'

'Impounded?'

'Driving without insurance.'

She stepped back. 'You?'

I nodded. 'Technically, though, it was Nick's fault.'

Her eyes widened. 'Nick, oh, my God, how rude of me. I didn't ask how things were going with you two. Any news?'

I laughed. 'It takes him six months of research to buy a TV, so I'm not holding my breath for a proposal anytime soon.'

'It's best not to rush into things,' she said, scooping up Henry in her arms. 'I wish Jeremy and I had waited and, well, you know, got to know each other a bit better first.'

The door to the club swung closed behind them. As I pulled on my coat and prepared to follow her out into the lukewarm drizzle, I wondered if the pendulum of love, initially swinging from high to low, was always destined to settle somewhere in the middle.

'Perivale? I don't know, check Google maps. I really don't have time to talk. I've got an important meeting.' Nick's irritation seemed to amplify down the phone line.

'Where, at the gym?' I replied, marching along the pavement.

'No, with the CEO from New York, actually.'

'Oh, you're going to Gaucho with Frank, then?'

He huffed down the line.

'Anyway, I can't Google it because I can't access the internet since you interfered with my phone.'

'Interfered? I'm not a sex offender. I was trying to help.'

'Well, now it doesn't work.'

'So, sort it out yourself.'

'That's not the point. The point is that you said you would do it.'

'Since when did your phone become my responsibility?'

'Since you started fiddling with it.'

'Look, I have to go.'

'Yeah, me too. I have to trek across London to collect our car from the pound because you forgot to get it insured.'

'Me? I forgot?'

'Yes. You.'

'It's your car too. You're the one who drives it.'

'But you promised you would get it insured.'

'I offered. There's a difference between offering and promising.'

'So you don't mean what you say?'

'No, that's not what I said.'

'It doesn't matter what you say if you don't mean it.'

'Look, I really have to go.'

'Yeah, whatever. Enjoy your steak.'

Two hours later, the train pulled into a station called Perivale. Still unsure as to whether this was a real place or just an elaborate set—directed by Nick from the comfort of his steakhouse to prove a point about how irresponsible I was—I climbed onto the platform and looked around. Google maps, now resurrected thanks to a lengthy phone call to the network help desk, inked out the thirty-minute slog through semi-detached suburbia. Instructed by a random app that Nick had installed, a pop-up immediately informed me the concrete cul-de-sacs I was walking past were once a vast expanse of fields that used to grow hay for the working horses of Victorian London. It was, I mused, ironic that the fields had harvested the fuel that would lead to their own burial under a blanket of tarmac.

'The queue ends here, love,' a man with a tattoo on his forehead informed me.

Standing behind twenty others lined up outside a depressing Portakabin, I impatiently tapped my foot as I timed each 'customer': one in and, twenty-five minutes later, one out. I huffed and puffed like a sulky teenager and then looked around in disbelief when it started to rain.

Huddled against the railings, I shielded my phone from the drizzle and read my emails, hoping, like Harriet, for a way to escape the greyness of reality.

One immediately caught my attention. Emily Hawkhurst was so sorry to be bothering me and was hoping that I might remember her. Well her mum, Susan, that was, who drinks Lady Grey tea. I met her a little while ago Emily's email prompted me. *Yes, Emily*, I thought, *that was years*

ago and, if I remember correctly, our first and last conver-
sation ended with you instructing me to shoot you if you
ever got that desperate.

Another email, from my virtual office, informed me that
I'd received a fax. As it was such an unusual occurrence, it
seemed they weren't entirely sure how to deal with it. Following several frustrating phone conversations, a scanned
four-page legal document eventually appeared in my inbox.
It was from a legal firm representing Sharon, the canapé
quibbler from the masquerade ball, who had joined the
agency a few months ago.

'Sued for what?' Thea asked, after I had read it and called
her in a panic.

'From what I can gather, for failing to find her a husband.'

She laughed. 'Can't we just refund her?'

'I did, but now she's seeking damages.'

'Damages for what?' Thea asked.

'Time wasted using our service, diminished fertility,
something from a specialist about anal follicle count,' I
explained, reading from the fax.

Thea laughed. 'I think you mean antral.'

I continued. 'She's saying it's our fault she may never
have children.'

'She's insane.'

'She's got a good lawyer though.'

Thea let out a long deep sigh, which conjured an image
in my mind of a dragon breathing fire. Then it morphed
into Thea wearing a white coat and using a blowtorch to
perform some kind of makeshift sterilisation.

It was after nine p.m. when I finally arrived home, damp
from the rain. My muscles ached and my stomach rumbled

as though it were contemplating eating its very own parietal cells. I almost wished I was still Henry's age so I could have a tantrum until someone made it all better. Or at least gave me a custard cream and a cuddle.

'You won't believe the day I've had. I'm so tired.' I sighed at Nick and then slung my wet coat on the chair.

'Me too.' He glared at the coat and then picked it up and walked towards the radiator with exaggerated effort. 'I'm exhausted.' He always had to win. If I was tired, then he was exhausted. How did I beat that? Terminal illness?

'What's for dinner?' I asked, eyeing the Waitrose bag on the counter.

He tipped it up and two cartons tumbled out. 'Paella or pea risotto?'

'Paella, please.'

He huffed.

'Oh, you want the paella?'

'I don't really like risotto.'

'Why did you buy it, then?'

'Because I thought you didn't like paella.'

'What? I've eaten paella like five million times since we've been together.'

'Five million times. Really?' He glanced up at the ceiling. 'That's, on average, three thousand times a day.' Then he looked back down. 'No wonder you didn't get time to sort the insurance.'

'Fine. I'll have the pea risotto, then. Rice and peas. Delicious.'

'Paella is just yellow rice and peas. It's the same thing.'

'Well, if it's the same thing, then why don't you have it?'

We glared at each other, a stand-off which seemed to result in a truce.

'I'm sorry,' I said, plunging a fork into the film lid. 'I've had a horrible day.' I withdrew the fork and plunged it in again. Withdrew, plunged. Withdrew, plunged. 'And the tossers at the pound wouldn't release the car,' I said on the fifth plunge.

'Why not?'

'Because I didn't have the original copy of the insurance certificate.'

'That's fair enough.'

'But I only got the insurance today, so how could I possibly have the original certificate?'

'Get it couriered.'

I huffed. 'And I'm being sued.'

'For what?'

I explained, as best I could, the fertility case against me, but his look, instead of the desired empathy, seemed irritated and condescending.

'Everything's always such a drama with you.'

The incessant beeping of the microwave plunged through my eardrums and into my brain like my fork through the film. I lunged forward to open the door.

'You'd make a trip to Tesco sound like you've undergone open-heart surgery.'

I threw the paella carton onto the counter and ripped off the lid.

'And,' he continued, 'I told you not to drive the car until the insurance was sorted.'

The hot steam burned my hand.

'You bring these things on yourself.'

The burn throbbed, radiating up my arm.

'And getting sued, in the midst of a recession, you know, that could take your business down.'

Throb. Throb. Throb.

He shot me a petulant glare. 'You really need to grow up and start taking responsibility for your life.'

'Right,' I said, slamming down the carton, paella oozing down the sides like molten lava. 'So let's get this straight. You're saying that it was irresponsible of me to get sued by an opportunistic menopausal loon? And it was irresponsible of me to trust my boyfriend when he'd promised to do something? If that is, indeed, what you are saying then, yes, you're right. I'm totally and utterly irresponsible.'

The tears lined up, ready to spill out.

'You rely on me too much. You need to stand on your own two feet.'

'We're supposed to support each other.' I sloshed the paella onto a plate. 'Not me do everything while you're eating steak with your wanky mate.'

'You don't do everything.'

'I run a business. It's hard work.'

'If it's so stressful, why don't you go get a proper job like the rest of us.'

The throb of the burn merged with the throb in my head. 'Oh, here we go. Why slog my guts out trying to help people when I could sell my soul for a big fat bonus? Like you do.'

Throb. Throb. Throb.

My body had had enough and decided to override my senses. I looked down to see my fist closing in around some paella, arm swinging back, slowly, purposefully before propelling the contents, catapult-style, towards Nick. His jaw dropped and his eyes widened as the yellow gloop slid down his face and onto his favourite Thomas Pink shirt.

He looked at me, looked down at his shirt and then back at me.

'That's it. I've had enough of you,' he said, lips thin, teeth gritted. 'Get out. Get out of my house.'

'Your house?' My eyes bulged, my muscles tensed.

'I paid more, so I'm the majority shareholder.'

'Oh, yes. Of course. Mr Billy Big Balls earns more than his irresponsible matchmaking girlfriend. And don't we all know it. Well done, you!' I noticed I was clapping my hands like a crazy person. 'But,' I said, the applause fading to a stop, 'I contributed towards this house so part of it is mine too. 'This bit.' I marked out an area on the ground with my foot. 'So I'll stay if I want to.' I plonked down on the sofa and folded my arms. 'You leave!'

'I'm going!' he shouted and then marched into the hallway to grab his coat, which was under several of my coats and required some wrestling to free. 'But I want you out of here when I get back.'

'Fine!'

'Good!' He slammed the door, leaving a trail of yellow rice behind him.

exchanged contracts on the house. Even the postcode ending with the letters N and E had our destiny stamped on it.

'I can't take any more,' Nick had said during our post-paella deconstruction.

'Fine. I'll go,' I said, my pride having answered before my heart could argue.

It was only now I'd come to collect my things, at the agreed time, while Nick was at work, that I realised I didn't want to go. My heart belonged here. All my dreams and plans for the future were here. But, short of chaining myself to the banister and claiming squatter's rights, I had no choice but to leave and to take my overfilled bags with me.

When I had rehearsed the moving-out scene in my mind, my behaviour had been dignified, mature and entirely appropriate for the demise of a significant and meaningful relationship. But when it came down to it, I found myself overcome by a juvenile urge to take *everything* that was mine, which included my toasted sandwich maker, my bath mats, my Christmas tree stand. Quite frankly, anything that I could recall having paid for. After I'd shoved my toilet brush into the car boot, I felt a twinge of shame though, and at the point when I'd considered unscrewing my doorknob and digging up my garden plants, I quickly closed the door behind me and posted the keys through the letter box.

During the drive home, as the toilet brush handle rattled against the rear window, the tears began to well and my chest began to heave. I quickly called Matthew, hoping his humour might somehow counteract my despair.

'Yes, exact your revenge.' Matthew laughed. 'He'll be sorry when he has to buy a new bath mat.'

'Okay, okay. I know it was childish. So, are you free tonight or not?'

Chapter 13

BAGS RAMMED WITH my life's belongings lay scattered across the floor like the aftermath of a battle. I slumped down on the stairs and took one last look around.

Aside from a few rice grains trodden into the rug, and a saffron splatter on the wall, it was like a poster for the perfect home; the sort of image that would be blown up and displayed on the hoarding around a building site. This scene in front of me, however, lacked the ubiquitous beautiful couple laughing and drinking wine. Her, languishing across a contemporary sofa, make-up as flawless as the white linen trousers she'd simply thrown on after a busy day as a city executive. Him, a successful financier and gym enthusiast, arriving home just in time to don Armani casuals and pan-fry monkfish on the brushed-chrome hob.

The sunlight poured through the glass pane above the front door, casting the shadow of a number seven across the floor. Lucky number seven, we'd joked on the day we

'Sorry, no can do. Date night tonight.' Since getting married and having two kids, Matthew was rarely available for anything that required less than six months' notice.

I sighed. 'All right, then, but any advice for me now? I could do with some.'

'Oh, I don't know, I thought you'd nailed it this time. Nick is a good guy.'

'He is.'

'So what happened?'

I tried the words out in my head first, to see how they sounded: *He wouldn't let me have the paella. He forgot to get the car insured.*

But that sounded pathetic. Finally I thought of something more convincing. 'He called me irresponsible.'

'Well, you are, a bit.'

I huffed. If I hadn't been driving, I would have folded my arms. 'You're supposed to be on my side.'

'Are you on your side?'

'And you're supposed to be making me feel better, not worse.'

'Nick isn't the one for you. You can do better. Plenty more fish in the sea. Is that what you want to hear?'

'No.'

'Well, what, then?'

'I want my fish. But.'

'But?'

'I want him to love me for who I am.'

I immediately pictured Matthew's eyes rolling, then I saw Thea's face, and her eyes were rolling, I could even picture Mandi's eyes rolling.

'That cuts both ways.'

'What's with the clichés today? What happened to my sharp, witty friend?'

He laughed. 'Well, if you want my two pennies' worth, I'll lay it on the line: at the end of the day, what it boils down to, the long and short of it is—'

I laughed. 'Stop beating around the bush and spit it out.'

'Okay, I'll cut to the chase. It's plain as day that you're making a mountain out of a molehill and cutting your nose off to spite your face. You should wait for the dust to settle, then lay your cards on the table and hope that this cloud has a silver lining.'

'And go back with my tail between my legs. I don't think so.'

'Pride comes before a fall.'

'Oh, put a sock in it.'

After I had hauled all my belongings into the hallway, feeling like a crazy bag lady, I retrieved the least creased dress from one of my suitcases and pulled on some suede boots. Then I ran a brush through my hair and set off for the club. This afternoon, along with Mandi and Thea, I was supposed to be delivering a training session for five newly recruited consultants. Due to Thea's propensity to fire more consultants than she hired, Mandi had put herself forward to run the recruitment campaign.

When I arrived, I was unsurprised to find five Mandi lookalikes, all lined up in one of the meeting rooms. Their eyes were wide, they had notepads on their laps and their pink pens were poised.

After formally welcoming Lucy, Susie, Daisy, Maisy and Minky to the team, Mandi stood up. She took a moment to smooth down her candy-floss pink dress and push back her blonde flicks, which were looking especially perky.

'Twelve thousand, four hundred and seventy-eight,' she said, tapping on her keyboard.

Suddenly, Jennifer Rush's 'The Power of Love' pulsed out of Mandi's pink laptop. The number was projected, in neon pink, onto a screen on the wall.

'That's the number of single people who have asked for our help.'

The Mandi clones looked on.

'Five thousand, two hundred and twenty-nine,' Mandi said, then tapped a key. 'Long-term relationships we've helped create.' Photographs of smiling couples appeared on the screen. 'Nine hundred and forty-eight—' Mandi clicked '—engagements.'

Images raced past my eyes: sparkling smiles, sparkling rings, more smiles, more rings. I was starting to feel dizzy.

'Two hundred and seventy-one—' she clicked again '—weddings.'

We saw more happy faces, smiles, hand-holding, kissing, more smiles, more hand-holding, more kissing, more kissing. I sat down, grabbing the sides of the chair for support.

Mandi beamed. 'And as of today—' she clapped her hands and bounced on the spot '—three hundred and seven—' one more click '—new lives!'

The screen filled with images of pink wrinkly faces: some wearing bonnets, some sucking dummies, one of Henry as a newborn, poking his tongue out. Each had doting parents, whose hopes for the future were clear through every crease on their face.

Just as the power ballad reached its crescendo, the Mandi clones, with beaming smiles and weepy eyes, all stood up and clapped. One of them, who I think was Minky, even whooped. Mandi basked in the glory as though she had delivered a world-changing presidential speech.

Next to me, Thea's eye rolling had reached an intensity whereby I was seriously concerned that she might be in the midst of an epileptic fit. When her eyes had settled back to their usual state—a vaguely bored glare—she stood up, switched off the music and addressed each of the Mandi clones with a silent nod.

'Relationships fail,' she said, her silhouette eclipsing the smiles on the screen. 'First marriages: fifty-three per cent. Second marriages: seventy-five per cent. Engagements: seventy per cent. Cohabitations: seventy-five per cent. And early relationships, those of six months and under, have a failure rate of around eighty-five per cent.'

My personal contribution to these statistics had been a formidable endeavour, I realised as soon as she'd said it.

Thea continued without blinking. 'The pictures you've just seen were all taken within the first two years of a relationship. That kind of love does not last.'

Mandi's recruits looked on dumbfounded, as did Mandi, who despite having heard Thea's speech many times before, never really accepted it as the truth.

Thea tapped on the keyboard and a graph appeared on the screen.

'Dopamine, phenylethylamine and oxytocin. These are the neurochemicals that drive the early stages of love. Psychologists refer to this stage as the collapse of ego boundaries. Neurologists say it fires off the same part of the brain as cocaine. Some psychiatrists believe behaviour patterns during this phase are comparable to being mentally ill.'

Mandi looked away as though the particularly scary part of a movie were about to begin.

Thea continued, her eyes fixed ahead. 'And when the hormones drop, which, just to be clear, they always do—anytime between three months to two years later—that's when most relationships break down.'

Susie, or it might have been Daisy, raised her hand and then swallowed. 'Why would anyone put their heart on the line if they knew they had only a fifteen per cent chance of making it?'

Mandi stood up. 'Because being in love is the most wonderful feeling in the world.'

She gazed down at the screensaver on her phone, of her and Steve grinning like the couples in the photos. Every day, since Steve had asked her out, Mandi's faith in love had seemed to multiply exponentially.

Usually Thea would tolerate Mandi's enthusiasm, but today it looked as though she was about to vomit.

'The reason people put their heart on the line is because most think they're immune to the rest of world's afflictions,' Thea said, glaring at Mandi.

'What do you mean?' Susie or Daisy asked Thea.

'They think they're special, that they'll be the fifteen percent that make it.'

Mandi interrupted. 'But, even if it doesn't work out, we all know it is better to have loved and lost than never to have loved at all.'

Although usually on Mandi's side, I was no longer in the mood to agree with her. I stood up and cleared my throat.

'For some perhaps, but for others, a life without love would be preferable to a life without heartbreak,' I said, my legs almost buckling beneath me.

Mandi lurched forward, but Thea blocked her, then frowned and cocked her head as though she were trying to decide if I were likely to break down, to start screaming 'Love hurts,' whilst throwing cushions at people in the manner of Jeremy at the masquerade ball. After seemingly completing her assessment of my psychological state, she walked towards me and then gently removed the presentation notes from my lap.

'Right,' she said, turning back to face the new recruits. 'Now, I'm going to talk about market value in dating.'

Mandi jumped up, pink marker in hand, and pushed past Thea. She began writing on the whiteboard.

'Twenty-eight,' she said, pointing at the number as though she'd just discovered *pi*. 'This is the most exciting age for women. It's the age we are most eligible for marriage.' She smiled and clasped her hands together. 'Anything below that is a little young. Above that age, er, well then, sadly—' her gaze dipped towards the ground '—things get trickier.'

'What she's trying to say,' Thea interjected, 'is that if you're a woman and you're not married, or at least engaged, by thirty, then you may as well slit your wrists. Or get a cat.'

'There's always hope,' Mandi added, scowling at Thea.

The Mandi clones scribbled down notes while Thea handed out a graph. 'As you can see, for women, the probability of marriage dips after thirty and then nosedives after the age of thirty-five. Down to thirty per cent.'

The recruits gasped in unison. Mandi, still brandishing the marker, walked back towards the board.

'Thir-ty-fiiiiive,' she said slowly as she wrote out the number on the board. 'This is the age men are most eligible for marriage. The peak of their curve.'

'I thought they peaked at eighteen?' Minky asked, brow furrowed.

'No, that's their sexual peak.' Thea shook her head, as

though she'd been set the task of teaching Pythagoras's theorem to a crèche.

'Men,' Mandi went on, 'are still in demand up until their late forties.'

'Especially the rich ones,' Thea added with a raised eyebrow.

'However,' Mandi continued, ignoring Thea. 'Many men over forty don't want to get married, which in turn removes many of them from the pool of availability, further increasing demand. In fact, from our research into men aged forty and over, who have never been married, only thirty-five per cent of them want to get married. Whereas, ninety per cent of single women over forty would like to get married.'

'So there's a deficit,' said Lucy or was it Susie? Probably, almost definitely, Lucy.

'Exactly,' said Mandi. 'And when there's a deficit teamed with a high demand, market value goes up.'

She drew big upwards-pointing arrows on the whiteboard.

'So men have a higher market value than women?' Lucy asked.

'Women's market value is high when they're younger, men's when they're older.'

Lucy scratched her nose. 'So that's why older men get to date younger women?'

Mandi nodded. 'Exactly. Thirty-five-year-old men want to marry twenty-eight-year-old women. So the thirty-five year-old women are left with the men who are over forty.'

'Can't they date the thirty-six-year-old men?' Lucy asked.

'No, those men want the twenty-eight-year-olds too,' Thea answered. 'All men want twenty-eight-year-olds.'

'Everything being equal,' Mandi said as though that made it all okay.

'And the twenty-eight-year-old women, what do they want?' Susie asked, scratching her head.

'Well, they want a man aged thirty to thirty-five, who wants to settle down and have a family,' Mandi said. 'Many men in their early thirties still aren't quite ready for marriage, so these girls end up with the thirty-five-year-old men. Eligible meets eligible.'

'There are always exceptions,' I interrupted.

'Not many,' Thea said. 'You need to memorise that graph. Because when you meet all the thirty-five-year-old women who want to date a thirty-five-year-old man, you'll need to tell them straight without wasting their time.'

Mandi chipped in, 'And it's important for the twenty-eight-year-old women too. They need to know that now is the time to make it happen, to get married and settle down.'

I stood up, wagging my finger at the new recruits.

'Yes. Tell them to hurry. Find a husband quick. Time's running out. Tick-tock. Your ovaries are shrivelling. Tick-tock. No one wants you. Tick-tock. Come to one of our parties when you're ovulating, give a guy a blow job, spit his semen into a container and inject it with a turkey baster after he's gone home.'

'That happened?'

I nodded and then dropped back down onto the chair.

'Did she get pregnant?'

'Twins.'

Five pairs of manicured hands flew over five open mouths and I decided it might be time to call the session to a close.

* * *

I arrived home to a heap of suitcases and the musty smell of emptiness. My flat had been vacant since the last tenants had abruptly moved out, lured most probably by the glossy brochure of a new development, and now it was as though it had given up hope and accepted its fate. All those years ago, when I'd first moved in, it had seemed like a blank canvas welcoming my imprint. But now, the curtains hung listlessly, the blinds drooped like heavy eyelids and the carpet looked as worn down as I felt.

Like an ant tackling a resistant crumb, deserted by the rest of its colony, I pushed the sofa, inch by inch, to the other side of the room. I was hoping a different perspective might help. It didn't. So, I sank down into the cushions and considered my odds. If being happy meant being in a successful long-term relationship, then, according to the statistics, only a few of us stood a chance. Could I be happy if I never got married? What about if I never had children? What became of all of us who were on the wrong side of the statistics?

Maybe it was time to rethink my life plan? Maybe, instead of living as one half of the beautiful couple in an advertisement for a luxury riverside development, I was destined to be on my own. To live a life of solitude ruminating over the one that got away and wondering how different the outcome would have been, had I graciously accepted that pea risotto.

An outlier in society, I could retreat to the country to live off the land and perhaps make chutney. I would take in stray dogs, love them like people and let them sleep in my bed. In an attempt to fill the gaping hole in my heart, I might start hoarding things. It would begin with the odd newspaper, perhaps a few ornaments I'd picked up at the local jumble sale, then, in no time at all, my house would be filled with fermenting chutney, useless bric-a-brac and festering dog litter. My family might stage an intervention, perhaps with the help of Dr Phil—knowing I was a fan—but it would be fruitless. By then I would have lost my mind, muttering profanities under my breath and throwing dog poo at anyone who came near me. I might even be on TV: crazy ex-matchmaker and her pack of dogs.

Nick would watch, as would Robert, both counting their blessings; they got out while they could. Before she turned thirty-five.

Chapter 14

IT HAD BEEN twenty days since the door of number seven had clicked shut behind me. Since then, every morning had been the same: I'd wake up, rub my eyes and for a brief moment believe that everything was okay. I'd stir a little, stretch and then extend my right arm across the mattress, feeling for him, reaching for comfort. But instead I'd find a cold, flat sheet, an unruffled duvet, an empty space. That was when the realisation would make itself known. At first, it would feel like a nudge, then a pinch, then a slap around the face, a punch to the jaw, a blow to the stomach. Then another. Each time with increasing intensity. I'd curl up to protect myself, but at the same time knowing that there was no way to escape the pain.

That morning was no different. After checking my phone to see if there'd been any texts from Nick since the one eleven days ago wishing me well in my 'future endeavours', I dragged myself out of bed. My muscles stung and my body felt heavy as I lumbered to the bathroom, each step more painful than the last. I had to keep focused. I needed shampoo, body wash. A lazy gaze around the room could set me back again. Just when I thought I'd made it, my concentration lapsed and my gaze lingered on a space in the cabinet where his Mach3 razor blade used to rest. Before I could do anything, my mind had raced back to a time before. Before Gillette had declared to the world that three blades were no longer enough. When my oxytocin, phenylethylamine and dopamine were at their peak. Before he'd decided I was irresponsible. Before I'd questioned how much he cared.

In the shower, the water was scalding but I didn't move. I let it wash over me, let my skin burn. The sting of each drop felt like a brief release, as though my nervous system was grateful to have been diverted elsewhere.

It wasn't until I arrived at the club, and walked down the staircase and into the lounge bar, that the dragging feeling in the pit of my stomach subsided. Stepping into the lives of others had given me a way to escape mine. By the time I saw Jeremy, seated at the table with an untouched coffee in hand and studying the *Financial Times* like a fundamentalist might study the Koran, my attentions had been fully diverted.

'Morning, Mr Blatch.' I greeted him in my best Miss Moneypenny voice.

He lurched backwards, spilling coffee over the paper. 'Don't creep up on me like that.'

He dabbed the pages. I edged towards him and slid into the seat opposite, feeling like a negotiator called in to retrieve the financial publication.

'So, how are you?' I asked.

'Stressed,' he said, gripping the pages as though they were wired to explosives.

'So, work not going so well?'

His temples pulsed. 'Down another million today. The entire fund is fucked.'

A sharp shrill erupted from his phone. He looked at it for a moment then smashed it on the table until the noise stopped.

'There's a silent button you can use instead.'

He didn't laugh.

'So,' I said, leaning forward, elbows on the table, 'you're obviously not here for my advice on the markets.'

He dragged his eyes away from the headlines and picked up the coffee. 'Might have a better idea than me.' He took a sip and I noticed his fingernails were bitten down to the beds. 'Actually, I wanted to talk to you about Harriet.'

'I thought as much. You know we met the other week?'

He nodded, rubbing his temples. 'I think she should go back to work.'

I frowned. 'I thought you said mothers should be at home with their children?'

'I did. They should. But she's no good for Henry if she's depressed. She needs to work.'

'Have you discussed it with her?'

He shook his head.

'Do you think you should?'

'Probably,' he said, pinching the bridge of his nose.

'And if you don't?'

He looked up at me. 'We'll get through it.'

'She thinks you don't fancy her any more.'

His eyes narrowed. 'What?'

'She said you haven't had sex in eight months.'

He leant back in his chair, his hand losing contact with the newspaper. 'She told you that?'

I nodded.

He ran his fingers through his hair and his fringe flopped back down like overcooked spaghetti. The skin on his face was pale, transparent even, stretched over his sharp bones like rawhide over a frame.

'It's my problem. It has nothing to do with her.'

'She thinks it has.'

He sighed. 'Maybe we just need a night away from everything. She said you offered to babysit.'

I nodded, though I knew a night of obligatory sex was not the solution. Harriet dolled up in a French maid's outfit and Jeremy in furry handcuffs strapped to a hotel bed, while I, a few miles away, plied Henry with custard creams was not going to save their marriage.

'I think you need more than a night away.'

He looked at me blankly.

I pulled myself up in the chair and leant towards him.

'You had a plan. An idea of how you wanted marriage and family life to be. But it's not working. Is it?'

He shook his head.

'So you need to adapt. Do you have a Plan B?'

He shifted in his seat. 'Not really. My plan's always been the same.'

'Which is what?'

'To make as much money as possible.'

'Okay, so forget the money. Think about what you want; what makes you happy. Both of you. Then make a Plan B. Together. And if Plan B doesn't work out, make a Plan C.'

He looked up to the ceiling for a few seconds and then looked down again, colour flushing back into his cheeks.

'Okay, I'll give it a go.'

When the old Jeremy smile had just about reached half-mast, his phone began vibrating violently on the table. A glance at the screen drained the blood from his face faster than a knife through the jugular.

'Got to go,' he said, before bolting up the stairs, clutching the *FT* like Henry would a custard cream.

I sat back in the leather armchair and tapped a pen on my notepad. Although the page was blank and I had no intention of making notes, it kept my hands busy. Lacking any other distractions, physical movement was the only method I had to prevent my thoughts from spiralling into darkness.

When pen-tapping was no longer functioning as a diversion, I looked up to see a brunette in a brightly patterned wrap dress edging down the stairs. Below her thick dark chocolate fringe, were a delicate nose, a pointy chin and a rosebud mouth. She looked like the sort of flower fairy I imagined as a child to be living at the bottom of my garden.

I stood up to greet her. 'Emily?'

She studied me with inquisitive hazel eyes. 'You're Ellie?'

I smiled, gesturing for her to take a seat.

'You don't look like I thought you would,' she said, leaning her elbows on the table.

I laughed. 'What were you expecting?'

'I dunno, someone a bit older.'

I laughed again. 'What, like your mum?'

She giggled. 'I can't imagine her here. In this place. Must've been hilarious.'

I went on to relay the conversation I'd had with her mother, carefully omitting any reference to Oompa Loompas. Afterwards, she covered her face with her hands and apologised profusely, before daring to peer through a gap in her fingers.

'I think I was born to be humiliated,' she said.

'Anyone with parents was born to be humiliated,' I replied.

Moving the conversation on, I asked why she'd changed her mind about meeting me, as opposed to her stated preference for instant death via a lead bullet through the cranium.

Her shoulders drooped and her chest sunk in. 'My best friend just got engaged,' she said.

I looked on, waiting for the rest.

'She and I were the only single girls left in our group. Now I'm the only one.'

I continued to wait.

'All they talk about is weddings and babies. They don't want to go to bars or clubs any more. They just go around each other's houses for dinner parties and bang on about interior designs and landscape gardening. Honestly, it's like they're in their fifties, not their twenties. One of the girls has even started an antiquing club.'

I frowned. 'Antiquing?'

'She's American,' she said as though it explained everything.

I laughed. 'Okay, so you don't want to hang out with them any more, maybe you just need new friends to go to bars with?'

'Don't really want to do that any more either,' she said, 'although I could do with a drink now.'

I smiled and then nodded at Steve.

'I thought I'd be married by twenty-eight,' she said.

I smirked. 'Have you met anyone you'd like to marry?'

She shook her head and then peered at my left hand. 'Are you married yet?'

I shrugged my shoulders. 'Not yet. But if there's one thing I've learned, it's that the best laid plans have a nasty habit of backfiring.'

Steve laid two glasses of wine on the table. She swiped the one nearest her and took several gulps. Straight away, I noticed her purple nail polish. Aside from a few chips, it reminded me of a colour I used to wear myself.

'My mum says if you don't have a plan, then life will find someone who does.' She took another gulp. 'But Dad left her when I was seven, so what does she know anyway?'

'She probably knows a lot more than you think.'

'He said she'd let herself go.'

'Do you think that was fair?'

She stared into her glass. 'What—leaving her or telling her it was because she had a fat arse?'

I laughed.

She took another swig. 'But he's divorced again now, so clearly he knows shit too.'

I put my notepad and pen on the table. 'Well, it's obvious you don't want to be like your parents.'

'Who does?'

'And you don't want to be like your friends.'

'No way.'

'So what *do* you want?'

She leant back in her chair. 'To fall in love, get married and be happy.'

'How about to be happy, fall in love and then get married?'

'That's the same thing.'

'No, it's not.'

She blinked. 'But if I meet the right guy and he loves me, then that will make me happy. I know it will.'

She sat with her arms crossed in front of her chest, eyes narrowed, jaw jutting out in defiance. It felt almost as though I were looking back at a reflection of my younger self. Only then did I realise that I should know better than to try to teach a lesson that we all must learn for ourselves.

'Okay, then.' I picked up my notepad and clicked my pen. 'Tell me all about this knight in shining armour.'

She went on to describe the same man that every female client had also described: thirty to thirty-five years old, over six feet, intelligent, good sense of humour, solvent, never married, no children. But this time with the added stipulation of 'must like rock music and poetry' and a preference for tattooed torsos.

Once Emily had left, I completed my notes, feeling as though I'd been subjected to a four-year detention assignment: describe Mr Right in your own words, several thousand times. When I'd finished, I flung my pen on the table and sunk my head into my hands.

'Need another drink?' Steve asked, peering down at me.

I looked up. 'Yes, please, something strong. But not too strong, I have to babysit tonight.'

He raised an eyebrow. 'You?'

I followed him back to the bar and pulled myself onto one of the stools. 'Henry, you remember. Ephenant?'

He laughed and then poured some whiskey into a tumbler, followed by five cubes of ice, which I assumed were his childcare dilution allowance. 'So who did the elephant trunk belong to?' he asked, smirking.

'An international entrepreneur looking for pink nipples.'

He laughed. 'The guy with the dodgy highlights?'

I nodded and gulped down the whiskey. It burned my throat.

'So what's his story?'

'Not sure yet.' I put the glass back down on the bar. 'Thea's client, we matched him with a glamour model.'

Steve nodded.

'Didn't go so well though.'

He shrugged his shoulders

I checked my watch. 'She's coming here in a minute.'

'Right.'

'I've got to call him first.'

'Yeah.'

It was clear he wasn't listening to me. 'You all right?'

'Um hum.'

'Sure?'

'Yeah, go and call trouser trunk.'

I stood in reception, watching Brigitte grinning sadistically while punching staples into a Barbie doll, which looked uncannily like Mandi, and I dialled his number. The ringing tone was international.

'Hey, gorgeous,' he answered without even knowing who I was.

'It's Ellie, I'm a colleague of Thea's.'

'And how is the devil's Cupid?'

'She's fine, thanks. I was just calling to ask about Kerri. Is it a good time to talk?'

I heard a girl giggling in the background and something that sounded like the light slap of flesh. 'Yeah sure, I'm in Marbella on my yacht. Chilling. Wanna join us?'

'Er, no,' I replied.

'Shame. So, you got any more hotties you can send my way?'

'I want to talk about your date with Kerri.'

He laughed.

'Well?' I asked.

'Hang on.' I heard a girl's voice in the background saying something that sounded Slavic.

'Is that Russian?'

He laughed. 'So what do you want to know?'

'The date?'

He laughed again and I heard some more flesh-slapping.

'Hello?' I asked.

'Yeah, sorry.'

'So?'

'So, what?'

I took a long and laboured breath. 'How. Did. It. Go?'

'Okay, okay, calm down. And I thought Thea was the angry one.' He paused and it sounded as though he were slurping a drink. 'Okay, yeah, Kerri. Where do I start?'

'What did you think when you saw her?'

He wolf-whistled. 'Hot.'

'And?'

'Nice tits.'

'Apart from that?'

'Not a keeper.'

'Why not?'

'Too many issues.'

'What does that mean?'

'I dunno.' Another slurp.

'Give me an example.'

'Hang on.' I heard another girl's voice in the background. This time it sounded Chinese.

'Is that Mandarin?'

'Yes.'

'I'm not even going to ask what's going on.'

He laughed. 'We're playing chess.'

There was more giggling in the background.

'Sure you are. Anyway, back to Kerri.'

'Where were we?'

'Example.'

'Oh, yeah, okay, here's one. We were at my villa, on the terrace, champagne, sunset…everything you birds love.'

I sighed.

'So I suggested we have a drink in the hot tub.'

'And?'

'She went all psycho on me.'

'Psycho?'

'Yeah, freaking out.'

'About what?'

'I dunno. All I did was point out that the chlorine levels might damage her bikini, and that it was probably best she leave it on the side.'

'Hmm.'

Another slurp. 'Then she started ranting on about how I just saw her as a pair of tits.' He laughed.

'Why are you laughing?'

'Because it's all bollocks.' He paused to laugh again. 'She was happy for me to fly her out here and pay for everything, and she turned up with her massive tits, flashing them every chance she got. Then had a go at me for looking at them.'

There were more giggles in the background. 'Are you sure you actually want a relationship? Because this isn't Rent-a-tit.'

He laughed again. 'I think you mean tits. I can't see anyone would want just one. But there's definitely a business idea there. I'll give Stelios a call, he's a mate of mine. Easytits, I can see it now.'

He slurped again. When I heard another voice in the background, this time in Spanish, I hung up the phone just as my mind attempted to reconcile nationalities with nipple colour.

Outside the club, my heels dug into the softening tarmac. The stuffy inner city air slid into my lungs like treacle from a spoon. Taxis and buses sighed like packhorses ready to drop, while red-faced office workers, sweating into their suits, funnelled between and beside them.

Just when I thought nothing could distract them, one by one, their heads swivelled, and the pavement cleared, like the sea parting for Moses. It was as though the city held its breath while Kerri's tiny frame—and double Fs squeezed into a child-size white linen dress—were carried on four-inch Manolo Blahniks towards me. Women's eyes narrowed to a toxic green, men's jaws unhinged as their spellbound gaze followed her path, heads bobbing in time with her chest as it bounced braless towards the club. As she skipped towards me with a broad grin, my phone vibrated. It was a text from Nick.

I have your spare car keys. Want to meet up to collect?

I opened the door to the club and bundled Kerri in, partly to shield her from further pervy glares but mostly so I could reread the text from Nick.

'You okay?' she asked as I stared at the screen.

I nodded, trying to decide whether Nick was engineering a reason to see me or if he was simply being practical. I ignored the stomach flip and reminded myself that, knowing Nick, it was most likely the latter.

Once I'd settled Kerri at the bar, after introducing her to a now chirpier Steve, I bolted up the stairs. I would have liked to take more time to consider Nick's motives but I had work to do. Out on the street, men were still dithering on the pavement as though they'd just witnessed some sort of supernatural phenomenon, so I switched on the Dictaphone I'd purposely concealed in my bag that morning and approached the first group I came to.

'Hi,' I said breathlessly, in an unfit rather than sexy manner. 'Mind if I ask you about that girl you just saw?' My question seemed to intensify their trance. 'What did you think of her?'

Following a moment of unified bafflement, one of them eventually answered. 'Hot,' he said, staring ahead.

'Hot as hell,' another one added, blowing on his fingertips.

I turned back to the first one. 'Would you date her?'

'Fuck yeah.' His eyes darted around as though he were envisaging the scenario.

'Would you marry her?'

'Most definitely.'

I frowned. 'Why?

'Er, because she's hot.'

'What if she was stupid?'

'Even better.' The finger-blower laughed.

I let out a deep sigh. 'What if she was diagnosed with breast cancer and had to have a double mastectomy?'

For a moment, their grins subsided, but then the finger-blower's laughter rumbled up again.

'Still, she's got a great arse.'

They laughed and globules of saliva scattered like shrapnel across my face.

I wiped it off with my sleeve. 'But then you were diagnosed with testicular cancer and had to have your balls chopped off?'

The laughter stopped.

I stepped towards them, my eyes narrowing. 'The surgery went wrong. There was necrosis. Then gangrene. It spread to your penis. It had to be amputated. What then?'

They stepped back, smiles fading.

'Would her arse matter then, eunuch boys?' I continued, inwardly justifying my approach as hard-hitting journalist rather than mentally unstable matchmaker.

One of the men stared at me, while the others started to back away, mumbling various excuses about returning to work. He stared at me for a little longer and then smiled.

'You're Nick's ex, aren't you?'

Suddenly the other men began to gather around again.

I nodded.

He clapped his hands together. 'I knew it.' He looked back at the others. 'She looks much fitter in person than she does in that photo Nick's always waving around. Doesn't she?'

The others agreed, before going on to explain that they were clients of the finance company Nick worked for. They each looked me up and down as though considering a purchase.

'Still, not worth forfeiting Candice for, eh, lads,' the spokesperson for the group announced.

I raised both eyebrows and my stomach tightened. 'Who is Candice?'

He smirked. 'She's a dancer, at the Windmill Club,' he said.

The others laughed.

'My favourite one, as it goes,' the spokesperson continued.

He must have read my expression because his smile soon dropped.

'Don't stress out though, darlin'. None of the girls, not even Candice could persuade Nick to have a private dance. He's a right mopey git at the moment.'

'Oh, that's reassuring,' I said, rolling my eyes. *Was I supposed to be flattered? What was Nick even doing at a strip club?* He'd always told me he hated those places.

While they went on to mutter amongst themselves about what Candice had persuaded *them* to do, I looked back down at the text Nick had sent. Immediately, I pictured him surrounded by pert-breasted strippers and champagne bottles in ice buckets. When my daydream progressed to Candice peeling off her thong right in front of Nick's face, I swallowed the bile rising up into my mouth and quickly replied to his earlier text:

Post the keys, please.

Suddenly I remembered the Dictaphone was still recording so I made my excuses and quickly moved on. Still trying to clear the image of a grinding Candice from my mind, I noticed two men standing outside a prestigious law firm and wearing pinstriped suits and red braces. I hoped I might glean a more sensible assessment of Kerri's appearance from them.

'Gentlemen,' I said, forcing a smile. 'Would you mind if I asked you few questions about the girl who was just here, the one in the white dress?'

As soon as I mentioned 'white dress', it was as though their brains shut down and the contents of their testicles took over.

'That dress,' the fifty-something man remarked. 'Spectacular.'

The younger man, in his mid-thirties, was staring straight ahead.

I turned to him. 'What did you think of her?'

A smile crept across his face. 'X-rated,' he said, and then they both smirked.

I rolled my eyes. 'So I take it you'd date her, then?'

'She looks expensive,' the older one said, flashing his wedding ring. 'But so long as she was discreet, I'd happily give her a pearl necklace to match her dress.'

His laugh escalated, his eyes squinted to a close and his mouth gaped open, revealing years of disease and decay. I felt an urge to ram the Dictaphone down his throat, pushing it all the way into his stomach so that his acid bile could digest his words.

When I returned to the club, having left their lecherous laughs to merge with the rest of London's toxic emissions, I wondered if I should show Kerri my findings. I wanted her to understand that, when presented with a body as sexy as hers, men lost their ability to focus on anything else. And that introducing herself boobs first was tantamount to burying a Rembrandt in the boot of a Ferrari. But after I'd played the recording, fast-forwarding through the conversation with Nick's clients, her face crumpled and I wondered if my approach might have been a little too radical.

'They really said all that? They're disgusting,' she said, wiping a tear from her cheek.

'You must know the effect you have?' I asked. 'Every man looks at you. And that's with your clothes on. What about all those photos of you online? The one of you in the purple knickers: How did you even get into that position?'

Suddenly Steve popped up from behind the bar.

'I like men to look,' she said.

'Why?' I asked.

She shrugged her shoulders. 'It makes me feel good.'

'Look, love,' Steve chipped in, 'men don't want to think of every Tom, Dick and Harry wanking over their future wife.'

She looked at him and then back at me. 'But that's who I am. I'm a glamour model.'

I shook my head. 'No. That's not who you are, that's what you do.'

While she, and Steve, processed what I had said, I checked my watch, conscious that time was passing and aware that a small child was going to be deposited at my house in half an hour.

I was about to call our meeting to a close, but she looked lost, and I didn't want to leave her in such a state of confusion. 'What are you doing tonight?' I asked her, while I was packing up my things.

Her eyes widened. 'Nothing, why?'

'I have to go home now, but why don't you come with me? We can chat more there.'

'I'd love that,' she said, flinging her bag over her shoulder.

'I hope you like kids,' I said.

She grinned and then skipped after me.

We arrived at my flat to find Harriet and Jeremy's Range Rover pulling into the driveway. Jeremy, still wearing his angst-ridden expression from the morning's meeting, jumped out of the car. Without so much as an appreciative glance at Kerri, he handed me a bag overloaded with items essential for Henry's stay. Harriet, unfastening a wailing Henry from his car seat, began the first round of negotiations to extract him from the car.

'Here's the lovely elephant lady, Henry. You liked her, didn't you?'

'No. Nooooo. I want Daddy. Daddy. Daddy.'

Without introduction, Kerri climbed in the back of the car. After a short interim of face pulling, and an impressive repertoire of farmyard animal noises, she lifted Henry out of the car.

'I don't know what it is, but kids seem to love me,' she said, patting his back while he clung to her like a koala.

Harriet walked towards them, smoothing down her evening dress and then kissed Henry on the head. She looked stunning. Her hair was swept up in a chignon and her make-up was subtle enough to let her features shine through. Kerri stepped back as though she were in the presence of an A-list movie star.

'Remember Plan B!' I shouted to Jeremy as the driver's door swung shut.

I crossed my fingers, hoping he had heard me.

After Kerri had expertly fed and bathed Henry and then sung him to sleep, we sat down on the sofa with a bottle of wine.

'Right, you remember when we met,' I said, pouring her a glass

'Yeah, at the players' party.'

'And you said you wanted more.'

She nodded.

'That was three years ago.'

She nodded again.

'Well, we tried it your way.'

She nodded.

'It didn't work.'

She shook her head.

'So, are you going to trust me now?'

She nodded again and then took a large gulp of wine.

Three hours later, after we'd rifled through the unpacked suitcases that were currently housing my clothes, Kerri stood before me with a make-up free face. Her hair was tied up, and she was wearing a simple gypsy top, skinny jeans, pumps and a pretty bracelet.

'I think I like it,' she said, twirling in front of the full-length mirror in my hallway. She ruffled her blonde fringe and giggled. 'Do you think I would suit Harriet's colour? Her hair is beautiful. I'd give anything to look like Harriet. She's stunning. And so classy. Do I look like her with my hair like this? Can I have her life, please?'

Be careful what you wish for, I imagined Harriet might warn her.

Once I'd piled my clothes back into the suitcases, Kerri looked at me, head tilted.

'Aren't you going to unpack?' she asked.

I sighed. 'Nope, I'm going to live in denial for a few more weeks.'

Her expression softened and she stared at me for a moment. 'He'll come round,' she said. 'And if he doesn't, he's an idiot.'

I shrugged my shoulders, then zipped up the final suitcase, before preparing myself for yet another sleepless night.

Chapter 15

'Mewwwk. Meeeeewk!'

Henry's shouting woke me at five a.m.

I found him bouncing off the sides of his travel cot as though it were a wrestling ring. My assumption that 'mew-wwk' was Henry for 'milk' was proved correct when he snatched the bottle from my hand, threw his dummy to the ground and thrust the teat in his mouth as though he hadn't been fed since birth. I sat down beside his cot and began rummaging in his overnight bag for entertainment ideas. Kerri had left last night, so now Henry was stuck with me, a novice of epic proportions, until Harriet and Jeremy returned. Unimpressed by my suggestions of book reading or puzzle solving, he decided his improvised game of pelting me with random objects was much more enjoyable.

Two hours later, following an onslaught of dummies, toys, bottles, sippy cups, wooden farm animals and ultimately porridge, I sat him down to watch his favourite TV show, starring a family of pigs, who appeared to be cooking sausages on a barbecue.

Keen to maximise my productivity during his downtime, I turned my attention towards the search for a solicitor to defend me against my alleged crimes against follicles. After whizzing through the online directories, I left garbled messages on answering machines and submitted multiple 'anal follicle count' entitled online enquiries.

'I'll be happy to represent you for a nominal fee,' offered David, a solicitor who called me, presumably after receiving one such an enquiry.

When I asked him about his experience with similar cases, he laughed and went on to explain that he was the founder of a firm who had won ninety-five per cent of their instruction and had covered most of the high-profile cases in this field.

'This field? Is it common, then?'

He chuckled. 'The first case in history, I suspect. We'll undoubtedly be breaking new ground. I'm sure the *New Law Journal* will be certain to cover it.'

'You're being sarcastic, aren't you?'

He chuckled again. 'You have nothing to worry about. Her claim is preposterous.'

We were interrupted by a wail from Henry, which had an intensity that led me to think one of his limbs had been ripped from its socket.

'Sounds like you've got your hands full,' David said. 'Leave it with me. I'll take care of everything.'

His voice was soft yet authoritative and I couldn't help thinking that this was the sort of guy that Kerri should be dating. Not some boob-obsessed playboy but a grown-up man, one who would take care of her and treat her the way she deserved to be treated.

Noticing that the pig family had been replaced with an overexcited man dressed as a chicken, I realised the cause of Henry's distress and changed the channel.

'Before you go, can I ask you a quick question?' I said to David.

'Of course.'

'Are you single?'

He cleared his throat. 'Well, er, yes. Yes, I am actually.'

It was two p.m. by the time Jeremy and Harriet came to collect Henry. Not that I was clock watching. By now, Henry and I were having a blast. When I'd realised that all he needed was my undivided attention and access to everything in my flat, then we'd started to get on a lot better.

'Look who's here,' I said as Jeremy and Harriet walked in. Henry threw down the remote control he was dismantling and then launched himself into Harriet's arms. She swung him around and he squealed with delight.

Jeremy stood beside her, looking as though he'd sidestepped the ten-ton truck that had been on track to wipe him out.

'We needed that break,' he said, lifting Henry from Harriet and onto his shoulders. 'We had a long talk and we're going to make some changes.'

'That's great,' I said, gathering Henry's belongings, which appeared to have infiltrated every corner of my flat.

Harriet stepped forward, grinning and swinging her arms by her side. 'We're moving to France,' she said.

Henry's sippy cup fell from my hand to the floor.

'We're going to buy a farmhouse and plant vines,' she explained.

I looked at Jeremy. He was smiling. 'After all, I am a big-eared farm boy.'

He dug Harriet in the ribs.

'The fresh air and countryside will be so good for Henry,' Harriet went on and then paused to stroke Henry's leg, which was dangling over Jeremy's shoulder.

'And Rusty,' Jeremy added. 'He'll love it too.'

Harriet sighed then stared at Jeremy. 'And we'd like to build some bridges with my family out there.'

'Bien sûr, ma chérie,' he said, wrapping his arms around her waist.

I smiled, almost feeling the warmth of their embrace. 'Well Plan B sounds like a winner.' I looked around the room at my unpacked belongings. 'Could do with one myself.'

Jeremy and Harriet glanced at each other. 'Need a hand with those?'

I stepped over a suitcase. 'Not yet,' I said, before leading them out.

Once they'd piled into the Range Rover, which was already brandishing GB stickers, I waved them goodbye. As they pulled out of the driveway, sunlight bounced off the rear windscreen and straight into my eyes. I wondered if this would be the last time I'd see them. Back in my flat, I scooped up the post. There was a small package among the letters. I tore it open and my spare car keys fell to the ground. My heart raced as I felt inside the envelope to see if there was a letter. I found a piece of paper: a compliments slip from Nick's firm. On it, he had written:

Keys as promised. Hope you are well.
Nick

'Hope you are well?' I muttered to myself, wondering how someone who had once retrieved a lost tampon from my most intimate regions, would now choose to communicate in such benign and formal terms. I turned over the paper and read the other side.

P.S. You made quite the impression on my clients...

I shook my head, baffled why Nick was readily associating with a bunch of genetically compromised twits. I threw the note in the bin and went to get changed for work.

There was a chill in my flat when I dressed, so I put on a black polo neck and black wool trousers. I brushed the porridge from my hair and then, once again, I closed the door behind me and marched out of my life and into the lives of others.

When I reached the station, I stood on the platform and looked up into the sky; it was clear. There were no clouds, no birds, nothing but air stretching up and away towards the end of the atmosphere. I wondered if we would ever truly understand what was beyond. Or why we would even want to. Without the comfort of winter's low thick clouds draped around the world like a blanket, I felt vulnerable and exposed. I wrapped my arms tight around my body and boarded the train.

The first scheduled meeting was with Cassandra, and I hoped to arrive with enough time to down a double espresso before she joined me.

'Oh. My. God. It's been too long!' she screamed across the bar as I came down the stairs.

'You're early,' I said, hauling myself onto a stool next to her.

'Red eye.' She twirled a glass of whiskey in her hand. 'Just landed, in from JFK. Winds were favourable. You joining me?' she asked and then took a glug.

'Bit early for that, thanks. Double espresso, please, Steve.'

Steve's head appeared from behind the bar. The dark circles under his eyes made it looked as though he was the one who'd just flown in from New York.

Cassandra looked me up and down. 'You in mourning or something? It's like twenty-five degrees outside.'

I laughed and said I was fine, but neither she, nor the eavesdropping Steve, looked convinced.

'More importantly, how are you?' I said.

'Oh, I'm just fine too,' she said, taking another glug. 'Other than the fact I haven't had a second date in three years.'

I narrowed my eyes. 'That's because you refuse to listen to my advice.'

I had matched her with, on average, one man per week. Allowing for holidays and, following the advice of a Buddhist guru, a year's abstinence, it had amounted to one hundred and seven dates. None of which had progressed to a second.

'But I've been a good sport, haven't I? Most people would've given up by now,' she screeched, before downing the rest of her drink.

'So,' I interrupted, 'if you were an athlete and you had been training for the hurdles for three years, and every day you tripped over the first one and fell flat on your face, would you keep doing it your way? Or would you perhaps try a different technique?'

'Okay. Okay,' she said, waving the question away. 'But

who's to say that I just haven't met the right man yet? They're not all the same, like hurdles, now are they?'

I rummaged in my bag for my notebook. 'Right, here are some of the feedback notes from the men you've dated. Do you want to hear them?'

Steve nodded first, then Cassandra.

'Scary, intimidating, wild, aggressive,' I began, 'too much, full on, overbearing, loud—' I turned the page '—opinionated, boisterous—'

'All right, enough already.' She lifted her hand to stop me. 'Did anyone say "fun, bubbly, outgoing"?'

'Not really,' I replied as Steve refilled her glass. 'Look, it's clear that these men don't know you, but these are the first impressions you're giving, so you have to change your behaviour.'

'Why should I? I want a man to love me for who I am.'

'You don't have to change who you are, just how you behave.'

She took another glug of whiskey.

'Look if a hurdler tweaks his hurdling technique, he's not changing who he is. Is he?'

'What's with the hurdle analogy?'

'Sorry, it's the best I can do today.'

She laughed and then turned to Steve. 'What do you think?'

He put down the whiskey bottle.

'Well,' he began. 'It's pointless pretending to be somebody you're not just to keep your partner happy.'

She slammed her hands on the bar. 'My point exactly.' She then turned to me.

'But,' Steve continued, 'you can't go through life without

changing or evolving, saying fuck you, this is who I am, take me or leave me.'

Cassandra frowned at Steve, seemingly angry he hadn't fully validated her argument.

'What would you know anyway?' she said.

Steve looked down, then back up at me, his skin devoid of pigment and the shadows below his eyes darkening.

Once Cassandra had left, having once again refused to compromise on her ideals, I turned to Steve. His mouth was downturned and his gaze was fixed on the carpet.

'You and Mandi?' I asked.

He shook his head like a doctor to a relative. I could almost hear the faint hum of a flatline.

When I called Mandi, her phone went straight to voicemail for the first time in three years. Before I had a chance to leave a message, Victoria came striding down the stairs, all tan legs and swinging ponytail.

'Hi, darling,' she said, waving her hand in the air from across the bar.

I stood up, eyeing her beige tailored shorts and cream satin shirt. 'You look amazing,' I said and opened my arms wide to hug her, wondering how she was emerging from her break-up like a butterfly from a cocoon, while I was still crying myself to sleep in Nick's old T-shirt.

She removed herself from my embrace and looked me up and down as though she were searching for a way to return the compliment.

'You look,' she said and paused, 'black. Why are you wearing black? We're in the middle of a heatwave.'

I shrugged my shoulders.

She shuddered. 'Anyway, drinks.' She clicked her fingers at Steve. '*Garçon*. Champagne.'

From the expression on his face, it seemed Steve had had enough of Victoria's finger-clicking. He stomped towards us and slammed an unopened bottle of Moët on the table, followed by an opener.

She smiled a tight closed smile. 'You know you can't spit in it if you don't take the cork out?'

He glanced back at her. 'What made you think it was spit?'

She screwed up her face. 'Vile creature,' she said.

I picked up the opener.

'They're all vile,' she continued, snatching the opener from me and throwing it to the ground. 'And stupid. What sort of barman thinks you need an opener for a champagne bottle? Moron.'

She pulled out the cork and let the bubbles gush out.

'He's not himself today,' I said.

'Oh, why? Has Rapunzel finally realised he isn't going to rescue her and decided to climb down all by herself?'

I went to pour her some champagne, before realising Steve hadn't brought any glasses, so instead I just handed her the bottle. After a moment's consideration, she took a large swig.

'So what happened with you and Patrick?' I asked.

She grimaced, as though I had suggested we swap outfits. 'You mean Ratprick.'

'Last I heard from him, he was about to propose?'

'I told him not to bother.'

'Why would you do that?'

'If he wasn't already having an affair, it would have only been a matter of time until he was.'

I frowned. 'What? Where did you get that idea from?'

She shrugged her shoulders and took another swig from

the bottle. 'All those girls fawning over him. And he loves it, swaggering around like a *Men's Health* model.'

'He is a *Men's Health* model.'

She sniffed. 'That's not the point.'

'What is the point?'

'He's a flirt.'

'Doesn't mean he's going to cheat on you though.'

'What would you know?'

I sighed. 'Maybe the fact that he has repeatedly told me you're the most amazing woman he's ever met, that he wants you to be the mother of his children and the fact he spent six months planning a proposal.'

'Oh, I forgot, you're best buddies and know everything about him.'

'He's a client.'

'So I suppose he's been asking for matches again?'

I shook my head. 'He loves you.'

'You wouldn't tell me anyway, would you?'

'Look, do you want me to talk to him?'

She scowled. 'No. Absolutely not. Why would you want to talk to him?'

'Because I want to help you.'

'So are you after him now?'

I laughed. 'Me? I'm not after anyone. I'm going to make chutney and hoard things.'

'What?' She looked at me as though I were losing my mind. I wasn't about to correct her.

She handed me the champagne bottle. 'So, you and Nick?'

I nodded, taking a swig.

She continued, 'He told me all about it.'

'You spoke to him?'

She smoothed down her ponytail. 'Yes, we went out for dinner.'

'Dinner?' The bottle almost slipped from my grasp.

'I thought it might cheer him up.'

My eyes narrowed 'But you're *my* friend. If anyone needs a cheer-up dinner, it should be me.'

'You were busy. Anyway, I bumped into him at the gym.'

'Since when do you go to the gym in Moorgate? You live in Chelsea and you work in Green Park.'

'I fancied a change.'

I slumped back in my seat while my mind filled with images of Victoria, the gym bunny. Her perfect bottom in body-con shorts, her cheerleader ponytail swinging enticingly as she bent over in front of Nick. He may have rejected Candice in her tacky seven-inch platforms, with her Essex spray tan, but Victoria was a different breed entirely. And if Victoria deemed him eligible enough to pursue then what about the rest of the female population? I felt sick. Sick and panicked that it was real. That I had lost him for ever. To a world of beautiful women. Women with perfect bottoms who would love him unconditionally while enthusiastically renewing insurance policies and actively encouraging social dining at steakhouses. They would stroke his brow or another unspecified body part while he exorcised the demons from his previous relationship: 'She threw paella at you, you poor thing. You know I would never do that.'

'So, what did he say? How is he?' I asked, unsure if I wanted to know the answer, to be reminded of his existence beyond me, beyond us.

'He's good,' she said. 'Job is going well.'

My stomach churned, bile rising up into my throat.

She flicked her ponytail. 'He looked great. Been working out it seems.'

I needed some air.

'We speak every day.'

I couldn't breathe. I stood up and leant against the table, feeling as though the walls of the vaults were closing in on me.

'He wanted you to have this.' She handed me an envelope, my name scrawled across the front.

Another envelope? I only received one this morning. I thought we were supposed to be the digital generation.

'It's important,' she said. 'It will explain a lot.'

I didn't want anything explained. Nick had already made it clear that I was too irresponsible for a grown-up relationship. What more needed to be said?

'I have to go,' I said, shoving it in my bag, before bolting up the stairs, flinging open the door and then gasping for air.

'Victoria went for dinner with him?' Cordelia bellowed down the phone as I paced along Embankment trying to disperse the adrenaline.

'It could have been innocent.'

'Yeah, given her track record, totally innocent,' she said. 'And what is Nick playing at?'

My mind flicked through its archives, retrieving all relevant files: the time Victoria bumped into Nick in her underwear when she'd stayed over, the way she squeezed her boobs together when she leant across the table towards him, how she touched his leg when she talked to him. I remembered finding her behaviour entertaining at the time, but perhaps I'd been naive. Maybe I should have been less amused and more vigilant.

'You know the fable about the scorpion and the frog,' Cordelia said.

'Yeah, yeah. She's the scorpion and I'm the frog and I'm going to get stung.'

'She can't help it; it's in her nature.'

'Or maybe Nick is the frog?'

'He's no frog. He knows better than to trust her.'

It might have been the comfort of her voice or the fact I hadn't seen her in months. Or because I was feeling especially alone but, without any warning, my eyes filled with tears.

'When are you coming home?' I asked, rooted to the spot.

She didn't answer. I leant against the building next to me and slowly looked up to the sky. A sign creaked on an iron bar above me and when my gaze came back into focus, it was as though the image slotted into my mind like a key into a lock. My gaze widened, taking in the glass front, the oak door. Then my focus shifted to inside the building, beyond the stainless steel bar, beyond the bamboo screens, to the table. It was the table Nick had led me to three years ago. Our table. The memory seemed to drag me back in time: the taste of the gin and tonics, the saki, his smile, his laughter, the warmth of his hand, the smell of his skin. But, now, as the afternoon sun beat down on my back, another couple sat in our seats. Laughing and joking as though their time would never end.

Eventually, she spoke. 'I'm not,' she said. 'I'm not coming home.'

I slid down the glass and onto the pavement.

After a short time had passed, I pulled myself up, dusted

myself off and found a pile of change on the pavement beside me.

'Aren't you hot in that get-up? It's boiling outside,' Dr Stud asked when I walked into reception.

'Bad judgement call,' I said. 'Didn't really think it through.'

Since our first meeting, he'd make an appearance every year or so to discuss his reasons for terminating the most recent of his relationships. Or, more importantly, to redefine his criteria for the next one. Today, though, I wasn't in the mood to tolerate any of his nonsense.

'Fancy a beer?' I asked as we sat down at a table.

While we sipped Coronas, he described his latest break-up and subsequent enlightenment.

'So, now I'm ready to settle down.'

I sighed. 'You've been saying that for the past three years.'

'What's that supposed to mean?'

'What you say and what you do. They don't match up.'

'But it's different this time. Now I know exactly what I want.'

I took another swig. 'Okay, then, go on.'

'Did you know I was a bit of an artist in my spare time?'

I shook my head.

'Well,' he said and began riffling in a bag he'd brought with him, then handed me a piece of paper. 'There you go.'

I looked at the sketch: a thick fringe, small nose, rosebud mouth and pointy chin.

'Emily,' I said.

'Who's Emily?

'That,' I said, pointing at the sketch, 'is Emily. Have you met her?'

'I don't know what you're on about. This is my perfect woman.'

'You don't happen to have a tattoo, do you?'

'Well, yeah, how did you know?'

That night, slumped on the floor and surrounded by suitcases, I looked at the letter Victoria had given me, at my name scrawled by his hand across the envelope and I wondered what it contained. Was it an apology? An admission of guilt, concluding with a Jeremy-style limerick proposal? Or perhaps a legal letter demanding the return of his lemon squeezer, which had inadvertently found its way into my suitcase? Or maybe it was a declaration of love for Victoria and her perfect bottom. Maybe they were running off to Spain to be with Cordelia, and to live in a giant commune, or government-funded halfway house for people desperate to escape me. But, whatever it said, I knew I wasn't ready for the truth just yet, so I tucked it away at the bottom of a drawer, wishing, as I did every night, that I'd wake up in the morning to find Nick in the shower and to realise that it had all just been a terrible *Dallas*-plot type dream.

Chapter 16

'I THOUGHT ONLY gay weddings had ice cocks.' Kat leant forward, stroking the length of the sculpture.

I knocked her hand away. 'It's supposed to be a racket and two balls.'

Of all the weddings I had attended, the prospect of William and Mitzi declaring their vows on a tennis court was possibly the oddest setting, although I knew it was entirely perfect for them.

Kat swiped two glasses of champagne from a passing waiter dressed as a ball boy, then handed me one, before downing hers.

'Yummy,' she said, her gaze lingering on his buttocks.

We were surrounded by a brilliant white marquee, which was flapping in the summer breeze. Above, the fabric of the ceiling was gathered up to the centre in pleats, looking like a rosette awarded to the triumphant couple. The sides of the marquee were tied to pillars like the curtains of a four-poster bed. A red carpet runway, lined with the purest of white lilies, led up to a small platform under the scoreboard where the words 'William + Mitzi' flashed in yellow lights.

'Oh, this is so exciting. So wonderful. So lovely, lovely, lovely!'

I recognised Mandi's voice from the first 'lovely', as her chatter resounded around the marquee, harmonising with the string quartet. The sweetness of her perfume wafted towards me, merging with the scent of the lilies. I turned around to see her twirling on the spot. Wearing a magenta tunic dress with thick pleats around the hem—her homage to the tennis theme—she looked stunning, radiant even. It seemed almost as if she were the bride. She rushed towards me and flung her arms around my neck.

'Oh, Ellie. I'm just, so, so, so—'

'Excited?' Kat suggested. 'Yes, we can see that. Would you like some champagne?'

Mandi took the glass Kat handed her. 'Happy. That's what I was going to say. I'm just so happy—' she looked down and then sniffed '—for them, at least.'

Clearly sensing the moment was about to degenerate into relationship talk, Kat wandered off, towards the ball boy with the tightest shorts.

I turned to Mandi. 'You okay?'

She blinked rapidly.

'Steve?'

Her bottom lip quivered.

I put my arm around her shoulders. 'Want to talk about it?'

'No,' she said, brushing me off.

'Sure?'

She downed her champagne and handed me the empty glass. 'We're worlds apart. It's for the best.'

Before I had a chance to respond, she had thrust her shoulders back and stormed off towards the red carpet runway. By the time she had reached the end, her march had softened to a skip. I watched as she gazed at the scoreboard, at William and Mitzi's names lit up together, as though they were written in the stars and I wished that I, too, could still believe.

The sight of a tall, pigeon-toed man tripping up and stumbling towards the champagne fountain interrupted my thoughts. At first, just the one glass toppled over, but then an unfortunate domino effect ensued. It seemed that the more he tried to rectify his blunder the more calamitous it became, finally culminating in a pile of broken glass, a collapsed table and a malfunctioning drinks fountain, spurting champagne into the air like a burst water main.

William's brother, I thought. When he tripped over the table for a second time and fell into the ice sculpture, gripping its girth as though it were a life raft, I began to wonder if we could ever really fight our destiny. Were we all direct products of our genetic coding? Our fates sealed from birth?

The music stopped and a ball boy, perched on an improvised umpire's seat, began thrashing a cymbal as though he were trying to summon the gods.

'Ladies and gentlemen, please make your way to your seats. The ceremony is about to commence.'

Following a moment's confusion as to whether we were on the bride's or groom's side, Kat and I, directed by the overzealous ball boy, who had quickly rebranded himself as an usher, moved along a row of white-covered chairs. We sat down directly behind William's father and brother.

The violinists' bows bobbed in unison to a gentle rendition of 'Here Comes the Bride'. William, standing at the front, clasped his hands together and looked back down the aisle. His gaze darted around until he saw her. His eyes widened and his bottom lip began to tremble. Through her veil, Mitzi looked as delicate as the lilies lining her path, the dress sprouting from her waist like petals from a stigma. Beside her, puffed up with pride, her father tightened his grip and fixed his eyes forward.

Distracted by what sounded like a pig foraging for truffles, I turned around to see Mandi, seated in the row behind us. Mascara tracks ran down her cheeks and there was a pile of soggy tissues in her lap. I wondered if she was going to last the day. When I turned back, I saw Mitzi's father let go of her hand and stare at his shoes. There was another whimper but this time it came from Kat. I reached out and squeezed her arm, but she pushed me away, sniffing and blinking until she'd regained her composure.

Aside from the moment when William dropped the ring, and became entangled with his brother during an unfortunate episode trying to retrieve it, the ceremony went without a hitch. At the end, when William's lips locked with Mitzi's, the Nazi usher resumed his duties and began a bellowing narration of the table plan, after which, we were promptly escorted back to the marquee. Straight away, Kat circled the perimeter of our table and inspected the place cards.

'Maureen,' she said, reading from one of the cards and then screwing up her face. 'She sounds like a laugh a minute.' She moved around. 'And Walter, he must be her equally riveting husband.' She picked up the next card. 'And who have we here.' Suddenly her face turned as white as the marquee and then she bolted off with the card in her hand.

I shrugged, assuming she was engineering a reason to speak to the ball boy and went on to examine the wedding favours in front of me. Grappling with the drawstring tennis net, I lost my patience and tore it open, spilling tiny sugared tennis balls across the table and onto the floor.

'Bollocks,' I said, bending down to pick them up.

'I think they're supposed to be tennis balls.'

The hairs on my neck stood up and a cold shiver shot through my spine. 'Robert?'

I turned round and he held out his hand to help me up.

I stared at him blankly while my mind fuzzed and crackled like an old TV set tuning into a channel. He gazed back at me. His eyes still had the intensity of a stormy sky, but the skin around them seemed thinner, more creased. His smile was just as broad, but his lips seemed narrower. It took me a moment to reconcile the memory I had in my mind with the man standing before me. He seemed as alien as he did familiar.

Suddenly, a ball boy approached the table. Kat stood behind him, pushing him forward. 'Sir,' he said, addressing Robert, 'there has been a mix-up with the seating arrangements.'

Robert raised one eyebrow. 'I was told to sit here.' He nodded in the direction of the usher, who was frog-marching guests to their seats as though his role were the fast-track to a dictatorship. 'You want to tell him he made a mistake?'

'It's okay, Kat. I'm fine,' I said, sitting down and pouring wine into my glass until it reached the rim. I'd drained it by the time the ball boy had left and Maureen and Walter had joined us at the table. A plump lady with a ruddy face, she introduced herself as William's aunt and her husband, Walter, a skinny, bulbous-eyed professor-type as William's uncle.

The moment she sat down, she stared at Robert and then at me. 'So, are you two married?' she said, her beady eyes unblinking.

I shook my head and then refilled my glass.

She looked at Kat and then back at Robert. 'So, are you two married, then?'

'No,' said Kat.

She looked at Kat then back at me, then covered her mouth with her hand and whispered something to Uncle Walter.

'We're not lesbians,' I said.

She sat back in her chair and frowned as though she were trying to solve a murder mystery.

'I'm single,' I said, folding my arms.

Her eyes widened as though she found her first clue.

'Divorced?' she asked.

'No, never married,' I replied resolutely.

Her eyes widened further.

'I'm single. And bisexual,' Kat interrupted.

Uncle Walter nearly choked on his wine.

'I'm single too,' Robert chipped in. 'You're surrounded. Best leave, it might be contagious.'

Aunt Maureen sniffed and smoothed down her blouse. 'We don't mind singles. Or bisexuals. Or lesbians. Or gays. Or even Chinese people. William's marrying one and we don't mind at all.'

'She's Japanese,' I said, topping up my glass. 'Mitzi is Japanese.'

'Same thing,' she said, snatching the bottle from me.

'Not really,' said Robert, snatching it back. 'China and

Japan are over three hundred miles apart. Japan is an island. China is not. The population of China is 1.3 billion.
Japan has only a tenth of that. In terms of land size, China
is twenty-five times bigger than Japan. They speak different languages, have entirely different cultures, different
political regimes and—'

'Entirely different views on dating,' I chipped in. 'Ninety-
eight per cent of men and women in China marry, but in
Japan, nearly thirty per cent of women, aged between thirty
and thirty-nine, are unmarried.'

'So Mitzi's a lucky girl to have met William, then?' Maureen concluded, pouring herself a glass of wine.

Robert looked at me with the bemusement of a presi-
dent whose speech had been interrupted by an enthusias-
tic intern.

'Since when did you become a love guru?' Robert asked
me, while Maureen pressed Kat for a more comprehensive
definition of bisexuality.

'Since when did you play tennis?' I asked Robert after
he'd explained how he knew William.

During the five courses that followed, Robert asked me
all about my life after our break-up. Just as I was about to
enquire if he still dedicated two hours a day to webcam porn
or if such recreational pursuits had been compromised by
his recent enrollment in William's tennis club, the dictator
usher, now acting as Master of Ceremonies, rapped a spoon
on a champagne glass.

'Quiet, please,' said the usher. Instantly, the room fell to
a deathly silent. 'Ladies and gentlemen. We hope you've
enjoyed the food *served*—the *game* or pheasant that is.
And you like the *set*-ting for this *match* made in Heaven.'

The guests, seemingly too fearful to groan, smiled politely. Then giggles spilled out from behind a collection of empty wine bottles lined up on a nearby table.

'You. Behind the bottles. Shush,' the usher said and Mandi's head popped up, followed by that of William's brother.

The usher resumed, yet kept his eyes on the offenders.

'Ladies and gentlemen, the groom.'

We all clapped and William stood up tentatively, smoothing his tie.

'My wife and I,' he began, his voice wavering, which made the applause grow louder, 'would like to thank you all for sharing our special day. Each one of you has played your part in helping us along the path to happiness.'

He turned to Mitzi. 'I have never been a confident man.' The guests laughed. 'But from the moment I saw you, sitting on that chaise longue, amongst all those cushions, I wasn't going to let anything stand in my way. I knew we were meant to be together.'

Gradually, William's voice seemed to fade into the background and I found myself imagining Nick in his place and myself in Mitzi's. Wearing a classic Vera Wang gown, I would smile demurely while my new husband relayed paella and toilet brush anecdotes with candour and affection. Tears would well in his eyes as he described to our guests, how, in a moment of self-centred madness followed by an uncharacteristic trip to the Windmill Club, he almost lost me. He would then go on to express heartfelt gratitude to all of those who helped guide him along the path of accountability, steering him away from Victoria's Spandexed bottom and then back into my arms with renewed appreciation and unwavering devotion.

'I used to fear everything,' William continued, the conviction in his voice dragging me out of my daydream. 'Now I fear nothing. Except failing you, Mitzi. And I promise I will never fail you.' He lifted his glass in the air. 'To Mitzi, for opening my eyes and my heart to the world.'

'To Mitzi.' The crowd toasted and she flung her arms around William's neck.

Robert rested his hand on mine.

'I'm sorry I failed you,' he said. Aunt Maureen raised her eyebrows as though she'd been presented with another clue.

Before I could respond, there was a collective gasp from the guests. I turned to see William, who had been thrown off balance by the ardour of Mitzi's embrace, lurch forward and plunge towards a folding table. As it was about to snap shut, swallowing him up, William's brother dived in after him, sending the cake spiralling into the air.

Mandi shot out of her seat, and began darting from side to side until eventually the three tiers of sponge stopped spinning and all at once plummeted towards the dance floor. Mandi pushed past the bridesmaids, and, with one desperate lunge, caught each tier in her arms and then held them aloft as though she had seized the bouquet.

Meanwhile, the usher, having freed William and his brother from a painful-looking encounter with a spring hinge, started behaving like a detective at a crime scene. Once he had sealed off the area with what looked like tennis racket grip, he announced that there was 'nothing to see' and with what looked like some kind of formal hand signalling, directed the guests towards the bar.

Several strawpedos and some vodka shots later, I found myself embracing the celebratory frenzy and began dancing 'The Monster Mash' with Uncle Walter. Following a surprisingly coordinated finale, which had drawn quite a crowd, Aunt Maureen stepped in. She looked panicked by Uncle Walter's open fraternisation with 'the singles' and dragged him away.

'That was quite a performance,' Robert said, after I'd stumbled off in search of the bar. 'I'd forgotten you had moves like that.'

I laughed, steadying myself against the counter.

He leant towards to me, slipping his arm around my waist. 'Can I buy you a drink?'

I pushed him away. 'It's a free bar, you muppet.'

'Well, in that case, order anything you want.'

'I'll have a coffee, I'm feeling a bit squiffy.'

'Squiffy?' He laughed, leaning in closer, hands resting on my hips. 'God, I've missed you.'

Suddenly a blur of pink and blonde flashed in front of us. 'Aren't weddings the most, wonderful, fabulous, amazing things ever!' Mandi threw herself against the bar, seemingly attached to William's brother.

Robert and I stepped back.

'Everyone should get married,' she slurred. 'Let's get married, William's brother. Forgot your name. Sorry.'

He looked startled.

'We should celebrate.' She hoisted herself onto the bar like a seal onto the shore. 'Champagne. I'm getting married,' she said to the barman and then pulled William's brother towards her. 'To William's brother.'

She turned to the barman. 'Want to know something interesting?' She let go of William's brother and he slid to the ground. 'Did you know, on average, a woman has sex with seven men before getting married? Seven.' She held up eight fingers.

The barman nodded thoughtfully as he poured the champagne.

'For men, it's double that.' She looked at her fingers and then realised that she didn't have enough.

I stepped forward to intervene, but before I could do anything she spun around, laughing like a baddy from *Batman* who was about to press a button that would destroy Gotham City.

'Guess how many for Steve?' she said, prodding my upper arm.

I stepped back but she leant in closer.

'Come on, guess!' she shouted, eyes like a rabid dog.

I shrugged my shoulders. 'Thirty?'

She shook her head and then drum-rolled her hands on the bar. 'One hundred and three.'

I raised my eyebrows, wondering how he had smuggled so many women passed Brigitte's watchful glare.

By now, Mandi was clapping. 'Super-stud Steve. Come on everyone, a round of applause for super-stud Steve.'

Again, I reached for her hand, intending to lead her away, but instead she grabbed William's brother's tie and pulled him towards her. 'You can be my number two.' She locked her lips onto his.

Following several failed attempts to wrench them apart, I gave up and sat down at one of the tables. Robert handed me a cup of coffee along with three sambucas, just in case I changed my mind.

'You threw paella at him?' He laughed. 'That takes me back.'

'I never threw paella at you.'

'You tipped a pan of Brussels sprouts over my head.'

'Oh, God, I'd forgotten that.' I held my head in my hands.

'So it's me? It was me all along? I'm a serial food-thrower. A madwoman.'

'I probably deserved it,' he said.

I lifted up my head and looked at the blur that was his face. 'I love him so much,' I said and then slumped back down onto the table. 'But he doesn't want me any more.'

He pushed the hair back off my face. 'I want you,' he said. 'I never stopped wanting you.'

I sat up and looked at him. 'Yeah, along with every other woman you could imagine shagging.'

'So, this Mr Perfect is squeaky clean, then?'

'Well, he doesn't have an account with bushybeavers. com.'

Robert laughed. 'Are you sure? It's a great site.'

I raised my eyebrows.

Robert smirked. 'Come on, Ellie, all men love porn. How else is it a hundred billion dollar industry? Girls enjoy it too. Surely you've had a few cheeky views.'

I rolled my eyes. 'Yes, you've got me. I'm addicted. I barely leave the house.'

Robert smirked. 'No substitute for mine though, I bet.'

Suddenly I felt the urge to laugh, and once I started I couldn't stop.

'Why are you laughing?'

'I'm sorry,' I said, before discarding the coffee and downing one of the sambucas. "I'm really sorry.'

He leant in closer, taking my hands in his. 'For what?'

I looked him in the eye. 'Expecting you to make my life perfect.'

He stared at me for a moment. 'I never stopped loving you, Ellie.'

'Yes. Apart from the day you called off our engagement.'

He squeezed my hands tighter. 'I was having a bit of a wobble. It was the commitment. The house. The wedding plans. It freaked me out. I'm over that now. Come on, Ellie, you know I'd marry you in a heartbeat.'

'Well, I'm over it now too. And I wouldn't.'

I stood up, steadying myself on the table and looking round the room for Kat, as best I could, given my inability to focus. I eventually located her entwined with one of the ball boys.

Suddenly, Robert was beside me. He slipped his arms around my waist. Before I had the chance to process what was happening, he pulled me towards him, his lips almost brushing mine. I looked up at him, feeling his body pressing against me. He muttered something about there being no substitute for the real thing then went to kiss me. All at once, a surge of panic welled inside. It started in my stomach then quickly spread through my limbs. I pulled away.

We stared at each other for what seemed like eternity.

Then I took a deep breath. 'Goodbye, Robert,' I said.

He called after me but I didn't look back.

Chapter 17

THAT NIGHT I couldn't sleep. I'm not sure if it was the strawpedos or the giant plate of pheasant I'd wolfed down prior, but my mind wouldn't rest. At one point though, I must have dozed off because I had a strange dream in which I was attending a wedding with Uncle Walter as my plus one. The bride was Victoria, the groom was mainly Nick but sometimes Robert, and at one point Kat. I managed to wake myself up just as the entire congregation, led by William's brother, began dancing 'The Monster Mash' out of the church.

Fuzzy-headed and perturbed, I dragged myself out of bed and into the bathroom. Following a confusing encounter with the shower control, which resulted in several aggressive blasts of ice-cold water, I abandoned any further attempts to wash myself and slung on a pair of jeans and a jumper. As I looked in the mirror, I recalled the days when I could spring back from a hangover like B. A. Baracus from a punch. Those were the days when I would throw on a T-shirt, add a touch of blusher, then face the world with a fresh and youthful complexion. But now it was as if, almost overnight, my skin had decided it was time to unveil the abuse I'd inflicted on it. And today, etched onto my face, was every unit of alcohol I had ever consumed, as though my body were desperate to tell the world of its suffering at the hands of its crazy alcoholic food-throwing mistress. The frown lines were deep, the laughter lines deeper. That at least, I concluded, meant I should be in credit for happiness. Following a slapdash application of mascara, which only worsened the situation, I grabbed my phone and called Kat.

'Morning,' she answered with a giggle.

'Where are you?'

I heard the ruffle of a duvet. 'With Tom.'

'The ball boy?'

There was a gasp and then a nasty slurping sound in the background.

'If you want a lift home, I'm leaving in five.'

Kat bounded into the car park five minutes later, like a puppy summoned by a squeaky toy.

'So?' I asked as I pulled onto the motorway.

She smiled like a newly converted cult member, the same smile that seemed to accompany every one of her toy boy barman-waiter-pilot encounters.

'How old is he? He looked about twelve.'

'He's twenty-three.'

'Kat, honestly. They're getting younger.'

She huffed and then turned to face me. 'So what? It's not like I'm going to marry him, so what does it matter?'

I sighed. 'As long as you're happy.'

'Well, I'm smiling and you look like someone just

drowned your kitten. So I'd say, out of both of us, I'm the one who's got it right.'

The car began to drift into the wrong lane. I swerved back on course and gripped the steering wheel tighter. 'Studies have proven that people in long-term relationships are happier than those who aren't.'

'Studies rely on people being honest with themselves. I'm going to take happiness where I can get it.'

'Where? Under a teenage barman in tennis whites?'

'On top, actually. And don't knock it until you've tried it.'

I scowled.

'You need to lighten up a bit. Go and get shagged. Robert couldn't get enough of you last night.'

'I don't want to get shagged. Certainly not by Robert.'

'Are you sure about that?'

'Yes. And you know why.'

She sighed. 'We all know you still love Nick. But do you really think he's practising post-break-up celibacy?'

I slammed my foot on the accelerator. 'It doesn't matter—' the car swung across the motorway and into the fast lane like a jet-propelled rocket '—what—' cars swerved out of the way as images of Victoria straddling Nick flooded my mind, with her perfect bottom and her perfect boobs and her stupid shiny ponytail '—he's doing!'

'Jesus! Slow down will you?' Kat yelled, clinging to her seat and mock braking in the passenger footwell.

'No!' I yelled back and then undertook the Porsche in front of me. 'This is making me happy. And you said I should take happiness where I can get it.'

My jaw tensed as I swerved back into the fast lane and began tailgating the Range Rover in front.

'Move over, knobhead!' I raged and punched my horn.

After the driver moved aside, I roared past and poked out my tongue at a child sitting in the back.

'Will you calm down?' Kat said. 'Let's pull over and have a coffee.' She sounded like Harriet trying to placate Henry. 'Look there's a service station. It has a Costa.' She pointed enthusiastically.

'Get out of my way, Fuckwit!' I shouted at the next car along that was impairing my progress.

'Hazelnut mochaccino,' she said, licking her lips, 'with whipped cream on top.'

Suddenly thoughts of a naked orgasmic Victoria were replaced by images of swirly cream floating on thick sweet coffee. A light dusting of chocolate.

'Okay.'

With one tug on the steering wheel, we were on the exit road towards the service station. When we arrived at the car park with a handbrake stop, Kat was clinging to her seat like a cartoon character who'd just driven off a cliff.

'I am never, ever getting in a car with you again. You're a lunatic.'

'Oh, lighten up,' I said and stomped off in search of coffee.

One hazelnut mochaccino and a pep talk from Kat later, I was feeling much saner and ready to continue the journey as a responsible lady driver in her early thirties. However, when I walked towards the driver door, Kat ushered me away as though I were an elderly relative who couldn't be trusted near a stove.

'I think it's best I drive,' she said, after grabbing the wheel. 'Come on.' She patted the passenger seat. 'You can check your emails and do some matchmaking while I'm driving.'

As soon as I clicked on my inbox, I crossed over into the parallel world, where finding happiness for others was no different from finding it for myself. The first email I read was from David, the lawyer who'd offered to help me with my case. He informed me that the other party had backed down and all threats of legal action had been retracted. I sighed. I should have felt vindicated, but I didn't. I felt as though I'd let her down. I knew she wasn't the peri-menopausal loon I'd initially thought her to be. She was just a woman who desperately wanted a family, and probably felt as though the choice had been taken away from her. Short of an overnight transformation of societal perception, coupled with further biological advancements, there wasn't much either she or I could do about it. But I couldn't help feeling irritated with myself for not intervening during the canapé quibble at the masquerade ball all those years ago. Maybe if I'd told her the truth back then—that we were un-able to present her with a Colin Firth clone, along with the canapés, to immediately impregnate her—she'd have faced reality while she still had time to do something about it.

Fortunately, the latter part of the email had cheerier news, and the match between David and Kerri had, it seemed, been a resounding success.

'So, let's get this straight,' Kat said after I'd explained. 'He's some random solicitor who called you up and offered to represent you for free?'

'Barrister. Yes.'

'Why would he do that?'

'Don't know. Because he's nice?'

'No one's that nice. And now you've matched him with a glamour model.'

I nodded. 'Kerri.'

'And you've never met him?'

I shook my head.

'And neither has she?'

'Nope, but they've spoken on the phone for hours.'

Kat shook her head. 'He could be a right minger. Hasn't Kerri asked for a photo?'

'No, she trusts me.'

Kat burst out laughing.

'What's so funny? Wouldn't you trust me?'

'Certainly not to drive.'

'Wouldn't you trust me to match you?'

'I don't see why you would do a better job than I would, and, besides, I don't think you really understand what I'm looking for.'

I laughed. 'I do understand. I just don't agree.'

She took her hand off the wheel and dug me in the ribs. 'So, what if he is a minger? This guy? And they've fallen for each other on the phone and then she doesn't fancy him. Why didn't you suggest they meet first? Before talking?'

'Because she needs a man to get to know her before he sees her. She's gorgeous and that's all men see.'

Kat nodded.

'It's like when you wear your teeny-tiny bikini top to Inferno's nightclub. No man listens to a word you say.'

'No one talks at Inferno's,' she said. 'And no one says nightclub any more.' She paused for a minute, staring ahead at the road and then lifted her finger in the air. 'And he doesn't know she's a glamour model?'

'No.'

She scrunched up her mouth.

'What?'

She opened it to say something, then closed it again.

'Come on.'

'You don't think that will bother him?'

'Of course I do, that's why I didn't tell him.'

She laughed. 'Oh, I get it. If you can override their better judgement and they fall in love before meeting, then magically the rest of their relationship challenges dissolve into insignificance.'

'That's the idea.'

She laughed.

'And what's wrong with that?'

'Nothing, if it works.'

'It might not, but at least it gives them a chance.'

She shrugged her shoulders. 'Yeah, let me know on that one.'

'Ah hah.' I leant forward and poked her in the arm. 'See you do care.'

She smirked.

'And I saw you crying at the wedding.'

'I had something in my eye.'

'Yes, a tear.'

It must have been an hour or so later, following Kat's compensatory snail's pace driving, when I looked up to see we'd reached the M25, the electric fence of London. Only those prepared to suffer attempted entry or exit. From here, I knew it could take anytime between thirty minutes and a lifetime to reach our destination.

As we slowed to a stop, cars crept up behind us. Soon we were just one tiny segment in the queue of traffic, which winded lazily along the motorway like *The Very Hungry Caterpillar* after it had polished off an entire book of snacks. A digital sign informed us there had been an accident on the other side. I realised that our queue must be due to drivers slowing down to look. What was so compelling about the suffering of others? Was it that it validated our own pain and made us feel less alone? Or perhaps it was the relief that it hadn't happened to us: that we had survived, that our lives were not as bad as we had thought, and that, in fact, we were the lucky ones.

Seconds later, my phone rang. It was Dr Stud, calling to tell me about his date with Emily.

'You were right. She looked exactly like the picture I'd drawn,' he said and then paused. I waited. 'And we had a lovely time.'

And waited.

'She's a lovely girl.'

I was still waiting.

'Very pretty.'

Oh, come on, I thought, *get on with it.*

'But…'

Here we go.

'I'm not sure she's my type.'

And lift-off. 'You drew a picture of her. And told me that was your type.'

There was a prolonged pause. 'Maybe my type isn't right. Maybe I need to change my type.'

I laughed. 'I think I liked you more when you didn't have a type.'

He sighed.

'Shall we start again?'

'Maybe we should.'

'Okay, instead of telling me what you want, why don't you tell me what you don't want? What was it about Emily that didn't work for you?'

He inhaled slowly. 'Actually, I've given it a lot of thought.'

'Okay.'

'When you and I first met, you told me to be more polite.'

'Less offensive, yes.'

'Well, I'm fed up being on my best behaviour all the time. It's exhausting.'

I sighed. 'So you're saying that—'

'I want a girl who loves me for who I am.'

'Right.'

'Preferably with a nice arse.'

When the call had ended, I drummed my fingers on the dashboard, trying to think of someone who would tolerate his inappropriate comments, someone who might actually find them amusing, endearing even. As the traffic ahead of us started moving again, thoughts of Cassandra flashed through my mind, her loud New York drawl drowning out any of her competitors.

Immediately, I texted Dr Stud.

Would you date someone in her late thirties?

He texted back:

Too old.

We'll see about that, I thought, as an idea popped into my head.

By the time we arrived back at my flat, the clouds had drawn a curtain over the sun as though putting it to bed for an early night. Kat skipped off with a vague plan to meet the barman from Zuma. I made my way up the stairs and thrust my key into the lock. The door creaked open like the lid of a coffin and I shivered as a gust of cold air blew past the unpacked bags that littered the corridor.

I looked down at the bulging suitcases and then sat down next to one, running the zip along the side. When I flipped it open, the memories came spilling out, like trapped souls from a burial ground.

Two hours later—with puffy eyes and a heavy heart—I hauled the final empty suitcase into the loft. I looked back down at the two piles I'd created. One for items I couldn't live without, which comprised my hairdryer, my passport and little else. And one for the things I knew I could no longer live with: dresses and shoes, piled on top of each other, each riddled with nostalgia and sentiment. Teddy bears professing a love for me equal to their arm span. Valentine's cards with broken promises and photographs flaunting lost moments. The toilet brush and the Christmas tree stand wobbled precariously on the top and looked as though they might tumble to the ground at any moment.

An entire roll of bin bags later, my flat was empty. It had been stripped of its soul, like an old country manor gutted for restoration. Once grand and spectacular, it was now just an empty shell. Lacking a team of jolly builders, a flamboyant interior designer and a signed blank cheque, I knew the daytime TV cure was not an option. So I opened my cleaning cupboard and armed myself with dusting equipment, a vacuum cleaner with impressive-looking attachments and a bag full of clinically proven cleaning products. I swept away every bit of dust, sucked away every speck of dirt, and wiped away every smear, smudge and stain.

When I pulled up the blinds and drew back the curtains, I noticed the clouds had cleared and the crescent of the moon glowed like a smile in the sky. Its radiance spilled through the window and onto my skin. My body felt drained, but for the first time in years, my mind felt quiet, still even.

'Darling? Are you in there?'

Her voice broke the silence like a scream from a fox in the night.

'Victoria?'

'Yes, let me in, silly!'

I sighed and edged open the door. She flung it wide open and strode in, wearing impossibly skinny jeans, nude patent stilettos and a caramel tank top. Her ponytail swung almost smugly, as though it knew its creamy blonde tones coordinated perfectly.

She looked me up and down. 'What on earth have you got on?'

'I've been cleaning,' I said and wiped my hands on the pink polka-dot apron Mum had given me for Christmas.

'Now it just gets worse. Stop talking and get rid of it.' She peered under the apron and scrunched up her nose. 'Of course I'm working from the assumption that what you have on underneath is preferable.'

I brushed her hand away. 'What do you want?'

'I've come to see you. That's what friends do.' Her mouth smiled but her eyes betrayed concern. 'Besides you haven't been returning my calls.'

I folded my arms. 'Why don't you go and see Nick, he's your friend now, isn't he?'

She flicked her ponytail. 'No need to be like that, Ellie. Nick and I have been seeing quite a lot of each other lately, but I don't want you to be all funny about it.' She opened my fridge and then scrunched up her nose again. 'Is that *Californian* chardonnay?'

I sneered at her. 'We can't all afford—'

'Puligny Montrachet?' She opened her bag to reveal three bottles.

By seven-thirty, the first bottle was empty and by eight-thirty, the other two bottles were also empty and lined up beside it. Victoria was now wearing my apron and we were working our way through an ancient curdled bottle of Baileys that I'd taken out to the bins earlier.

'I'm a drunk alcoholic spinster,' she slurred as she refilled her tumbler.

'You can't be a drunk alcoholic can you? Isn't that an oxy-thingy?'

'Moron.'

'I'm not a moron.'

'An oxymoron, I meant. But sometimes you are a moron.' She hauled herself up in front of the mirror in the lounge. 'An alcoholic isn't always drunk.' She pulled at the skin on her face. 'So it's not an oxymoron.' She lifted her jowls. 'I need a facelift. No wonder Patrick didn't want me.'

'Patrick loves you.'

'Patrick loves women.'

'He didn't…doesn't want anyone else. You were just being paranoid. And what are you worried about, you're gorgeous.' I stood behind her in the mirror, hunched my shoulders and stuck out my rabbit teeth. 'Look at me.'

She laughed, then looked back at her own reflection. 'My therapist says I'm a narcissist,' she said.

I slumped back down on the sofa. 'Therapist?'

'Yes.'

'Since when do you have a therapist?'

She spun round from the mirror, lifting her skin up in an improvised facelift.

'Since I was five.'

I sloshed some Baileys into my mouth and the rest down my chin.

'My parents wanted me to be perfect.' She pulled her ponytail up tighter. 'Is that better? Have my jowls gone now?'

I laughed. 'Your parents thought a therapist would make you perfect?'

When we'd drained the rest of the Baileys, we sat slumped on the sofa next to each other, the apron tied around both of us.

'So did you?' I asked, slipping off the cushion towards the floor.

'Did I what?'

Tied to me, she too began to slide towards the ground.

'Have sex?'

'Sex?' She clung to the arm of the sofa.

I hit the floor. 'With Nick?'

Her grip was stronger than I'd anticipated and eventually she hoisted me back up.

'No, silly.' She giggled. 'Nick loves you.'

Chapter 18

STRAINING AND CREAKING with complaint, the train seemed to pull away from the station with the same reluctance with which I had left my bed that morning. I was on my way to meet Thea, to discuss her negative attitude and the numerous complaints it had elicited from clients. The most recent one having been prompted by her instruction to a twenty-something idealist to 'go get a life'.

She was waiting for me outside the club.

'Good morning.' I greeted her with my best cheery smile, relieved to see she had just finished her cigarette.

'Is it?' she replied and stamped it out on the pavement. 'Let's get this over with, then.'

She strode down the stairs, looking like a very beautiful military commander wearing skinny jeans. If I hadn't known otherwise, I would have thought she owned the club, though I suppose in a way she did. As I followed her, I tried to copy the way she walked, but the result was more camp Royal Guard than supermodel strut. As we passed the reception desk, Brigitte bowed her head. When we reached the bar, Steve put his hands behind his back and stood upright as though he were awaiting orders.

As we sat down, her dark eyes narrowed.

'So?' she asked.

'So...' I replied.

It was as though we were in a relationship that we both knew must end, yet neither of us could muster the courage to make the first move.

I met her gaze. 'It's not working, is it?'

She shook her head, and for the first time since I'd known her, she broke eye contact first, then looked down into her lap.

'So, what's changed?'

She looked up. 'People. I can't work with them any more. They're a nightmare.'

I frowned. 'I don't think there's a market for matchmaking any other species.'

She smiled. 'Other animals don't have our issues though, do they? They just find a mate, do a little dance and that's it. Job done.'

'Well yes, we're a bit more sophisticated than that.'

Her eyes narrowed further. 'The only difference between us and other mammals is that we have free will. Well, at least we're supposed to have free will, but we don't.'

I frowned, wondering if she and Matthew had been having clandestine meetings to discuss the fate of the human race.

She looked up to the ceiling. 'We're all clones. We all want the same things. We want to date the same men or the same women. Have the same house, the same car, the same

clothes, the same holidays. Even the same fucking kitchens. We don't know how to think for ourselves any more.'

I shuffled in my seat, inwardly trying to justify the
Poggenpohl catalogue I'd snaffled away in my bedside
drawer.

'Marriage is a dying concept. Year on year, the numbers drop,' she continued. 'Finally, people are catching on
that it doesn't make them happy. But we're angry because
we were lied to. We were told that it would make us happy.
That happiness was something we were entitled to. That
we deserved. It's all bullshit.'

She looked at me. Her face was flushed and her jaw
seemed tensed.

'Thea. Breathe,' I said quietly.

'And now we've created a self-serving, narcissistic and
spoiled society. People expect to get everything, yet they're
not prepared to give anything. No wonder relationships are
doomed to fail.'

'We're not all that naive, Thea. Some find fulfilling relationships.'

'And what exactly is a fulfilling relationship?' She looked
at me, eyebrows raised. 'Relationships are either sadomas-
ochistic dependencies or idealised projections which, at
best, fizzle into the bland, mutually irritating interaction
that people call friendship.'

I sat back in my seat. 'So what if they are? So what if
no one actually achieves the idealised happy-ever-after? If
people find happiness along the way, in whatever form it
takes, then surely that's something?'

Straight away, I realised that was, in essence, what Kat
was trying to tell me the day before.

She laughed. 'People don't find happiness. It's not lying

on the ground somewhere waiting to be snatched up or handed to you by your friendly matchmaker. Happiness comes and goes. And with it comes pain. Equal measures of both. The perfect match.'

I stared at her for a minute, wondering whether she was right. 'But you can't go through life without feeling anything. You may as well give up now.'

Her expression was blank. 'I gave up a long time ago,' she said, 'but this job is like lining up cows for the slaughterhouse.'

I laughed.

'But especially stupid cows, who have a choice, yet we still want to join the queue.'

The first rumblings of laughter echoed down the staircase, like the warning tremor before an earthquake.

'Talking of stupid cows,' Thea said, 'here's a herd now.'

The laughter spilled into the lounge bar, followed by the five Mandi clones charging down the staircase.

I smirked at Thea.

'Actually, I think a more appropriate collective noun would be a murder,' Thea said.

'Or a gaggle?' I suggested.

'More like a giggle,' Steve said as he cleared away the coffee cups.

The new recruits sat around our table, each modelling a different shade of pink like a Mr Marbella nipple colour chart. With their pens poised, and their blonde hair styled in perfect flicks, they looked at me expectantly.

'Where's Mandi?' one of them asked.

I had given up trying to guess who was who. I shrugged my shoulders and turned to Thea, who looked equally baffled.

'She's supposed to be training us today,' another one said.

'On what?' Thea asked.

They all raised their hands as though it were a test. Thea pointed to the nearest one.

'Transactional relationships,' she said.

Thea smiled drolly. 'Might stay for this one.'

When we were seated in the meeting room, the door swung open and Mandi burst in to a collective gasp. Her hair was scraped back in a black scrunchie, and she was wearing black jeans and a black French Connection T-shirt with the words 'fcuk Love' emblazoned across it. Her skin was lacking its usual pink blush and gloss, and under her eyes were coordinating black circles.

She marched to the whiteboard, scrawled the letters 'T' and 'R' in black marker and then turned to face us.

'Transactional Relationships,' she began. 'Or Tits and Rich, as Thea says.'

The new recruits gasped.

Mandi continued. 'Trading something you have for something you want that is valued equally by both parties. What's the oldest transactional relationship in history?'

One of the recruit's hands shot up.

'Prostitution,' she said and then looked up to the heavens as though she had committed blasphemy.

'Yes,' Mandi said, nodding. 'Sex for money. What else can sex be exchanged for?'

The recruits looked puzzled.

'Gucci handbags?' Thea suggested. 'A Cartier watch, Michelin star dining, a new pair of boobs, luxury holidays, a mock Tudor house in Essex.'

Mandi mimed a stop sign. 'They're just other variations of sex for money. What else can sex be exchanged for?'

The collective frown of the recruits deepened.

'Why would one hundred and three girls have sex with a barman? What are they getting out of it?'

In the corner of my eye, I saw what looked like Steve's shadow loitering outside the meeting room. One of the recruit's hands shot up and blocked my view.

'Pleasure,' she said.

Thea sneered.

'Intimacy?' another one suggested.

Mandi rolled her eyes. 'From a one-night stand?'

'She means pseudo-intimacy,' Thea chipped in.

Mandi's eyes were still rolling. 'Anything else?'

'Self-esteem?' one of the recruits suggested.

'Comfort?' another said.

'Fun?' another added and then blushed.

Mandi walked towards the board and began writing: 'fun', 'comfort', 'self-esteem', 'pleasure'. Then she stood back.

'It is widely recognised that one-night stands erode self-esteem,' she said, drawing a black line through the word. 'As for fun, I doubt there's much fun from being banged senseless and then asked to leave.' She drew another line through that one. 'Ditto for comfort.' Another line. 'And as for pleasure, well, a recent survey reported that over ninety per cent of women fail to orgasm during a one-night stand.'

She spun around and waved her marker in the air. 'The real reason women have one-night stands is because they're drunk and think they'll be empowered by acting like men. Or because they secretly hope it will lead to more. But it won't. Sex cannot be exchanged for love.'

The recruits looked on, dumbfounded.

'Nothing except *love* can be exchanged for love. Not beauty, not wealth, not intelligence, not power, not lies, not manipulation. Nothing. For a relationship to last, the only transaction possible is love for love.' Mandi wiped away the list. 'But for that to happen, love must be equally valued by both people.'

Brandishing the marker again, she slowly wrote out the words 'The End' on the whiteboard. Then she gave one more glare to the recruits, threw down her pen and stormed out of the room.

Chapter 19

THE SKY WAS indigo with streaks of magenta and the balmy air sent a shiver down my spine like hot breath on my neck. In front of me, the pool glowed turquoise, its surface rippling like a satin sheet, and beyond office windows glowed like eyes in the night. Tonight, we were hosting a White Party on the roof terrace of Shoreditch House.

Tables cloaked with pristine white tablecloths were nestled in the corners. Beside each were two chairs, and on top, suspended in oversized crystal vases were a pair of flickering candles. A glossy white grand piano stretched out next to the pool with the nonchalance of a lazy cat, while jazz bounced into the air with predictable irregularity, the faint hum of traffic providing a comforting base note.

'If people can't fall in love here, then there's no hope for them.'

I turned around and then stepped back, narrowly missing the edge of the pool.

'Thea?'

She smiled. 'Thought you might need some help tonight.'
I frowned.

'Seeing as Mandi's lost the plot,' she finished.

Wearing a plain white slip, with her hair loosely tied
up, Thea's sharp edges seemed to have softened. Her face
looked rounder, younger even. I smiled at her.

'I haven't changed my mind, though,' she said, pulling
a cigarette out of her bag.

Sighing and gasping, the five recruits swept in and began
twirling around the roof terrace, their near-identical dresses
spinning up and out. I almost expected fluffy white wings
to sprout from their shoulder blades. I turned to Thea, anticipating frenetic eye rolling, but instead, I saw her darting
from table to table, decanting chocolates into heart-shaped
bowls I was about to say something, but my attention was
diverted by Mr Marbella swaggering across the terrace
with enough confidence for all the single men in London.
Teamed with white linen trousers and a short-sleeved shirt,
his fake tan and highlights for once looked almost appropriate for the setting, albeit overshadowed by his Hublot
watch, which snatched the light at every opportunity like
a wannabe at an *X Factor* audition.

'Evening, ladies,' he greeted us all, but focused most
of his attention on the larger breasted of the recruits, who
I think was Minky, although the identical white dresses
weren't helping.

'Can you stop looking at her tits, please?' Mandi seemed
to appear from nowhere. She pushed past me and then
glared at Mr Marbella.

With re-glossed lips and the return of her perky flicks,
she appeared to have shaken off last week's blackness, but,

as she turned to face me, her eyes looked misty as though a cloud had drifted over her corneas.

Mr Marbella turned away from her and towards me.

'We need to talk,' he said, nodding towards some chairs alongside the pool.

Once we'd sat down, I wondered if, finally, he was prepared to have a serious conversation.

'This really isn't working for me,' he said.

I sighed, disappointed there had been no epiphany on his part. 'No problem. I'll arrange a full refund.'

'You're not supposed to agree.' His dark blond eyebrows knitted together. 'You're supposed to fix it.'

'Fix what? You don't seem to require anything to be fixed.'

'I want to meet someone.'

I laughed. 'For what purpose?'

'To get married and have kids. What else?'

'Do you really think you're going to find that in a bikini on a yacht?'

He laughed. 'I don't wear bikinis. Maybe that's where I'm going wrong.'

'You know what I mean.' My mind forged a disturbing image of a string bikini bottom superimposed onto the self-portrait of his genitals. 'The way you act, the way you look, most women, well, the decent ones anyway, wouldn't consider you for a serious relationship.'

He leant forward.

'And why does your future wife have to have perfect tits? They won't stay that way for ever, you know. In a few years, they might be swinging around her ankles like a basset hound's ears. What would you do then?'

'Surgery?'

I sighed and then went to stand up.

'Look, I like big tits. It doesn't mean I'm a bad person.'

'I'm sure that's true.' I paused.

He leant forward further. 'But?'

'You have to look and act like a good husband before you're allowed the chance to be one.'

He sat back. 'But if she's the right girl, she'll love me for who I am.'

Thea approached, obviously in earshot and rolled her eyes. For a moment, I was almost tempted to do the same.

'There's someone who wants to speak to Ellie,' she said, pulling me up from the chair by my arm.

Mr Marbella jumped to his feet, swiped a glass of champagne from a passing waiter, and then sauntered off into the crowd.

'We'll talk later,' I shouted after him, but my words seemed to bounce back like a failed SMS.

I turned back to Thea, but she was gone. In her place was a tall, dark-haired man with green eyes and a soft smile. He was wearing a white fitted shirt tucked into suit trousers.

'David,' he said, holding out his hand for me to shake. 'I popped by to give you a copy of all the paperwork.'

I smiled, thankful for his help, though mildly baffled as to why he chose a singles' party rather than an office for a formal exchange of legal documents. Once he had handed me the papers, he stood staring as though he were expecting me to say something.

'So why haven't you called Kerri?' I asked, assuming this to be the question he was anticipating.

'Sorry,' he said. 'I should've called her.'

'Well, why didn't you?' I noticed my hands were on my hips, so I quickly removed them.

He smirked. 'I—'

'Yes?'

'I feel like I'm in the stand.'

'Where you are legally obliged to answer.'

He laughed.

'So?'

He scratched his nose. 'You didn't tell me she was so attractive.'

'That's good though, isn't it?'

'Well, for most men, I suppose.'

'But not you?'

'No, not me, I'm afraid.'

'Why not?'

His faced creased. 'When we spoke on the phone, we really clicked. I felt as though I could tell her anything—' he paused '—but then in person, she looked nothing like I'd imagined she would.'

'Which was?'

He puffed out his cheeks. 'I don't know, I expected her to be more girl-next-door than *Baywatch* babe, I suppose.'

'*Baywatch?*' I asked, wondering why his benchmark image for a large-breasted woman was nearly twenty years out of date.

I then imagined Kerri arriving for the date, wearing a late-eighties red swimsuit and carrying a float.

He ran his fingers through his hair. 'Every man was gawping at her and then looking at me as though they were trying to figure out how I did it.'

'Are you sure you weren't just being paranoid?'

'No. One man actually followed me to the toilets and asked me how I did it.'

I raised my eyebrows.

'Next to me in the urinal, he looked up and said: "Well, it had to be one of two things, so from the look of it, you must be rich."'

I stifled a laugh. 'What did you say to that?'

'I just walked out. But when I got back to the table, there was another man trying to chat her up. And another one sent champagne over while I was sitting there. It was absurd.'

Just as I was beginning to see his point, an attractive woman started bobbing up and down behind him, seemingly trying to get my attention. It wasn't until I noticed her dove-grey eyes that I realised who she was. I did a double take.

'Joanna?' I asked.

She smiled and then bounced towards me. David stepped sideways. Her hunched apologetic shoulders had lifted and it seemed that finally the body mix-up had been resolved. Now in receipt of her intended slim, toned figure, she was modelling tight white trousers and a white off-the-shoulder mesh top. Her hair, now a rich brown with honey-blonde highlights, hung heavy and shiny around her shoulders. For a few moments, I stood staring at her.

'Come on, I wasn't that bad before was I?' she said, before winking at David.

I forced a smile, feeling oddly disappointed. 'No, of course not.'

She cocked her head. 'But?'

'You said all that gloss wasn't you?'

She laughed, revealing an intricately engineered Hollywood smile. 'I'm still the same person underneath.'

I noticed David visibly processing her words, a puzzled expression creeping across his face. I turned to him.

'Out of interest, what did Kerri wear on your date?'

His puzzlement faded in an instant. 'Red dress. Short and tight. Very tight.' He seemed to drift into another state of consciousness as he recalled the image.

Short and tight, I thought as I watched him walk back into the crowd, swiftly followed by Joanna. *That's not exactly what Kerri and I had agreed.*

Feeling the effects of the champagne I had guzzled in honour of Joanna's transformation, I stepped back to a quiet corner of the roof terrace and watched as couples began the familiar fumbled first stages of contact.

Was Thea right? I wondered. Were they all just lining up for the slaughterhouse like cattle? Couldn't they see they were destined for as much pain and anguish as they were love and happiness?

'You're looking a bit thoughtful,' Mandi said, after she'd tottered over to join me. 'Are you having one of your philosophical moments again?'

I smiled. 'It was just something Thea said about happiness and pain being dished out in equal measures.'

Her smile faded. 'As much as I hate to say it, I think she might be right.'

'So you've really lost faith?'

She shook her head. 'I'll never lose faith in love,' she said, looking down and slipping her foot in and out of its sparkly shoe. 'It's just hard to accept that it's not as perfect as I thought it would be.'

I exhaled a laugh. 'Disappointing, isn't it?'

Tears began to slide down her cheeks, glistening like Swarovski crystals.

'Devastating, more like.'

I leant in and wiped them from her face. 'Shall we play guess who?'

Predicting who would leave the party with who was Mandi's favourite game and she followed my forecast like a trader follows the FTSE.

She smiled.

'Right,' I said, scanning the terrace. 'Those girls there—' I pointed to a group of svelte, bronzed blondes in their mid-twenties all wearing micro-minis '—with the legs.'

'Yes.' She nodded.

'They'll end up with the traders lined up at the bar.'

'How do you know they're traders?'

'I just do. Then see the two entrepreneurs over there?' I pointed at two men standing by the door to the kitchens. 'They'll end up with the two girls over there. They work in TV production.'

Mandi frowned. 'How do you know that?'

'I just do.'

'But how?'

'And that guy over there.' I pointed at a tall Greek-godlike figure in white linen, his shirt unbuttoned to reveal a sculpted and waxed chest.

She nodded. 'Yeah, the fantasy man, every woman wants to walk hand in hand with across a white sandy beach.'

I giggled.

'Where he would pull her to his rippling torso, kissing her roughly while the waves crash violently against the shore,' Mandi continued, almost reverting to her previous starry-eyed self.

I laughed. 'His large manly hands tearing at her bodice, freeing her heaving bosom, while his member throbs against the soft flesh of her inner thigh.'

She giggled. 'His tongue probing purposefully, savouring her scent, the curves of her flesh, the taste of her juices.'

'Then he fills her, thrusting with the vigour of a thoroughbred stallion—'

'Until their bodies stiffen, giving way to a tidal wave of a simultaneous orgasm—'

'Then they collapse into each other, exhausted and spent, limbs and souls entwined.'

We laughed.

'Okay,' she said. 'Whose heaving bosom does his throbbing member end up with tonight?'

'No one's,' I said. 'He's a perfectionist and he'll be followed around all night by women he's not interested in. The girl he likes—and there is only one—her.' I pointed to a long-limbed, fresh-faced model type. 'She will be locked in by an alpha male who won't let Mr Mills and Boon anywhere near her.'

Sure enough, as I spoke, the girl was being virtually pinned against the wall by one of the traders.

Mandi smirked. 'And what about her?' she asked, pointing at a pretty brunette.

I looked on, trying to identify the woman. 'Oh, yes, Joanna.' I almost failed to recognise her again. 'She'll probably be following Mr Mills and Boon around all night, when she should be talking to a more...' I leant forward, squinting. 'Who is that?'

'That's Greg, he's a chiropractor. Such a lovely guy. They seem to be getting on, don't they?'

We watched as Joanna flicked her hair and stuck out her chest.

'I tried to match them years ago. But she was having none of it.'

Mandi giggled. 'Good to know you don't always get it right.'

'What, the matching or the—'

'All of it,' she said and then walked away, glittering and shimmering as only Mandi could. But something else caught my eye. Something was shimmering a lot more than the rest of her. I peered closer. It was her left hand. A ring.

'Mandi,' I called after her, but my voice was lost in the buzz of the party. I stepped forward to follow her, but inadvertently collided with a girl who was walking at speed.

'Look where you are going, will you?' a voice said with familiar disdain as its owner swept past towards the toilet door.

'Victoria?' I asked after I'd recognised her perfect contours in a backless white jumpsuit.

She spun around. 'Oh, gosh, sorry, Ellie. I didn't realise it was you.'

She looked me up and down, clearly unimpressed with my fifth-hand Karen Millen eBay purchase. 'Is the zip-up look coming back already?'

I forced a laugh. 'It's white and it's a dress. Anyway, why are you in such a rush?'

'Some imbecile thought chocolate hearts would be a good idea at a White Party,' she said, turning around and pointing at her bottom. 'I only sat down for a second. And now it looks like I'm incontinent.'

I tried not to smile.

'And it's not just me. One of your Barbie brigade has sat on one too.'

I frowned, wondering if this was Thea's parting shot: a strategically placed chocolate heart on the seats of those who had offended her. As the host and therefore enabler of crime, I knew it was up to me to check the posterior of all those who could be on Thea's hit list, so I left Victoria to

sponge her bottom in the Ladies' and began to move stealth-
ily around the party.

After receiving several protests, a few propositions and
some alarmed looks, and aside from what appeared to be
one genuine incontinence problem, I found most bottoms
to be clear. However, I had yet to assess Mandi or her un-
derlings. Once I had located Mandi, in full matchmaking
mode between Mr Marbella and one of the micro-minis, I
crept around behind her. Just as I was about to zoom in on
her sacrum, my mission was thwarted by a tug on my arm.

'What are you doing?'

The hairs on the back of my neck pricked up. I turned
around to face a man decked out in a white tuxedo and grinning widely. It was Robert.

'You again?' I said.

His grin widened further.

'You're always creeping up on me.'

He raised an eyebrow. 'Always? I'm *always* creeping up
on you?'

'Well, the past two times, yes. And since there have only
been two times in the past five years, then I think that con-
stitutes always.'

He smirked. 'Okay, I'll approach from the front next
time.'

'That is the socially accepted method,' I replied. 'If I
were a feral animal you would have received a nasty bite.'

'Or a pan of Brussels sprouts,' he said with a wink.
'Though, it appears that, you too prefer the approach-from-
behind method. I've been watching you look at people's
bottoms for the past half-hour. What's that all about? Is it
a new matching strategy?'

'Long story,' I said with a flick of my wrist. 'Anyway, what are you doing here?'

He stepped towards me, taking my hands in his. 'I'm single and I want to meet a beautiful girl—' he looked me up and down, frowned a little and then gazed into my eyes '—who's wearing a white dress.'

I brushed him off. 'Well, off you go, then. There are hundreds here.'

He leant back towards me, zooming in on my chest. 'Did I mention my preference for a retro zipped cleavage feature?'

'Go,' I said, waving him away. 'But watch out for the chocolate hearts.'

He glanced back over his shoulder, still grinning. 'Is that supposed to mean something?'

I waved him away again. 'It's not a riddle. They look like poo if you sit on them.'

A determined recruit, who I think was Minky, must have noticed Robert was alone, so she grabbed his hand and swept him away. Seconds later, he turned back to point at her bottom, which was exhibiting a substantial chocolate smudge. I quickly relocated Mandi, keen to resume the investigation.

'Right, let me check your bottom. Then we'll talk about your ring,' I said as I turned her around.

'What?' she asked, startled. 'My bottom ring?'

'Ah ha, just as I thought,' I said in the manner of a TV detective. 'You have been targeted.'

'Are you okay?' Mandi asked, her face expressing genuine concern.

'You have chocolate on your bottom,' I declared as if it should make perfect sense to her.

'I know. I sat in some earlier. A real nuisance.' She didn't seem bothered at all. 'But what about my ring? Surely you don't need to look at that?' She backed away from me.

'On your finger, dopey. The ring on your finger.' I grabbed her hand. 'Ah ha, there we go.' Still in detective mode, I examined the pretty, princess-cut diamond sparkling on her finger. 'Since when were you engaged? Why didn't you tell me?'

Mandi went mute. Her silence seemed to be amplified by the sudden hush from the terrace. The lounge music had been replaced by the faint tinkering of piano keys and I looked around to see Robert brandishing a microphone and standing next to the piano. The guests stared at him, expressions ranging from bafflement to wonder. The pianist continued with the unwavering integrity of a seasoned professional. I imagined him, on the *Titanic*, committed to finishing his piece before quietly dismounting in search of a lifeboat. My daydream was broken by the sudden realisation that the pleasant melody—that everyone was now bobbing their heads to—was in fact the intro to Chris de Burgh's 'Lady in Red'.

Robert shimmied around the makeshift stage, looking like the hired entertainment, before belting out the first verse as though he were Pavarotti at the O2 arena.

The traders exploited the opportunity and moved in to close the deal with the micro-minis. Following their lead, the entrepreneurs held out a hand to the TV production girls. Soon everyone was slow dancing. Joanna pushed past Greg the chiropractor to collar an unclaimed twenty-something with over-gelled hair. Mr Mills and Boon struck a pose next to Thea while she rolled her eyes repeatedly with the precision of a Swiss watch mechanism.

Roaring out the chorus, Robert moved across the floor like a pro and I blinked twice. The evening had somehow transformed from sophisticated roof terrace soirée to bizarre cruise-ship karaoke.

Tracking across the crowd, his eyes searched out mine while he crooned something about a lady in white, who should be dancing with him, cheek to cheek. The blush began at my neck and spread to my face quicker than ink through water. At the point when I was radiating more heat than Mr Mills and Boon's torso, Victoria emerged on the makeshift stage, seemingly having bullied one of the Mandi clones into swapping outfits. She moved towards Robert and slipped her arm around his waist, the skimpy dress skimming her braless breasts. As he continued to warble that he hardly knew this beauty by his side, Victoria pressed her cheek against his, but his eyes were still locked on me.

Mandi scrunched up her face and turned to me.

'Isn't that your ex-fiancé?'

I nodded.

She laughed. 'Bloody hell, for a matchmaker, you really know how to pick them.'

'Well, at least I don't have chocolate on my arse.'

She giggled. 'And at least you haven't agreed to marry a Cockney barman.' She looked down and began fiddling with the diamond. 'The clarity is terrible.'

'You love him though, don't you?'

She twirled the ring round on her finger. 'Is love enough though, Ellie?'

'It's something,' I said, just as Robert fell to his knees and delivered the final line in a stage whisper.

'I love you.'

I shuddered as though a stream of Arctic air had funnelled towards me. For a brief moment I imagined Nick standing in Robert's place, though the white tuxedo was doing neither of them any favours. I shook my head to clear the image then turned back to Mandi.

'Love is something, Mandi. Hang on to it with everything you've got.'

Then the crowd erupted into applause, the duo lapping it up as though they were the prom king and queen.

Chapter 20

VICTORIA SLIPPED FROM Robert's grasp and into the pool. Her arms were flailing and her head went under. She was drowning. I jumped in and swam towards her. She grabbed me, but, as she pulled herself up, she pushed me down. My head was submerged. I held my breath and tried to wriggle away, but she was too strong. Eventually, my muscles relaxed and my airways dilated, letting the water fill my lungs, gurgling as it did. My nerves twitched. Gurgle, gurgle, gurgle.

I woke with a start, my heart racing as I gasped for air. I quickly realised that I was, in fact, alive and in my bedroom, rather than the subject of a sensational 'Pool Party Tragedy' newspaper headline.

Gurgle. Gurgle. Gurgle.

When my breathing and heart rate had normalised, I noticed that the sinister rumblings were coming from my en suite. I peered around the doorway to discover that, while my subconscious had been fighting a premature and unjust death, my lavatory had been decorating the bathroom tiles with a sludgy sewage residue.

I grabbed my phone, typed a quick search for plumbers into Google and scanned the list. When I'd discounted Putrid Plumbers for the unsettling claim that no hole was too deep, too dark or too dirty, I settled on Pete's Plumbing. It promised old-fashioned plumbing at old-fashioned prices. I hoped old-fashioned meant pre-war rather than pre-Eastern European immigration. Pete answered within one ring and said he'd be there within the hour. 'Prompt Pete promises punctuality', as the small print of his ad said.

After I'd pulled on some old jeans and a T-shirt that I wasn't opposed to getting sewage on, I washed my face in the kitchen sink. Then I collapsed into the sofa and thought back to the surreal events of the night before. What was Robert doing there? And Victoria, what was she up to? And the chocolate hearts, I would have to get to the bottom of that. I rested my head on the arm of the sofa and gazed out of the window, frustrated to find that the grey morning fog was thickening rather than clearing. On a quest for clarity, I reached for my phone and began scanning the post-party texts and emails.

There was a text from Robert at 01.23, who, or so it seemed, was now communicating exclusively via Chris de Burgh lyrics. After I had scrolled down through his poignant extracts, I began to feel nauseous. All my flat needed now was a pile of vomit to complete its Tracey Emin–style display of bodily fluids. The next instalment came at 02.14 via which he informed me that he had never seen the dress I had been wearing. Then, there was something about my highlights and me shining so bright, and he concluded with the rather extravagant declaration that he had been blind.

Had there been a full moon perhaps? I deleted it and moved on to the next, hoping the complete works of Chris de Burgh hadn't been transcribed to text.

It took me some time to finish reading the deluge of emails from the overexcited recruits, who had whipped themselves up into a who-hooked-up-with-who frenzy. I then moved on to deal with complaints about clothing damage caused by the irresponsible placements of chocolate hearts. Finally, I noticed two suspiciously similar texts from Kat and Cordelia. They had both booked an impromptu flight back to London in order to 'pop by and see how I was'. Concerned that perhaps they knew something I didn't, I quickly checked my body for any tumours, growths or other signs of impeding death. Confident there was no immediate cause for concern, I moved onto a text from Victoria, which comprised a list of strange questions about Robert, then a bizarre text from Joanna referencing our 'male screening process', and then finally, and the only one to make any sense, was a text from Prompt Pete informing me that he was on his way.

'So do you or don't you screen your men?' Joanna asked after I had called her.

'What for STDs?'

'No, for singleness.'

'Singleness?'

She huffed. 'You know what I mean.'

'If you're asking if we check our clients are single, then yes of course we do as far as we can.'

'But your men don't want relationships.'

'My men?'

'Men don't want relationships.'

'All men?'

'Yes. All men.'

'All the men you meet, you mean?'

She huffed again.

'Okay, so what happened?'

'When?'

'Last night.'

She sighed. 'I met a guy.'

'And?'

'We seemed to get on really well.'

'And?'

'He walked me to the station.'

'And then?'

'And then nothing, he didn't ask for my number or anything. So, he's obviously not looking for a girlfriend, is he?'

I sighed. 'That really isn't much information to go on.'

'I bet he's not even single.' She huffed. 'You say all your clients are single. I bet he's not.'

After harnessing the collective detective skills of the Mandi clones, I tracked down the man in question. His name was Alex, he was ten years Joanna's junior and a broker. He was a friend of one of the traders. I gave him a ring.

'Joanna, who's Joanna?' He sounded hungover and baffled.

'The girl you walked to the station.'

He sniffed. 'Oh, yeah, her.'

I heard a knock at the door, which I suspected to be the plumber arriving promptly, as promised. I opened it and ushered a round jolly-looking Pete towards the bathroom.

'Hang on a minute, it's coming back to me.' Alex paused and then laughed. 'Yeah, yeah. So how much do you wanna know?'

'All the gory details, please.'

'All right,' he said.

He went on to explain that he'd been chatting up a girl he liked for most of the night, but she'd wandered off chasing 'some white-linen-clad knob end'. Then, at the end of the night, 'when the twat in the tuxedo started singing', Joanna had caught his eye, smiled at him and held her hand out to invite him to dance.

'She seemed well up for it, so I wasn't going to say no.'

'Okay,' I answered, while I attempted to sign *blocked toilet* to Pete.

'But, then she started grilling me.'

'Grilling you?' I asked, wondering if it was a new kind of dance move.

'Yeah, all these questions about my job, relationships, ex-girlfriends, properties, investments, pension.'

I cringed. 'So, what did you say to that?'

He laughed. 'I told her what she wanted to hear.'

'Which was what?'

'That I'm solvent, single and looking for love.'

I sighed.

'Oh, come on, I'm not going to tell my life story to some girl I've just met.'

'I see. So what happened next?'

'We snogged and, when the party was over, I offered to walk her to the station.'

'Why?'

'Because she was up for it. And she wasn't bad-looking either. Not my usual type. I normally go for really hot girls.'

'I'm sure you do.'

'But you know what they say: if you've got an itch that needs scratching.'

'You should go to the clinic?'

'What?'

'Nothing, sorry. Carry on.'

Pete started waving a plunger around and pointing down the toilet. I nodded.

'And on the way home, she was all over me.' He paused. 'Kept grabbing my cock.' He paused again and then laughed. 'She wouldn't leave it alone.'

'Really?'

'Yeah, she was seriously cock-hungry, couldn't get enough. What more was I to do than offer my services?' His laughter peaked with a series of short breaths, and then ended with a sniff.

'Okay, and then?' I wanted him to stop saying 'cock' and get to the point.

'So when we were at the station, she dragged me into an alley, pushed me up against the wall and... Are you sure you wanna hear all this?'

'Yes, go on.'

'Then she started sucking my cock.'

And another one. 'What, just out of nowhere?'

'I sort of saw it coming.'

I forced a laugh.

'And then just as I was about to—'

'See it coming?'

'Yeah, she turned around, bent over and then shoved it up her—' he cleared his throat '—up her, you know, her...'

'Her what?' I took care to avoid the loudspeaker button. Prompt Pete looked perplexed enough as it was.

'Her behind.'

I laughed. Now was the time he'd decided to become prudish.

Prompt Pete raised his eyebrows before plunging his instrument down the toilet.

Alex continued. 'She was well into it, loved it, kept screaming for more, she—'

'Okay, enough, I get it.'

'You asked.'

'And then what? She just went home?'

'Yeah, then she went home. I went home. Everyone happy.'

'I don't suppose you'd want to see her again?'

He let out a long guttural laugh. 'Er. No.'

After I'd gladly hung up the phone—it was far too early in the morning for bottom sex—I sat down on the edge of the bath. I watched Pete continue to plunge his tool down the toilet, an act that did nothing to remedy the images flooding my mind. Was it me or had the world gone mad? How could Joanna think this would or even could lead to a relationship? Clearly it was my job to explain this to her, though usually I would delegate such a task to Thea. I wondered if I had it in me to tell her how it was.

Pete continued plunging until he cleared the blockage, and then sat back, letting his tool flop to the floor.

'Any chance of a cup of tea, love?' he asked. 'I'm parched.'

While Pete drank the tea, and tucked into my chocolate Hobnobs without washing his hands, I filled him in on the story. After all, he'd already heard most of it anyway.

When he'd finished chewing, he wiped his mouth and sat up. 'Marjorie and I tried, you know, the back canal, one time.'

I winced.

'On our anniversary, after a few bottles of Mateus Rosé.'

I nodded.

'Can't say it did much for me. Marjorie wasn't keen either.' He stuffed another biscuit into his mouth 'Afterwards, she kept asking me if I was gay.'

I snatched the now empty packet of biscuits from Pete and then dialled Joanna's number, rationalising that the conversation with her, no matter how awkward, would be infinitely more tolerable than this one.

'You offered him sex on a plate so he took you up on that offer. There was nothing more to it for him,' I explained, while Pete poked around in the cistern.

'What do you mean? So, he just wanted sex and not a relationship?'

'Yes, with you, at that time, he wanted sex, but definitely not a relationship,' I explained

'So, I was right. He isn't looking for a relationship.'

'That's not what I said.'

She sighed.

'Look, under all their silly bravado, men are secretly hoping to meet the girl of their dreams. Someone they think is gorgeous and sexy and with a personality they could fall in love with. However, if that doesn't happen, then the second best outcome is sex, generally with the hottest, most willing girl.'

Pete produced another tool from his bag.

'Oh, right, so he would just have sex with anyone, then?'

'Some men would, but not all. It depends how discerning they are. The key is to learn to give off the right messages to attract the more discerning ones. Talking of which, weren't you talking to Greg last night too? What happened there?'

'He didn't seem too keen.'

I laughed. 'He's probably a bit put off by the fact that every time he's tried to chat to you, you've blown him off.'

Pete looked up, a little alarmed.

'I mean, you've rejected him,' I said. 'And then to see you leaving with another guy...'

She sighed again. 'I'm not very good at this, am I?'

I laughed. 'Find me someone who is.'

When I'd hung up the phone, a pungent aroma wafted through the air. I put my hand over my mouth, but not after I'd already imagined tiny airborne sewage particles clinging to my skin, wafting up my nose, sliding down my throat, then crossing my lungs and percolating into my bloodstream.

'Sounds like your job deals with more crap than mine,' Pete said with a chuckle, as he donned some industrial gloves.

I smiled.

'It's a different world now,' he said. 'Women weren't like that in my day.'

'Yes, it's a funny world,' I said, adopting what I hoped was a brisk and conclusive tone.

I'd already spent over two hundred pounds of old-fashioned pricing, pouring him tea and feeding him biscuits, I didn't want to further increase the bill with an extended debate on relationship philosophy in a post-feminist era.

'Women these days. You want it all,' he continued, standing up and then wiping his apparatus on my cream towel. 'You want all the rights without the responsibilities.' He flushed the toilet. 'Like you, for example, you live on your own, but you still need a man to fix things around the house.'

My mouth opened, and then closed again, as I thought better of reminding him that I was paying him with money I had earned, not asking for help in exchange for bottom sex.

'In my day, it was easier. Roles were clear. Men and women knew their place.'

I laughed. 'They didn't have a choice.'

'Women need men.'

'And men need women.'

'Women aren't what they used to be. They used to cook, clean, keep a lovely home. Have modesty. Respect for themselves.'

'Cooking and cleaning is having respect for themselves?'

'Marjorie would turn in her grave if she could see the young women today—' he shook his head '—drinking like sailors, letting men take them up the alley on the first night. I don't know.'

After he'd relieved me of three hundred pounds and reiterated the point that I needed a good man in my life, Pete set off to rescue another misguided maiden from a leak she had no man to fix.

As he walked away, leaving the faint outline of sewage footprints on my carpet, a strange thought popped into my head. Well, it was more of an image than a thought: I saw Emily's mother enjoying a pot of tea and some chocolate Hobnobs, then perhaps a glass of Mateus Rosé? After my daydream had progressed to Prompt Pete plunging his tool into Emily's mum's cistern, I wondered if I should pass on the number of a good old-fashioned plumber.

After I'd scrubbed away the fallout from the toilet, I decided a soak in the bath might prepare me for a night of unsolicited concern from Cordelia and Kat. Further texts had informed me that the location of their intervention was to be the local *tapas* restaurant. This seemed somewhat of an anticlimax after their flamboyant channel-crossing gesture of friendship. From the apparent urgency of their return, I was almost expecting a televised intervention comprising a multidisciplinary team of experts, a shocking diagnosis and culminating in an enforced admission to a specialised clinic.

As I sank into the bubbles, watching them pile on top of each other and stretch out into rainbow arcs, I remembered my chemistry professor describing the millions of tiny surfactant compounds that held bubbles in place. He'd explained that one part loved the water, the other part hated it, yet both polar-opposite reactions were required to hold the structure in place. If the formation of a simple bubble had such complexity, then how could we even begin to grasp the dynamics of an interaction between two continuously evolving human beings in an uncontrolled environment. With an exasperated sigh, I popped the biggest bubble, pulled the plug and then climbed out of the bath.

When the residual foam had slid off my body, forming a small frothy puddle at my feet like the remnants of a snowman, I studied my reflection in the mirror, wondering if I might recognise the girl I had been five years ago. My body looked no different, albeit lacking the soft glow of youth. My hair was the same, though a slightly darker shade of blonde. But my mind—and the thoughts it contained—were like those of a different person. I looked down at the floor tiles, scrubbed to a gleaming white, knowing that it would be impossible to tell the state they had been in only a few hours earlier. I wished it were that easy with people. To wipe us clean and to start again, without holding on to the crap that life throws at us. When I wrapped a towel around me, watching the last of the bathwater spiral down the plughole, I decided that finally it was time to leave my past behind.

When I walked into the bedroom, a ray of sunlight seemed to bypass the clouds and shoot through the window and into my eyes. I closed them, but the yellow streak continued to pulse around my head, intensifying as it did. When I slowly opened my eyes, there was only one thought that remained: Nick. Recognising the familiar stabs of longing, I tried to conjure an antidote, an alternate plan for the future. But it was difficult to believe in anything else. I didn't really want to move to the country and hoard things. I didn't even like chutney. I wanted Nick, and everything that he was. I wanted us to have paella arguments or even failed attempts at bottom sex on our silver wedding anniversary. I didn't want to mould him into my perfect man. I just wanted us to be together again. There was no point in me moping around, hoping that at any moment he might abseil down from my roof and then burst through my window wearing a black onesie and brandishing chocolates.

I stared at my bedside table for a moment, at the bottom drawer where I'd hidden the letter weeks ago. Before I could stop myself, I pulled open the drawer and yanked out the letter. Just as my fingernail tore through the envelope, I was interrupted by Kat and Cordelia hammering on my front door.

'We're here!' they bellowed.

I opened the door and they barged in, dropping their suitcases to the floor and then flinging their arms around me.

I stiffened. 'I was about to open the letter,' I said.

I felt their grip loosen, then Cordelia stepped back, snatching the letter from my hand.

'Let's have a drink first,' she said in a bizarrely theatrical sing-song voice.

Kat, uncharacteristically silent, made a beeline for the bottle opener. 'Been on Facebook today?' she asked, then twisted the opener into the cork.

I frowned. 'No, you know I hate all that networking "talk about me, more about me" crap. I mean, who cares if some girl you haven't seen since junior school is "so excited it's the weekend".'

Kat wrenched out the cork and Cordelia looked at me with a quizzical frown.

My throat felt dry, my heart started racing. 'Why, what does it say?'

Kat looked to the floor, and Cordelia's expression changed from one of concern to one of panic, as she snatched the bottle from Kat and began pouring.

My hands started trembling and the arctic chill returned.

'He's met someone, hasn't he?' I asked, struggling to form the words. 'That's why you're here.'

Kat thrust a glass into my hand. 'Drink,' she said.

I stared at the glass, but was unable to move. 'Who is she?'

Cordelia leant forward and tipped some wine into my mouth. 'You're not going to like it.'

I swallowed. 'Who?'

Kat leant forward and tipped my glass again.

I swallowed again. 'Who?' I repeated.

'We never liked her.'

'Who?'

'I can't,' Kat said.

'Tell me.'

'I don't want to.'

'You have to.'

'You tell her,' she said to Cordelia.

'You're the one who saw it on Facebook,' Cordelia said, knocking back her wine.

'Will somebody please tell me!' I screamed.

'Write it down,' Cordelia said, throwing Kat a pen.

Kat looked around for some paper.

I flipped over the notes I'd made on Joanna's alley antics and then threw the pad at her. Kat wrote each letter, slowly and deliberately, as though it were an entry for a calligraphy contest. I downed my wine and then ripped the page away from her. As I read the letters one by one, my mind struggled to register.

'Victoria? What? But it can't be her. That can't be right.'

'Yes. Victoria,' Kat said, pouring herself a large glass of wine.

'But she was at the party last night. She was dancing with Robert.' I snatched the glass from her and began drinking. 'She's my friend.'

'She's no friend of yours,' Cordelia said.

'But she was all over Robert last night. It just doesn't make any sense.'

'Since when does anything make any sense?' Kat said, pouring herself a replacement glass.

Cordelia picked up my bag and coat. 'Come on,' she said, 'let's go eat.'

Kat loitered behind to finish her wine and then followed us out the door, stuffing the letter into her bag.

That night, it felt as though the world were turning without me. I listened, but I couldn't hear. I watched but everything was blurred. I ate, but could taste nothing. I drank glass after glass, but the numbness never came.

Chapter 21

'WELCOME TO THE CHALET!' the staff said in unison as they lined up to greet us. Their five-star smiles seemed fixed to their faces as though there were a sniper in the rafters, ready to take them out if they dared adopt any other facial expression.

The chalet manager, Kate, stepped forward to shake my hand.

'Welcome back,' she said. 'It's always a pleasure to host one of your trips.'

Her smile was the most inauthentic of them all. Over the years, I'd seen it range across the full spectrum, from manic child's entertainer to 'Here's Johnny' in *The Shining*.

While the suitcases and ski paraphernalia were unloaded from the coach, the guests waded through the deep snow and into the grand entrance hall. This year we had hired three chalets nestled at the foot of the slopes in St Anton. Guided by the results of a wall-sized ski-trip love-match flow chart that Mandi had spent months constructing, we had split the clients into three groups. Each group had been allocated either Mandi, Minky or me as their matchmaker.

'Nice pad,' Mr Marbella said, plonking himself down onto the enormous sofa that lined the perimeter of the lounge.

In the centre of the room, a glass flume reached from the polished floorboards to the oak-clad eaves. Inside, the fire roared like a caged animal, the flames burning fiercer and brighter with each crackle. Alongside the lounge, stood an imposing oak table, dressed as if for a royal banquet, silver cutlery laid out around crystal-encrusted candelabra.

'Oh. My. God. Hot tub!' screamed Cassandra, as she climbed onto the sofa and looked out the window.

Outside, against the star-filled sky, the hot tub bubbled away, lit up like some kind of disco cauldron.

'I'm going in!' she squealed, her New York mega-volume bouncing off the cladding, and started unzipping her case.

Mr Marbella flinched and Emily who was sitting on the sofa put her hands over her ears.

'Don't tell me I have to *share* a room?' Victoria flounced down the staircase, ponytail swinging violently. She looked at me with narrowed eyes.

We hadn't really spoken since her Facebook declaration that she was dating Nick, aside from a brief conversation during which she'd enraged me further by asking me to explain in detail how I felt about it. After I had slammed the phone down and then texted Nick an angry 'have a nice life' sort of message, I'd tried to bury both of them in the back of my mind. That was until, claiming she was now single, she booked a place on the ski trip, and then turned up at the airport acting as though nothing had happened.

Mike rushed towards her and picked up her suitcase. It

had been several years since I'd met him at the champagne bar on my first night of headhunting, but despite his unwavering appreciation of the opposite sex, he'd been insistent that he was still not ready for a long-term relationship, instead preferring to focus his energies on enjoying the journey. I watched him gazing up at Victoria and wondered if that might be about to change.

'So, do we really *have* to share?' Victoria asked again.

'I thought it would be a good way for everyone to get to know each other,' I replied.

'You can share with me,' Mr Marbella said with a wink.

Mike sneered at him. Then Cassandra bolted past in a bikini, heading towards the hot tub.

'Wait for me,' Dr Stud shouted, chasing after her, swimming shorts flapping wildly.

'Why don't you share with Emily?' I suggested, having noticed Emily slumped on the sofa sporting a sullen expression.

'Fine,' Victoria said sniffily, before flouncing back upstairs.

Mike grabbed her bags, along with his, and sprinted up ahead of her.

With everyone else out of the room, I walked over to Emily and sat down next to her on the sofa.

'You okay?' I asked.

'Yeah, I suppose,' she replied.

'Are you sure?' I asked, looking out the window at Dr Stud as he plunged into the hot tub after Cassandra. 'Isn't a bit weird, you know, after your date with him?'

'Oh, I'm not bothered by that,' she said. 'He's cool. We're cool.'

'So what's up, then? And don't say "nothing".'

She laughed. 'You sound like my mother.'

I put my handbag on my lap and gripped the straps 'Oh, no, dear. I'm just worried about you, dear.'

She laughed. 'Honestly, I'm fine. It just takes me a while to get used to new people, that's all. I'll be fine tomorrow.'

'Okay,' I said, placing the bag back on the floor.

'So, what's with you and Victoria?' she asked, kicking off her boots. 'If looks could kill, she'd have arrived in a body bag.'

'Long story.' I sighed. 'Another time.'

'It's not fair,' she said, lifting her knees up to her chest. 'You get to know everything about us, but we never get to find out about you.'

I laughed. 'You're not missing anything.'

'You girls coming?' Mike interrupted, swaggering down the stairs, hot tub ready, muscles sculpted to swimwear-model perfection. Behind him, was Victoria, her limbs long and toned. Her stomach was flat and taut, boobs pert and perky. For all the tiny triangles of her bikini were masking, she may as well have been naked. No matter how hard I searched, it was impossible to find even the tiniest of flaws. Immediately, my mind, working with the expertise of a Hollywood editing team, forged images of her and Nick together: him watching her undress with a lusty half-smile, seeing her perfect body naked and then comparing it to mine. I could never compete. No amount of Pilates, power plates, mud wraps or wheat-grass detox would ever convert my body to hers. As her rounded little bottom wiggled its way towards the hot tub, I turned back to Emily. Her eyes were wider than the moon in the sky.

'Bloody hell,' she said. 'There's no way I'm getting my bikini on next to her.'

Just then, Kate burst through the kitchen door with a smile to rival the Joker in *Batman*. 'Champagne and canapés in ten minutes,' she said. 'Shall I send them out to the tub?'

I nodded, trying my best not to mirror Kate's expression. It was eerily contagious.

'We'll take ours in here, please,' Emily said, looking a little perturbed by my contorted smile.

Against her slouchy cream jumper, the flecks of gold in her eyes burned brighter than the flames in front of us. My image of Emily had since morphed from flower fairy into some kind of sci-fi creature that could either save me or kill me with only one glance. While we sipped champagne and consumed what I suspected to be more than our share of the canapés, we talked about men. I asked her if she liked anyone on the trip.

'There's a guy in the chalet next door,' she said. 'Tall, scruffy blond hair.'

I smiled. 'Ah, Zac. In Mandi's chalet?'

She nodded. 'I think so.'

'He's American. A graphic designer, thirty-two. Six feet three inches. Quite flir—'

'Stop,' she said, tugging at my arm. 'I want to get to know him myself.'

'Why?'

'It sort of spoils it when you know everything about someone before you really meet them.'

I laughed. 'Well, that is sort of the point of all this.'

'I know,' she said. 'But this time, let me get to know him first.'

'Okay,' I said, reaching for another canapé. 'So how about this chalet, any guys you like?'

She shook her head vigorously, as though I had suggested she stand naked next to Victoria. 'No way.'

'Why not?'

She laughed. 'They're all tossers.'

'No, they're not.'

She continued laughing.

'They're actually really nice guys once you get to know them.'

'Yeah right. Even the short one with the highlights? He's the biggest knob of the lot. Really rates himself.'

'Oh, I do, do I?' The voice came from behind us and we turned around to see Mr Marbella towelling his hair. It looked much better wet. The dulled down highlights made him look almost normal.

He cupped the contents of his shorts. 'Biggest knob of the lot. You got that one right.'

Emily giggled. 'Sorry,' she said.

He smiled, walking towards us, gown trailing on the floor like a bridal train. 'You're forgiven,' he said to Emily. 'As long as you promise you'll be in the tub tomorrow.'

Suddenly Victoria pushed past him. 'Can't you find a robe that fits?' she said. 'Maybe they have some kiddie ones here.'

'Only if you get a bikini that fits,' he replied, gesturing at the now opaque white fabric stretched over her nipples. 'Actually, on second thoughts, maybe not.'

Mike glared at him.

'Oh. My. God!' Cassandra squealed, opening her gown and looking down at her skinny frame. 'I'm all wrinkly!'

Dr Stud jumped in front of her. 'Want a professional opinion?' he asked, pulling her robe further apart. 'All looks good to me.' He grinned.

'Get a room,' Mr Marbella and Emily chanted in unison.

When we were all fully clothed, and seated at the dinner table, Kate kicked open the kitchen door and walked in with eight starters balanced on her arms. Her smile had now morphed into something like the acid house logo. Behind her was the on-site chef who described the menu as though his creations were a comparable endeavour to the Sistine Chapel. After we had devoured our minuscule scallops sprinkled with mushroom dust, as well as the teeny-tiny guinea foul breasts dipped in asparagus emulsion, Mr Marbella requested the chef prepare a large portion of fries, to share with Emily, after she'd expressed a preference for food that took less time to get ready than she did.

'So, how's that girl, Kerri, doing?' Mr Marbella asked when we were tucking into the selection of cheeses.

'Good,' I replied, surprised he'd even remembered her name. 'She's engaged now. To David, a barrister, lovely guy.'

'Engaged? Wow. Can't say I'm surprised though,' he said, plucking two grapes from the cheese plate. 'She's got a great pair of—'

'Yes,' I said, taking the plate away from him and passing it to Emily.

'What?' he asked. 'Why can't I say it?'

Emily slammed the plate down on the table. 'Tits,' she said. 'That's what you were going to say, wasn't it?'

'Yep.' He sat back and popped the grapes into his mouth.

'So predictable,' she said, stabbing her fork into the Stilton, 'so pathetic.'

I glanced round the table and saw Victoria and Cassandra smiling wryly. Mike seemed a little perturbed, as did

Dr Stud. But Mr Marbella, having swallowed his grapes, sliced into the Brie.

'So what if I appreciate a nice pair of tits? All men think it. I've just got the balls to admit it.'

'How do you know what all men think?' Emily asked.

'Because I am one.'

She laughed. 'That only qualifies you to comment on how *you* think. You can't prove all men think like you. That's utter rubbish.'

'She's got a point,' Cassandra interjected and Victoria nodded.

'Okay,' Mr Marbella continued, waving his fork in the air, Brie wedged on the end. 'Let's ask the men around the table. Mike? Studman? Do you like big tits?'

Mike, it seemed, knew better than to offer comment and kept quiet. Dr Stud, however, dabbed the sides of his mouth with a napkin and launched straight into his response.

'I like big ones, small ones, round ones, conical ones. All types. I like tits.'

'Conical ones?' Victoria asked with a puzzled expression.

'Yes, you know, the ones that are less round and more, well, more, you know…conical.' As he explained, his hands appeared to be trying to mirror the image in his head. 'Yours are round,' he added as though it were an afterthought.

Cassandra laughed. 'And mine?'

'Yours are small,' he answered. 'But a nice shape. Round I would say.'

Mr Marbella turned to Mike. 'So, mate, we haven't heard from you yet. You like tits?'

Mike glanced at Victoria. 'I appreciate the female form for all that it is.'

Mr Marbella laughed. 'He's just saying that because he doesn't want to piss off the girls. If we were on our own, he'd be honest.'

'Would he?' Emily asked and then took a swig of her port. 'If, as you say, he's lying to impress the girls, then he may lie to impress the boys. How can you prove honesty, even to yourself?'

Mr Marbella sat back in his seat. 'We've got a smart one here, better watch ourselves, fellas.' Finally he devoured the lump of Brie that he'd been waving around for the past few minutes. 'But it still doesn't change the fact that I like big tits. Anyway, I bet the only reason you're offended is because you've got small ones.'

'Yes, of course,' she said, knocking back the rest of the port in her glass. 'My entire self-worth rests on the size of my chest.'

'Well, you don't have much to balance it on, so that could be the issue.'

'I'm not the one with the issues here.'

'Well, clearly you are or you wouldn't be so angry at me.'

'Well, clearly you are or you wouldn't be so superficial.'

'Clearly I am what?'

'A twat.'

'Well, there we go.'

'There we go what?'

'You're obviously losing the argument if you're resorting to name calling.'

'It wasn't name calling. It was an observation.'

'Well, you've got no tits. That's also an observation.'

'Okay, okay,' I interrupted, 'let's change the subject.'

Cassandra leant forward and put up her hand. 'Okay, ladies. Let's talk about dicks. I prefer short, fat ones to long, skinny ones. Thoughts?'

Dr Stud burst out laughing and Cassandra joined in. Moments later, they were gripping their sides, tears streaming down their cheeks. The rest of us looked on as though we'd missed the punchline.

'And what's inside? Doesn't that count at all?' Emily asked, digging at the rind on her plate.

'Yes, of course,' said Mr Marbella. 'The tighter the better.'

Emily's face turned a deep red. She threw her fork down, pushed back her chair and then stomped up the stairs. I turned to Mr Marbella, wondering what I should do. Send him to his room. Arrange a flight home. But instead of leaning back, triumphant in the debate, he looked down, the colour draining from his face. He then dropped his fork and, before I could speak, he'd charged up the stairs after Emily.

While I was trying to sleep that night, next to Cassandra who, it seemed, made more noise dormant than she did awake, the strangest thoughts filled my mind. Images of boobs and their various forms: big ones, small ones, Dr Stud sporting a pair the shape of traffic cones. Mr Marbella with an elephant's trunk sprouting from his swimming shorts. Victoria naked, Nick looking at her, then touching her, touching her perfect round boobs. Mr Marbella pumping them up with a bicycle pump until they were so big they engulfed Nick, trapping him between them. He couldn't breathe. Emily lunged at them, plunging a fork into one. Air gushed out and then suddenly, I awoke to the sound of Cassandra's snores as they reached a terrifying crescendo.

Chapter 22

'BUT I TOLD you I'd never do a black run again,' Emily said, legs dangling from a chairlift suspended above a ravine thick with powdery white snow.

Dr Stud and I were sitting beside her. 'Don't worry,' he said, lifting the bar. 'Your knight with shining highlights will be here to rescue you.' He pointed his pole at Mr Marbella, who was already at the top of the run, and appeared to be shouting at Mike.

Emily huffed. 'I don't need rescuing.'

She skied off the lift, wobbling only a little.

It was four days into the trip and despite frequent bouts of bickering, and vastly differing ski abilities, our chalet group skied and après-skied as one. Following the first night's boob feud, Mr Marbella seemed appropriately repentant, coaching Emily through the icy moguls and even retrieving a glove she had dropped off the chairlift.

'Wait for me, Studs!' screeched Cassandra, before launching herself from the chair lift, towards Dr Stud, and then careering into him. They fell over, laughing, skis and limbs entwined.

'This way,' shouted Mike, ushering us over. Mr Marbella stood beside him with an expression as unforgiving as the slope before them.

We skied towards them. 'Shit,' said Emily, her face as white as the snow. 'Is there any other way down?'

Mr Marbella glared at Mike. 'No, let this lot go down and then we'll do it together.'

Mike giggled.

Mr Marbella glared at him again. 'Seriously? You're laughing because I said we'll do *it* together?'

Mike's smile faded.

'Go on, then,' he said to Mike. 'Now you've got us here, go on and impress old tarty arse with your slick moves.'

Victoria, virtually born on the slopes—apparently, her mother was skiing when she went into labour—had spent a lifetime perfecting her technique. However, she seemed more interested in skiing for an audience than challenging her ability. It was as though the slopes were her catwalk, and today she was modelling a white one-piece, purple boots, purple headband, and wraparound purple glasses.

Mike pushed off in front of her, zigzagging down the slopes with the simplest twist to his hips, his legs bending instinctively over the gradient. This was interspersed with jumps and subsequent glances over his shoulder to check Victoria was watching. Victoria moved down the slope, balletic and elegant like a gazelle springing down a hill. Dr Stud shimmied down after them, with the occasional off-balance wobble. Lastly Cassandra set off, hurtling towards him.

'I'm coming, Studs!' she shrieked, skimming the edge

of the run, beyond which the tips of pine trees swayed ominously.

At the foot of the slope, skiers piled onto the lift. I watched them and the hundreds who queued behind them. I'm sure they were each aware of the risk, of the high probability of being hurt, yet they were still willing to chance it for the pursuit of pleasure, an intrinsic urge that seemed to lie within all of us.

Mr Marbella positioned himself next to Emily. 'You ready?' he asked. 'Just take a deep breath and follow my path, okay?'

She positioned her skis into a downward turn.

'Keep your eyes focused on the sign down there. That's where we're going.'

'What, the one that says "Caution Hazard"?'

'No, the one behind it that says "Happy Hour".' He smiled before moving off slowly, carving out a route for her to follow.

I stood behind Emily and looked ahead. The bright white of the snow made my eyes water. I pulled down my goggles, but, even so, I could barely make out what lay ahead.

Mike sprint-skied down the final part of the run, concluding with a dramatic stop just in front of Victoria. He flipped off his skis and swaggered into the bar, a casual glance over his shoulder to check Victoria had witnessed. She followed nonchalantly, pulling up her purple glasses onto her head and unzipping her suit down to her waist. Cassandra and Dr Stud quickly joined them, their child-like giggles echoing up the slopes.

When a haze softened the light, and my eyes could eventually focus, I looked at Mr Marbella and watched his eyes track Emily. Soon clarity replaced confusion. I noticed the way he looked at her: the intensity in his gaze, the slight furrow of his brow, the gentle curl to his lips. My stomach flipped and my hands started trembling. I recognised that look. It was the exact same way Nick used to look at me, the way he looked at me as I devoured the sashimi on our first date, the way I'd caught him staring at me during the months that followed. The look that had waned with time.

Suddenly, though, Mr Marbella's expression changed. His half-smile dropped and his eyes widened.

'Achtung!' a voice shouted from behind us, accompanied by rumbling sound through the snow.

I glanced round to see a snowboarder ploughing down the side of the run, the side that Emily was just turning into. I looked on, my muscles paralysed, my voice mute. Mr Marbella sped towards her, but it was too late and his face contorted as the boarder smacked into Emily and sent her tumbling down the hill.

Before I could blink, Mr Marbella was by her side. He scooped her up and skied down to the bar with her in his arms as though he were the King of the Slopes. The crowd on the terrace outside, who had been drinking and laughing one moment earlier, were now silent, their mouths open and their faces creased with concern.

'Oh, my Gaaad!' wailed Cassandra, rushing over, as Mr Marbella laid Emily down on the decking.

'Emily, are you okay?' Mr Marbella asked, stroking her cheek.

'I'm fine,' she said, brushing him off and then trying to lift herself up. 'Ow, that hurts.'

Dr Stud looked on. 'They've called the medical team, they'll be here in a minute,' he said.

Mr Marbella frowned. 'You're a doctor. Can't you check her out?'

Cassandra stepped forward, hands on hips. 'He's a gynaecologist. I doubt now is an appropriate time for a Pap smear.'

Mr Marbella glared at Dr Stud and then began to feel Emily's neck, arms and legs. 'Where does it hurt, sweetheart?'

'My ankle,' she replied, collapsing back down, tears filling her eyes.

Mr Marbella's jaw tensed. He placed Emily's ankle gently down on the decking and then stood up and looked around the bar. He paced the terrace for a moment until his gaze locked on a tall man shoving a snowboard in the stand. He walked towards him, said something in German and then swung a punch upwards into the man's jaw. The man swayed for a few seconds and then fell face first in the snow. The audience gasped. Then Mr Marbella picked up the board and smashed it against the decking, breaking it in two.

'Uh-oh,' Mike said as three of the man's friends began striding towards Mr Marbella, pushing up their sleeves and clenching their fists. Mike put down his pint and walked towards them.

Before Mike could reach them, Mr Marbella, armed with a ski, hit the first over the head. The man dropped to the ground. The second he took down with an upwards flick of the ski to his jaw. When it came to the third, he threw down the ski, gripped the man's jacket, pulling him towards him. He stood on tiptoes and then smacked his forehead into the man's face. When the man collapsed into the snow alongside his friends, the crowd roared as though they had just witnessed a gladiator victory at the coliseum.

Moments later, Mr Marbella pushed through the now chanting mob, towards Emily who was being propped up on a deckchair by one paramedic, while another wrapped a bandage around her ankle.

She rolled her eyes. 'My hero.'

Mr Marbella turned to me with a smile. 'Is there no pleasing her?'

She laughed. 'Was I supposed to be impressed by that lame display of testosterone?'

He smiled. 'As displays of testosterone go, that was not lame.'

Emily's eyes twinkled through her smirk.

'See, she does like me really,' he said.

'Yeah, I also like my bulldog, Trevor.'

He laughed. 'Okay, then, Miss Hard-To-Get. I'm going to the bar, is it too non-PC of me to offer you a drink?'

'I'll have a Slippery Nipple,' she said, still smirking.

He raised his eyebrows.

'A pink, upwards-pointing one if you can get it?' she said.

He nodded and then walked away with a baffled expression.

After he'd left, I turned to her. 'How do you know about that?'

She looked down at the decking. 'I was there.'

'When?'

'When you met him. I was in the bar with you.'

I was still frowning.

She leant forward. 'I wanted to do my due diligence before meeting you, so I sort of spied on a few of your consultations.'

I laughed, realising that was exactly the kind of thing I would have done.

'Phew,' she said. 'Glad you're not pissed off.'

'No, not at all. But why?'

'Why did I spy?'

'No, why did you sign up, after overhearing his consultation?'

Just as she was about to reply, Mr Marbella appeared with a tray of Slippery Nipples.

Several trays later, Mandi and Minky joined us with their chalet guests, by which time the bar's clientele were dancing on the tables, the benches and various other improvised platforms, consumed in a Euro-pop frenzy. Cassandra and Dr Stud were drawing a crowd with a combination of moves that I suspected St Anton had never witnessed before and doubted would ever witness again. It was as though two forces had joined to create something unique, something disconcertingly greater than the sum of its parts. Mike was still trailing Victoria like a beagle after a fox, and Emily, despite her sprained ankle—and the fact that she was confined to a deckchair—was smiling a smile wider than anything the chalet staff could have mustered.

While I was ordering another tray of Slippery Nipples, Mr Marbella appeared next to me at the bar.

'Do you think I'm in with a chance?' he asked.

I scrunched up my mouth. 'You and Emily?'

He squinted. 'No, me and Mike.'

I laughed. 'Sorry,' I said. 'It's just—'

'Just what?'

I shook my head. 'Nothing.'

He lifted his hands. 'Look I never thought I'd fall for a girl like—'

'Fall for?'

He flushed.

'Are you blushing?'

'No.' He fanned his face. 'It's hot in here.'

I smiled. 'Yes.'

'Yes what?'

'Yes, you're in with a chance.'

He grinned.

'But—' I nodded towards Zac, the six-foot-three American from Mandi's chalet who was now helping Emily out of her chair '—you know you've got competition.'

'That little twerp?'

'Little?'

'He's a total wanker. I heard him ask the waitress for a threesome.'

'Maybe he was just ordering a drink? The cocktail menu lists some ambiguous creations.'

'No,' he said, his jugular twitching, 'there's no way he cares about Emily like…' He paused. 'Come on, help me out here.'

'Okay,' I said, taking the tray of drinks from the barman. 'You need to find a way to get rid of Zac, so you can tell her how you feel.'

He grabbed two Slippery Nipples from the tray and then glared at Zac, nodding slowly.

'Got it,' he said. 'Thanks, babes.'

After I'd distributed the rest of the drinks, I grabbed my ski jacket, pushed open the wooden doors and walked out into the night air. Its frosty glaze clung to my face as I stood on the decking and looked up at the mountains. Their peaks were kissed by clouds dense with snow. Snow that would drop tonight, billions of flakes all united in their purpose.

The morning would see the ground carpeted again, hazardous terrain softened once more. Away from the destruction and complications of human existence, nature's default was peace and harmony. Maybe I could hoard things in the Austrian mountains rather than the English countryside? 'Crazy bag lady and her canine companions relocate to St Anton.' I could swap chutney for *gluhwein* and maybe learn to play the accordion, though my hoarding of bric-a-brac would be more doily-centred and the dogs might need some fleece-lined coats.

I turned back to the bar and looked through the window. As I watched everyone drinking and laughing, I wondered if I was destined to be the spectator rather than the participant. The sound of footsteps crunching in the snow interrupted my thoughts and I turned to see a jacket-less Victoria staggering towards me.

'I kissed him,' she said, leaning against me. I pushed her back and she wobbled like a Weeble. 'I missed Kike.' She shook her head. 'I mean I kissed Mike.'

I looked ahead, saying nothing.

'You've got to talk to me at some point,' she said. 'It's physically impossible—' she paused and then frowned '—I mean humanly impossible to ignore someone for an entire week.'

'No, it's not.'

'Hah! Got you.' She clapped her hands together. 'Now we're officially talking again.'

I sighed, looking up at the clouds, and hoping they might intervene and drop a large block of ice on her head.

'He's the first boy I've kissed since Patrick.'

I turned to her. 'Really?'

'Oh, you just don't get it, do you?' Her face scrunched

up in an exaggerated frown. 'You always want to believe the worst of me.'

I noticed my hands were on my hips, but I left them there.

'You dated Nick, despite the fact that you knew it would hurt me, despite the fact that you knew I was still in love with him.'

She let out a deep sigh. 'I needed to do it to prove to you that you did.'

'What? You're not making any sense.'

'I'm a bit drunk.' She swayed from side to side as though further evidence were required. 'I needed to prove to you that you still loved him.'

'By dating him?'

'I didn't date him, silly. It was a test to see how much you still loved him.'

'What? I don't understand. So you didn't date him?'

'No.'

'So Facebook was a lie?'

'You do it all the time with your clients.'

'What, lie to them?'

'Yes, sometimes you do, if you think it will help them.'

'No, I don't.'

'You do.'

'I don't.'

'Do.'

'Don't.'

'Do.'

'Don't! Don't! Don't!' I shouted. 'And what about Robert, what was that all about?'

'I didn't want him messing everything up.'

'So, your plan was to date my ex-boyfriends in order to help me?'

'No, that's not what I said.'

'Well, what are you trying to say?'

'I was trying to help.'

'Help? What gives you the right to be meddling in my life?'

'It's what you do. You've made a profession out of it.'

'People ask for my help. They want me to meddle. They ask me to meddle.'

'Would you ever ask for help though?' She looked at me, her face almost pressing against mine. 'Would you?' she asked again, louder this time. 'No, you wouldn't, because you're too proud. Proudy, proudy proud pants!'

'Well, *your* help I can do without,' I said, turning my back on her.

'We'll see about that.'

She went to flounce off, but her foot was wedged in the snow and she lurched forward. Instinctively, I grabbed her arm to stop her from falling.

She looked up at me, her eyes wide. 'Did you even open it?'

'Open what?'

'The letter.'

I let go of her arm. 'No, not yet.'

She wedged each foot in the snow, presumably to stabilise herself. 'He thinks you cheated on him.'

My stomach flipped. 'What?'

'With the penis.'

'What penis?'

'The one you drew.'

My mind raced, flicking through all its phallus-themed files. 'Oh. The elephant. I wondered where that had gone.'

'Yes, so did Nick.'

'It wasn't me who drew it.'

'I know. But he said it wasn't the first time. He told me he'd found a penis photo on your phone when you met: a close-up with a dog in the background.'

'I hope you explained that one.'

'Yes, though not entirely. Anyway, I'd just about convinced him. And then photos of you and Robert popped up on Facebook.'

I frowned. 'Photos?'

She nodded. 'You were tagged at that wedding, didn't you see?'

I shook my head.

'There was one of you with some old guy doing a weird dance, and then one of Robert stroking your hair and trying to kiss you.'

I sighed. 'But nothing happened.'

'I know that,' she said, pulling her foot from the snow. 'And I think Nick knows it deep down too.'

I looked up at the clouds that had been capping the mountains to see they had lifted, exposing the peaks. I took a long deep breath.

'I'm so sorry,' I said, wrapping my coat around the both of us. 'I've been such an idiot.'

She smiled. 'I only ever wanted to help you.'

We linked arms and turned back towards the bar.

'Anyway, silly, didn't you wonder why the founding partner of a prestigious law firm represented you for free?'

I stood still and stared at her for a moment. 'That was you?'

She shook her head. 'Not me.'

My stomach flipped. 'Nick?'

She nodded. 'He never stopped loving you, you know.'

A smile swept across my face, that was until my thoughts caught up. 'Yes, so much so that he was lured to the Windmill Club to be consoled by Candice.'

Victoria laughed. 'He told me about that. Said he couldn't get out of there fast enough.'

I rolled my eyes. 'Yeah, right.'

She turned to me, her ponytail swishing through the icy air. 'Ellie. Nick loves you. Why is that so hard for you to believe?'

I looked up at the sky. 'Because when a man loves a woman...' I paused and sighed. 'I don't know, isn't he supposed to do anything for her? Move heaven and earth to win her heart? Not post back her keys and then write a lame letter.'

She burst out laughing. 'And what did you do to prove your love for Nick? Throw food at him, take his toilet brush and then nearly snog your ex?'

I looked at her, at her creased eyes and stretched smile, and suddenly I started laughing too. Once I'd started, I couldn't stop. After our moment of joint hysteria, Victoria leant towards me with her arms out, presumably for a hug, but she lost her footing and almost knocked me over. Following a little jostle to regain our balance, we linked arms again and made our way back to the bar, giggling as we went.

Once inside, our laughter quickly subsided. Zac was leaning against the table with a blurry look in his eyes. He was standing next to Emily, rubbing his head and wobbling from side to side. A sudden realisation hit me like a Mr Marbella ski-slap. *Move heaven and earth to win her heart?*

'Oh, no,' I said, waiting for the fall.

After a couple more wobbles, Zac hit the ground like a

felled tree. My gaze shifted to Mr Marbella, who was looking on, a sardonic smile creeping out from the corners of
his mouth.

'Gosh. It's almost like he's been drugged,' remarked Victoria as the crowd swarmed around him, Alice Cooper's
'Poison' infiltrating the airwaves.

Chapter 23

'TEA, COFFEE, BIRTH CONTROL, ANYONE?' The air steward patrolled the aisles, sneering at couples.

I couldn't really blame him. Since we'd boarded the plane, he'd been required to conduct an extensive seat-swapping exercise in order to accommodate the newly formed couples, then to service their incessant demands for Slippery Nipples from the drinks trolley. Then to tolerate hair-stroking, hand-holding, cooing, sighing, gasping and inappropriate fondling under blankets. However, from his current facial expression, and the tight grip he had on an open bottle of water, it seemed he was unwilling to overlook the squelchy noises coming from the seats behind me.

'Come on, guys. Give it a rest,' I said, leaning round my seat to the row behind. Cassandra and Dr Stud's tongues were entwined. They glanced sideways at me without breaking contact.

'Shhh,' Mr Marbella said, sitting beside them with his arm round Emily. She was asleep, snuggled up on his chest.

Mandi sat across the aisle with a furrowed brow and a pink notebook open on her lap. Her fluffy pink pen bobbed up and down, looking like some kind of exotic yet well-trained caterpillar.

'Psst, Mandi,' I whispered.

She lifted her hand without looking up. 'One second.' The pen bobbed up and down some more. 'Okay done.' She looked up, grinning. 'Guess what?'

'What?'

'One hundred per cent.'

'No way.'

She clapped her hands. 'For the first time ever, a one hundred per cent hit rate.'

'Shhh.' Mr Marbella held a finger to his mouth.

I grinned, giving her a double thumbs-up.

When I turned back in my seat, Victoria, who was sitting beside me, prodded my arm.

'So that means everyone on this trip met someone?' she asked.

I nodded, still grinning.

'What, even that hefferlump in the other chalet?' She scrunched up her nose. 'And the skinny geeky guy?'

I pointed to the happy couple who were two rows up across the aisle. 'How did you not notice them? They've been all over each other for days.'

She sniffed and then shook her head as if to clear the image. 'I have a filter for ugly people.'

Mike leant in from her other side and then squeezed her knee, flashing his knicker-dropping smile. 'Don't you ever change,' he said.

'Ever?' she asked.

'Never, ever, ever,' he said, twirling her ponytail and

gazing at her adoringly. I glanced at the sick bag, just to be sure of its location if the need arose.

When he leant in to kiss her, I, along with the steward, decided my voyeurism quota had been filled for the day. I picked up my iPod, plugged in the earphones and closed my eyes. The music washed over me like the sea over sand, the rhythm and the lyrics triggering thoughts and emotions, rolling, crashing and then pulling back. My muscles tensed then relaxed. I let out a deep sigh and images floated through my mind. The faces of all those I'd known. The people I'd helped, the people I'd failed. Those whom I'd loved and those whom I'd lost. I knew now that without sadness, happiness was meaningless. That one was dependent on the other. As I let the acceptance flow through me, it felt as though I were floating in the ocean, surrendering to the peaks and the troughs of the waves, letting the tide direct me. It was almost as though I could feel the spray from the sea, splashing on my face. Another splash. I opened my eyes to find the steward with a menacing glint in his eye and an empty bottle in his hand. Next to me, Victoria and Mike wore the contents with corresponding shocked expressions.

At baggage collection, the carousel chugged along with suitcases piled high, showcased to their audience. The passengers waited, eyes fixed on the conveyor, searching for their case. Occasionally, someone would identify the wrong one, then quickly toss it back, embarrassed by their misguided certainty. Others would fidget, shifting the weight from their feet, seemingly fretful their suitcase may never arrive. I supposed some cases would remain unclaimed, circling the carousel like unwanted dogs in a pound, eyed up suspiciously by officials and ultimately destroyed.

'There's mine!' squealed Cassandra, before springing onto the carousel and wrestling her suitcase as though it were a crocodile.

Meanwhile, Dr Stud was battling to balance his skis and an oddly shaped case on a trolley. Victoria stepped away from the scene, obviously keen to distance herself from any association, while Mike did his best to look unfazed by the weight of his suitcase, two pairs of skis and Victoria's Louis Vuitton trunk. Clearly not wanting to be outdone, Mr Marbella, skis balanced across his shoulders, heaved his entire Burberry suitcase collection into his arms and then carefully placed Emily's bag on top as though he were transporting a Fabergé egg. I directed them to the trolley park and explained that my liability insurance didn't include competitive lifting.

Trolleys loaded up, we loitered by the customs exit, waiting to say our goodbyes. Mandi broke the stand-off first with her clients, initiating a seemingly well-rehearsed group hug, which also appeared to include a team mantra and custom handshake. When they'd concluded with a bottom-wiggle high-five combo, Minky launched into an Oscar-style speech, thanking each of her clients for their role in the trip that would have undoubtedly changed their lives.

Our group looked at each other with the awkwardness of teenagers at the end of a date. Despite good intentions, I knew that, for most of us, it was the end of a journey. As much as they felt like family, I knew that now was their time to move on, to begin their lives together. Some would update me, invite me to their wedding, their baby's christening. Yet most would disappear, almost as though they were ashamed of any intervention. Ashamed that they had asked for help with something that was supposed to be easy and effortless.

Victoria broke the silence with uncharacteristic perkiness.

'Righty ho, let's go to Arrivals.'

Her tone and her choice of words seemed slightly bizarre: who says 'Let's go to Arrivals'? She ushered us through customs, checking her watch. After passing through, with only a moment's concern when a sniffer dog took a liking to Mr Marbella, we walked into the vast white space that was the gateway to London. It was teeming with people, all rushing to greet their loved ones. *There is no greater barometer for love than the arrivals area at an airport*, I thought as I watched some swamped by a deluge of hugs and kisses, while others were left to make their own way home.

Cassandra and Dr Stud skipped ahead, laughing raucously. Mr Marbella stopped in front and threaded his fingers through Emily's. She turned to him, pushed back the thick fringe from her eyes and smiled just as a busty blonde in a sprayed-on T-shirt wiggled past them. Mr Marbella didn't flinch. He looked straight through her and then back at Emily with a smile that was worth more than all the diamond-encrusted Rolexes in the world.

Moments later, standing alone at the edge of the concourse as the latest arrivals were announced via the Tannoy, I watched as each of our hundred-per-cent-hit-rate couples left the airport. I plonked down on my suitcase and wondered how many of them would last. If the statistics prevailed, then eighty-five per cent would end up single again.

My thoughts flashed back to the day I'd decided to become a matchmaker. When I'd been focused solely on the end goal of finding love for my clients and myself. However, now I'd learned the truth: that love's arrival wasn't accompanied by a magnificent fanfare. It wasn't the prelude to a dramatic conclusion or fading final scene alluding to a lifetime of happiness. I looked around me, at the people arriving only to depart again, and I realised that one journey's end was nothing more than the start of another.

I tore the tag from my suitcase, screwed it up into a ball and tossed it in the bin beside me. Then I looked up to see Mandi bounding towards me, her luminous pink suitcase trundling behind her.

'Fancy a victory drink?' she said, pointing towards the bar next to us. Then she nodded at the sandwich board outside, which promised a foot of onion rings and a glass of wine for a fiver.

When we were wedged in a faux leather booth, with two warm glasses of chardonnay in hand, Mandi and I looked at each other across the table. She smiled and then let out a deep sigh as though she were exhaling years of matchmaking accomplishments.

I lifted my glass. 'Cheers.'

She raised hers to meet mine, bypassing the imposing stack of onion rings. 'To us,' she said. 'Mission accomplished.'

I took a long slow sip and then put my glass back down on the table, wondering why it was that I still felt a few residual stabs of dissatisfaction. Just as the chardonnay began to seep into my veins, it suddenly came to me: I wasn't an altruist after all. All along, I had been secretly hoping fate might somehow reward me for my endeavours.

'What's up?' Mandi asked, picking up an onion ring and inspecting it. 'I thought this was what you wanted?'

I looked up to the airport ceiling, hoping that, beyond,

God might be in the midst of an emergency meeting, having summoned Eros and the angels, to debate the best compensation plan for a selfless matchmaker.

I looked back down to see a giant onion ring disappear into Mandi's mouth.

'You know that proverb about the doctor?' I asked.

She wiped her mouth with a napkin. 'Yes. I know it.' She pointed her finger in the air. 'The one where he tells the patient to pull himself together.'

I sniggered. 'That's a joke, Mandi. Not a proverb. I meant the one about the physician healing himself.'

She shrugged her shoulders and then grabbed another onion ring.

'But you're healed. You're happy. Aren't you?' she said.

I reached for the ketchup and squeezed an enormous blob onto my plate.

'Just because I *can* live without him, doesn't mean I want to,' I replied.

Mandi shoved the onion ring into her mouth, chewed for a bit and then swallowed.

'You'll find the answers, Ellie. You always do.'

I shrugged my shoulders and took another sip of wine. 'And you? Do you still think Aristotle was right about the one soul, two bodies thing?'

She shook her head, mumbling something about Celine Dion. 'Anyway,' she added, 'in Steve's case, it was more like one soul inhabiting the entire female population.'

I smirked. 'So what do you think now?'

She took a deep breath and then looked me directly in the eyes. 'There's no soulmate, no one special person for everyone. Love is what you make it. It isn't a feeling, or even a need.' She looked down and swivelled her engagement ring around on her finger. 'It's a choice.'

An onion ring slipped from my grasp and sank into the ketchup. I pulled it out and started dabbing it with my napkin. Mandi watched for a moment and then her gazed drifted behind me. Suddenly, her eyes widened, she jumped off her seat and ducked down under the table.

'Quick. Get down,' she said, tugging at my arm.

I dropped down next to her and we peered over the tabletop.

'Over there. Look,' she whispered, negating the subtlety of her tone with extravagant pointing.

A tall dark-haired man wearing white linen sauntered along the other side of the concourse. I noticed his shirt was unbuttoned, exposing a sculpted waxed chest.

'Is that Mr Mills and Boon?' I whispered to Mandi.

I turned to her to see her head nodding with the fervour of a pneumatic drill. When I looked back to Mr Mills and Boon, I noticed beside him, behind a curtain of dark hair, was a tall slim girl. She had her hand tucked into his back pocket. They were wearing matching outfits. I couldn't see her face but I recognised something about the way she walked. It reminded me of a military commander.

'That's not Thea, is it?' I said to Mandi.

Mandi nodded, even faster this time, to the point where I was concerned she might actually bore a hole on the concrete floor.

'Looks like they've been on a mini-break,' I said, admiring their stylish 'his and hers' overnight bags.

Once Mr and Mrs Mills and Boon had exited the airport in the throes of a climactic snog, Mandi turned to me, her mouth twitching at the sides. My smile broke first, and then hers, and in less time than it would take us to perform a Thea-style eye roll, we both collapsed into a fit of giggles.

'What on earth are you two doing?'

We looked up to see Victoria, peering down at us, her eyes narrowed, her mouth downturned.

Mandi and I jumped up and smoothed down our clothes.

'I thought you'd already left,' I said, suddenly acting like a teenager who'd been caught smoking behind the bike sheds.

Victoria looked us up and down, glanced at the onion rings and then scrunched up her face.

'If we're going to be working together, then I expect more professionalism than this,' she said.

'Working together?' Mandi asked, looking startled.

'I just bumped into Thea. She told me she's left.' Victoria swished her ponytail and her eyes narrowed further. 'So you'll need a new matchmaker then, won't you?' She leant forward and picked a piece of batter off my top, then flicked it onto the floor. 'Obviously I'm staggeringly over-qualified but now you've got a venture capitalist involved, it's doubtful you'd be able to manage without me.'

Mandi's jaw dropped. Mine quickly followed.

'What?' I asked.

Victoria sniffed. 'Thea just told me. She said some investor called her while she was away. Apparently, he wants to take your agency international.'

I stepped back and turned to Mandi, then back to Victoria.

Victoria flicked her hand as though offers of global expansion were a routine occurrence. 'Thea said she'd email you the details later.'

I stood still for a moment, wondering if the onion rings might have been laced with hallucinogens.

Victoria tapped me on the chin. 'Close your mouth. You look like a simpleton.'

I closed it, though Victoria's reciprocal expression implied the simpleton look was still very much present.

'Come along, then. Let's get going,' she said, grabbing Mandi's hand and mine before dragging us out of the bar. 'Leave your luggage. Mike can deal with it. We've got work to do.'

'Work? Now?' I asked, contemplating throwing myself to the ground and screaming 'Terrorist.' All I wanted to do was go home, open a bottle of wine and start planning my future as a universally revered businesswoman slash esteemed love guru.

Eyes down and striding forwards, she dragged us out through the airport exit and into the biting morning air. Just as she was about to haul us into the path of an oncoming taxi, I stopped and pulled her back.

'Victoria. What are you doing?'

'I want to go home. I'm tired,' Mandi said, looking as though she were about to stamp her feet.

'Oh, stop whining, the both of you,' she said. 'I'm a matchmaker and I have important work to do. Now wait here.'

Victoria took a few steps towards the taxi, which had just pulled up in front of us. I could just about make out the back of a man's head in the rear window. Victoria's ponytail, which had been swaying like a pendulum, suddenly slowed to a stop. Her expression softened and a smile swept across her face as the taxi door swung open.

'Ellie, come.' She summoned me as though I were a sheepdog.

I heard a gasp from Mandi. I glanced beside me to see her grinning and clasping her hands together.

When I turned back to the taxi, I drew a sharp breath. The man swung his legs out and then planted his feet on the ground. I recognised his shoes immediately. They were an upgraded version of the pair that had descended the spiral staircase years ago.

I exhaled a long deep breath. Instantly, it felt as though there was stillness all around me. As though the flights had been grounded, the Tannoy unplugged, and even the world itself had stopped spinning. All that remained was the steady beat of my heart and my chest rising and falling with each breath. I watched him climb out of the taxi. Straight away his brown eyes met mine. I took in one more breath and held it there. My stomach didn't flip, my muscles didn't tense. Instead, as we stared at each other in silence, all I could feel was the warmth of the sun soaking into my skin, as though granting each cell a vital component.

I ran towards him and let his arms envelop me.

'I missed you,' he said, the waver in his voice revealing just how much.

I nuzzled his chest and inhaled his smell. As my tears soaked into his shirt, I prayed that we had learned the hardest lessons already. But when I wiped my eyes and glanced over his shoulder, up at the sky, towards a cloud where I imagined Eros and the angels to be collating the minutes of their meeting, I had an inkling, deep inside, that there might be a whole lot more to come.

And I didn't mind at all.

* * * * *

'A fresh new voice in romantic fiction'
—*Marie Claire*

Everyone has one.
That list.
The things you were *supposed* to do before you turn thirty.

Jobless, broke and getting a divorce, Rachel isn't exactly living up to her own expectations. And moving into grumpy single dad Patrick's box room is just the soggy icing on top of her dreaded thirtieth birthday cake.

Eternal list-maker Rachel has a plan—an all-new set of challenges to help her get over her divorce and out into the world again—from tango dancing to sushi making to stand-up comedy.

But, as Patrick helps her cross off each task, Rachel faces something even harder: learning to live—and love—without a checklist.

If you enjoyed this book, try more from Sarah Morgan

Following the success of the Snow Crystal trilogy, Sarah Morgan returns with the sensational Puffin Island trilogy. Follow the lives and loves of Emily, Brittany and Skylar as they embark on new journeys and unexpected encounters.

Look out for these titles, coming soon in 2015!

Some Kind of Wonderful – July 2015

Christmas Ever After – October 2015

**Find out more at
www.millsandboon.co.uk/first-time-in-forever**

The fantastic new read from rom-com queen Fiona Harper

Claire Bixby grew up watching Doris Day films and yearned to live in a world like the one on the screen—sunny, colourful and where happy endings were guaranteed. But recently Claire's opportunities for a little 'pillow talk' have been thin on the ground. That is, until she meets Nic.

Sparks soon start to fly, but Claire's now questioning everything Doris taught her about romance.

Can true love ever really be just like it is in the movies?

Perhaps, perhaps, perhaps…

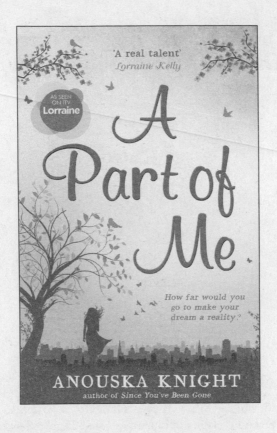

Anouska Knight's first book, *Since You've Been Gone*,
was a smash hit and crowned the winner of Lorraine's
Racy Reads. Anouska returns with *A Part of Me*,
which is one not to be missed!

Get your copy today at:
www.millsandboon.co.uk

She's loved and lost — will she ever learn to open her heart again?

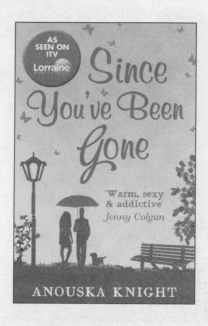

From the winner of ITV Lorraine's Racy Reads, Anouska Knight, comes a heart-warming tale of love, loss and confectionery.

'The perfect summer read — warm, sexy and addictive!'
—Jenny Colgan

For exclusive content visit:
www.millsandboon.co.uk/anouskaknight

PICTURE PERFECT

Movie stars aren't always picture perfect,
especially when it comes to secrets
from their past…

And in Hollywood, a town built on illusions,
believing you can escape might just be
the biggest deception of all.

Full of sex, secrets and scandal, *Picture Perfect* is ideal
for fans of Paige Toon and Lindsey Kelk.

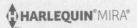

Bringing you the best voices in fiction
🐦 **@Mira_booksUK**